Grayslake Area Public Library District
Grayslake, Illinois

1. A fine will be charged on each book which is not returned when it is due.

2. All injuries to books beyond reasonable wear and all losses shall be made good to the satisfaction of the Librarian.

3. Each borrower is held responsible for all books drawn on his card and for all fines accruing on the same.

DEMCO

Stain of Guilt

This Large Print Book carries the
Seal of Approval of N.A.V.H.

HIDDEN FACES SERIES
BOOK TWO

Stain of Guilt

Brandilyn Collins

THORNDIKE PRESS
An imprint of Thomson Gale, a part of The Thomson Corporation

THOMSON

GALE

Detroit • New York • San Francisco • New Haven, Conn. • Waterville, Maine • London

ALL RIGHTS RESERVED

Thorndike Press® Large Print Christian Mystery.

The text of this Large Print edition is unabridged.

Other aspects of the book may vary from the original edition.

Set in 16 pt. Plantin.

LIBRARY OF CONGRESS CATALOGING-IN-PUBLICATION DATA

Collins, Brandilyn.
  Stain of guilt / by Brandilyn Collins.
    p. cm. — (Hidden faces series ; bk. 2) (Thorndike Press large print christian mystery)
  ISBN-13: 978-0-7862-9187-8 (lg. print : alk. paper)
  ISBN-10: 0-7862-9187-7 (lg. print : alk. paper)
    1. Fugitives from justice — Fiction. 2. Police artists — Fiction. 3. Women artists — Fiction. 4. Murderers — Fiction. 5. Large type books. I. Title.
  PS3553.O4747815S73 2007
  813'.6—dc22   2006035001

Published in 2007 by arrangement with The Zondervan Corporation LLC.

Printed in the United States of America on permanent paper
10 9 8 7 6 5 4 3 2 1

For my weekly prayer partners,
Carol Lee, Jacqueline Clark,
and Sally Ball.
Countless times, we have witnessed
God's power and grace.

*"For where two or three
have gathered together in My name,
there I am in their midst."*
— Matthew 18:20

AUTHOR'S NOTE AND ACKNOWLEDGMENTS

Once again, I must voice my thanks to some very wonderful people:

Les Caldwell, retired deputy sheriff, and his wife, Marilynn, helped me with some interesting law-enforcement and forensic issues, and he and Marilynn read the manuscript to catch my mistakes. Les, you're the best.

Niwana Briggs, for critiquing the manuscript.

My husband and family, for putting up with me. Especially during the obsessive final week of writing.

Karen Ball and Dave Lambert, my dedicated editors, who make my writing so much better. And all the talented folks at Zondervan, who make my books possible. Curt Diepenhorst deserves special mention for his awesome artwork on the book covers of this Hidden Faces series.

One note about the setting for *Stain of*

Guilt. Grove Landing is fictional, but the area in which it is located is very real. The *Record Searchlight* is a local newspaper in Redding, California, but no Adam Bendershil works for the paper, and all actions of the reporter in this book are entirely fictional. My apologies to the Shasta County Sheriff's Department for altering the outlay of its building in Redding for the sake of this story.

"Although you wash yourself with soda and use an abundance of soap, the stain of your guilt is still before me," declares the Sovereign Lord.

— Jeremiah 2:22

"Come now, let us reason together," says the Lord. "Though your sins are like scarlet, they will be as white as snow; though they are red like crimson, they shall be like wool."

— Isaiah 1:18

PROLOGUE

He should have called the police.

Emily Tarell stood in the wide entryway of her executive home, one hand on the staircase banister. The rich parquet floor gleamed under light cascading from the crystal chandelier. Emily loved that polished look of molten gold. But tonight it almost mocked her. Its sheen was too bright, too perfect for the stain that had soiled this house and the Tarell family business. A chill traced spindly fingers between Emily's shoulder blades. She watched as the carved wooden door to her husband's private study began to close. At the last moment Don angled his head through the narrowing space to give her one of his now-don't-worry-dear looks.

Little good that did. Emily could not shake the darkling premonition that hovered about her shoulders, ghost-whispering the approach of unseen evil. It rasped and sputtered, heard yet not heard, cautions uttered across a chasm.

Sometimes Don was just too bighearted. Too quick to forgive. If he'd listened to her, Bill Bland would be interrogated by the police in a dirty little room down at the station instead of settled into an easy chair in his boss's home study.

Click. The door latched, shutting off the four men.

Emily swallowed. What should she do now? She couldn't just stand there, waiting, haunted by the sibilance of broiling wrath. She'd already been far too obvious with her emotions, answering the door with a nervous hello to Peter Dessinger, barely able to look Bill Bland in the eye when he'd arrived a half hour later. If Bill hadn't known he'd been caught, he knew it now, just by her transparency. Her son, Edwin, had nodded to Emily, mouthing, *It'll be okay.* Just like his dad. Both soothing her, even as they refused to heed her sense that something, *something* slithered toward them, looking to consume. Hadn't the same feeling writhed in the pit of her stomach the day Wade had his accident?

Emily pushed away from the banister and headed for the kitchen, her flat-heeled shoes shushing against the hardwood floor. Some herbal tea was what she needed. Calming spearmint flavor. Then she would sit in the family room with a book. No television. That way she could keep an ear cocked toward the study for a raised voice, any sign of how the confrontation was going. She selected a tea bag from a glazed canister and dropped it into the bottom of her favorite mug. The one Wade gave her for a birthday when he was twelve.

Oh, Wade.

Emily steeled herself against the familiar wash of emotions as she filled the teakettle with water. Her youngest son was killed in a car wreck a little over a year ago. Just back from his sophomore year at college, he drove off to meet up with some of his high school buddies . . . and never returned. The pain of that loss would never subside.

Firming her lips, she pushed the heart-ripping thoughts away. She couldn't deal with them right now, on this night.

Not a sound emanated from the study. Emily strained to listen. The silence snapped and clacked in her ears. What were they doing in there? Had Don told Bill that they'd uncovered his embezzlement? That his sinful trail was undeniable?

Whatever would Bill *do?*

Tea made, Emily made her way into the family room, aware of her own breathing — of the catch she felt in the back of her throat. She lowered herself onto the couch, set her cup down on an end table, then stared at the brick fireplace. She'd forgotten to choose a novel from the bookcases lining the walls. No matter; she couldn't concentrate enough to read.

That premonition eeling through her . . .

Her last look at Wade's smiling face before he got into that car . . .

Stop it, Emily. You're overreacting.

She clenched her drink, staring without seeing at the plush blue carpet. The house was so still. What could — ?

Crack!

The furious sound shattered the air. Emily froze. What was that? It sounded almost —

"Nnno!"

The long, muffled cry squeezed her heart. Edwin's voice, but as she'd never heard it, raucous and distorted with shock.

A second bang split through her ears.

Emily dropped her tea. The near-boiling liquid leached through her slacks and attacked her legs with the bite of a thousand fire ants. Her mind scrambled to rationalize, to tell herself that what she'd heard could not be.

Get up, get up!

By some strength outside herself she shoved to her feet, stumbled around the end table, the couch. She raced across the shining parquet, nearly slipping, and jerked open the study door.

In a brain-searing instant, she took in the scene. Don, crumpled on the floor by his desk. Peter sprawled on the couch. Edwin on top of Bill Bland, her son fighting for his life.

Emily screamed.

"Mom, get away!"

Edwin's and Bill's hands flailed between their bodies, fighting over something. In the blur of movement, she couldn't see the object until it was knocked aside. *A gun!* It hit the floor with a dull thud, then spun. Bill's right hand scrabbled for it. Missed. Skittered again like a frenetic spider seeking prey, fingers closing around the barrel. He yanked the weapon up and smashed the butt end into Edwin's cheek.

"Aahh!" Edwin's face contorted, his hands flying toward the wound. Bill gave a mighty shove and pushed him off. Rising to a crouch, Bill scuttled for the door. Edwin caught him by an ankle, crashing him again to the floor. Bill's head hit the hardwood with a smack.

Emily melted away from him into the door frame.

Both dazed men lurched to their feet. Bill still held the gun by the barrel. Edwin lunged. With an awkward two-step, Bill swayed out of his reach and veered toward the door. His glazed eyes locked with Emily's, and in that split second she saw the fear in his murderous soul. He knew Edwin would kill him for what he'd done.

Before Edwin could launch again, Bill stumbled past Emily and through the hallway. He wrenched open the front door and pounded down the porch steps.

Edwin started after him.

"No!" Emily threw herself in his path. "He's got a gun!"

Her son hunched before her, breathing hard, indecision jagging furrows across his forehead. Outside, a car engine gunned. Tires squealed away. Edwin's shoulders sagged. He blinked once, twice, then turned toward his father. Grim resolve firmed his face. Together he and Emily staggered toward Don, sinking to their knees on either side of the still form. Emily had to shuffle backward as Edwin turned Don onto his back.

"Dad, Dad!" Edwin pushed fingers against

his father's neck, feeling for a pulse. A keen rose in Emily's throat. Blood stained the front of Don's shirt, a bullet hole over his heart.

"No, no, no, no, no," gurgled a voice that could not be her own, a voice that would leak from a drowning woman. Emily cast herself across her husband's chest.

"Mom, get back! Let me see if I can help him!"

Edwin pushed her shoulder, and she lifted away, hands up and trembling in the air. She waited for Don to say something, for his eyelids to flicker, for *something* to tell her he still lived. In vain Edwin again sought a pulse from his father's neck, his wrist. He grabbed his dad's face, fingers digging into the cheeks, and shook it.

"Dad! Come on, Dad, *come on!*"

Sobs gurgling in his throat, he tore open his father's dress shirt, popping the buttons. Deep red stained the T-shirt beneath. Edwin yanked it up, exposing a fatal wound. "No, no." He pressed his palm against it and rubbed, as if to erase it, erase the unthinkable events of the last two minutes.

It's so small. The thought echoed in Emily's head. *So small.* A wound this compact, this neat, could spill so much blood?

Could take away her husband, her life?

Edwin fell back on his haunches, blood on his hands. "He's gone." The words squeezed from his throat.

Emily blinked rapidly, trying to form words, to think. Cold acid dribbled through her veins, eating away her energy.

Edwin's chest heaved. He drew a palm across his mouth, smearing blood onto his mouth and chin. "I've got to . . . There's . . ."

Shaking his head, he pushed to his feet and made his way across the room. Emily crouched on the floor and hugged herself, dazed eyes following her son's movements toward Peter Dessinger. Peter slumped over on the couch, one hand trapped beneath his torso, the other dangling toward the floor. His neck twisted at an odd angle, his face half buried in the cushions.

He's dead too. The knowledge blew through Emily. *Don's dead. Peter's dead. Wade's dead.*

I'm dead.

Distantly, she watched Edwin ease Peter's body onto the floor, examine a bullet hole in the center of his forehead. Peter's eyes were wide open and fixed.

Nausea slimed into Emily's throat. She barely had time to turn her head away from Don before she threw up. When her stomach held nothing more, she dry heaved.

She could hear Edwin beating the floor with his fist, crying, "No, no." Then she sensed him pushing to his feet, his denials intensifying, anger mounting. Still she held her sides, jaw open and gagging. Edwin's cries churned into waves of rage that crashed him through the room, sweeping knickknacks off tables, throwing books, overturning a chair.

"I'll kill him!" A figurine smashed into a hundred pieces against the wall. "I'll *kill* him!"

Emily listed to one side, shrinking into herself. Trying to block out the guttural threats, the smell of vomit and blood. Through a blur she saw her son drag himself to the doorway of the study. "I'm going after him." The words cut from his throat.

"Edwin." Her voice shook, a mere whisper. "No."

"Call 911. I'm going after him."

"Edwin! *Don't!*"

Her son never looked back. He shoved himself over the study threshold and toward the open front door. Emily wailed as his footsteps slapped down the front sidewalk and melted into the dusk.

■ ■ ■ ■

TUESDAY, MAY 4

■ ■ ■ ■

CHAPTER 1

The grandfather clock chimed 1:00 P.M.

My visitors were all too prompt.

I stood in the great room of my executive-style log home, peering through an expansive window at the white Mercedes that had just pulled up to the curb. Pressing my knuckles into my chin, I watched the front car doors open. A man got out of the driver's seat. That would be Edwin. Midforties. Brown hair, slightly receding. My artist's eye took in the thick eyebrows, a strong nose. The natural upward curve of his lips, now weighted by downward furrows. From the passenger side emerged a stately looking woman in perhaps her late sixties. Her gray hair was well coiffed. She had a soft mouth and wide-set eyes. I saw little resemblance between mother and son. Perhaps Edwin looked more like his late father.

Falling into step side by side, they began a

purposeful walk toward my front door. Neither spoke.

I knew only a few details of what they wanted. These were enough to set me on edge.

With a deep breath I started toward the door.

"Mrs. Tarell." I forced a smile. "Mr. Tarell. Please come in."

"Thank you. Please call me Emily." The woman's voice poured over me like molasses, thick and sweet.

"And I'm Edwin." He shook my hand with the firm grip of a confident business-man. Seeing him up close, I thought him handsome in a melancholy sort of way. As if life had painted his features to profess the tragedy he'd seen. "You are so kind to see us on such short notice."

"Of course. And call me Annie, by the way." I gestured toward the couches and arm chair grouped around the massive rock fireplace. "My kids are at school so we can sit here. Would you like something to drink?"

"Oh, no, we're fine." Emily tipped her elegant head up, surveying the huge room and its twenty-five-foot ceiling. "Beautiful place you have. Absolutely beautiful. Have you been here long?"

"Only since last spring. My father had it built almost six years ago. My sister and I inherited it when he died unexpectedly. A heart attack."

Emily closed her eyes. "Oh, I'm sorry to hear that." Edwin murmured similar condolences.

As I nodded my thanks, Emily made her way to sit, straight-backed, on one of the oversized couches. Edwin waited as I chose the couch opposite Emily, a large, glass-topped coffee table between us. He sat in an armchair in the middle, facing the fireplace.

"Your children are how old?" Emily asked.

"Kelly's thirteen and Stephen's sixteen." I gave a little wince. "Two teenagers."

"Oh, boy, I remember those days. But you'll make it. We all do."

At the last comment her eyes drifted toward the fireplace, and I sensed she looked through a spiraling tunnel into the past.

"Mom?" Edwin's voice was gentle. "Do you want me to tell Ms. Kingston — Annie — why we're here?"

"No, no, I'll do it." Emily lifted her shoulders, suddenly all business. "I'd like to start at the beginning, if I may. So you can fully understand how important this is to me. First, as I told you on the phone, I've known of you since last summer, when all the news stories covered your daring face-off with that horrible murderer."

Face-off. Ironic way to put it.

"In the fall, Annie, I read the follow-up feature story about you — how through that experience you'd decided to become a forensic artist and were now taking classes. I was interested, you see, because in the back of my mind, my own plan was forming." Emily smoothed her skirt. "I told you that twenty years ago this spring my husband, Don — Edwin's father — was shot and killed. Along with his vice president, Peter Dessinger."

"Yes. I'm so sorry."

She nodded. "My husband was a keen-minded businessman. When we were newly married, he founded a small plastics manufacturing company. Over the years he built it into a very successful business — one he would pass on to his two sons. Since Don's death, Edwin has been running the company. He was very young when he took over so suddenly, but he's done well . . ." She glanced at Edwin.

"And your other son?"

Emily's mouthed pinched. "Our younger son, Wade, was killed in an auto accident shortly after his twenty-first birthday. Just a little over a year before Don died."

I swallowed, searching for an appropriate response. Losing a son and a husband in such a short span of time? I couldn't imagine the grief. Emily noted my stricken expression and gave me a sad smile.

Edwin looked at his hands. Even all these years later, he apparently found it difficult to watch his mother's pain.

"Peter Dessinger had been with Tarell Plastics for over fifteen years," Emily continued. "He and Don were not only business associates, they were the best of friends, and our families knew each other well. In 1980 Don hired a new chief financial officer who was quite young — only twenty-nine. This was the man I told you about over the phone. Bill Bland." Emily shook her head. "Can you believe a name like that? And he looked bland too. Average height and weight, light brown hair combed to one side. Glasses. Sort of a doughy face. Absolutely . . . banal. He had little sense of humor, few hobbies other than reading. He was very reserved, almost standoffish. In short, what one might consider a stereotypical accountant type."

Maybe, but he must have hidden a mind-boggling secret life. The stereotypical CFO didn't commit double homicide. I repressed a cringe. My overactive brain was already hurtling me down speculative paths. What would make a person like Bill Bland do what he did?

Edwin seemed to read my mind. "The man my father hired wasn't the same man I came to know. There was a dark side to Bill Bland. Even so, we never would have guessed what would happen. Not in a million years."

"People are often not what we think." I gave him a wry smile even as my ex-husband's face taunted my thoughts. Three years ago, out of the blue, Vic announced he was leaving me for someone named Sheryl — a girl much younger and prettier than I. Not in a million years would I have seen that coming.

Emily looked me in the eye as if sizing me up. For some reason she seemed to like what she saw. Maybe she'd made a fatal mistake about Bill Bland, but I sensed she still believed in her ability to judge people.

"So." She sighed. "Things went fine for the first three years. Then Bill began to have trouble at home. We didn't hear about it at first; he was so private. And when Susan, his wife, didn't show up for the company Christmas party, we believed his story that she needed to stay home with their sick one-year-old. But in time the truth started coming out. They were having trouble — real trouble. She'd left him for another man, who would soon be moving out of state. She'd taken the baby with her. By the spring she and Bill were divorced. Bill could hardly function. He loved his family deeply. I could almost say fiercely. Seemed to me he wanted to control his wife too much. And he was so meticulous, you see — every part of his life in a certain order. His work, his home, his finances. Now all was in shambles."

Edwin rubbed the arm of his chair — an unconscious gesture of concentration that I could imagine him making as he solved problems at work. "Bill was a control freak, all right. I knew him better than Mom did. Still, he was very private in a lot of ways. Later I learned from Susan that Bill didn't have the money to buy out her half of their house. And he really wanted to stay in that house."

"And he faced monthly expenses of alimony and child care," Emily added. "Susan was cunning, not planning to marry her new man, so the alimony would keep flowing."

That hit home. Sheryl had been cunning in her own way. Later I realized how she'd set her sights on Vic the moment she met him. Bill Bland, like I, had been left adrift, a castaway on a bleak and rugged island. *He'd* even had his child taken . . .

Watch it, Annie.

Ambivalence weighed my thoughts in equal balances. If the Tarells' request proved what I expected, such empathetic thoughts about this murderer would be necessary. But oh, so uncomfortable. Not that it mattered. I wouldn't accept their assignment.

Emily lifted a hand from her lap. "Of course, these are only our assumptions as to why he embezzled the money. We never did get a full explanation from him."

"Because he fled, you mean."

"Well —" Edwin's fingers now drummed the chair arm — "that's true. But he said enough that night when we confronted him about the money. So I'd say it's more than just assumptions." He drew a breath. "I think my mother told you I was in the room that night my father and Peter were killed. See, I worked for the company in the finance department. I was the one who discovered the missing funds in the first place. It was clear to me from the beginning there was only one person who could have done it."

Emily made a little sound in her throat. "And of course after . . . everything happened, and the detectives looked into the business side of things, the trail was very clear. It led straight to Bill's personal checking account, if you can imagine the stupidity of that."

She fell silent, fiddling with the hem of her skirt. For a moment, none of us spoke.

Emily looked up abruptly. "Tell me, Annie, about the forensic art courses you've been taking."

I blinked at the change in subject. "Okay."

I'd been fortunate that quite a number of courses were available in the past school year. I explained to Emily and Edwin that through various institutions such as the Scottsdale Artists' School in Arizona and Sam Houston State University in Texas, I'd taken weeklong workshops, including introduction to forensic art, basic and advanced facial reconstruction sculpture, comprehensive composite drawing, understanding the human face, the aging process, and advanced two-dimensional identification techniques. Many of the basic drawing concepts were already familiar to me, since I'd majored in art and had ten years' experience as a courtroom artist, but I wanted to start my new career from the beginning.

"That's a lot of time away from home and your children."

31

"Yes. But I have a terrific sister. Jenna. She loves to boss me around. She had a lot to do with pushing me into this field in the first place. So when I need someone to stay with the kids, I sort of . . . remind her of that."

Mild amusement played over Emily's lips. "Serves her right."

"Certainly does."

The grandfather clock bonged 1:30. Emily pulled in a breath. Her gaze lingered upon the clock, making me think of the painstaking passage of time during the last twenty years. Every day, week, month, spent healing from grief meant an equal time of Don Tarell's murderer evading justice.

"Do you believe in God, Annie?" Emily turned her eyes back on me.

Well. How was *that* for an unexpected question? I looked to Edwin, who turned his eyes away. Evidently, he'd leave any personal probings to his mother. For a moment I considered sloughing off the inquiry, but something in Emily's eyes stopped me.

"Yes."

"Good. And do you believe He wants to lead our lives?"

I hesitated. Did Emily somehow sense my private soul-searching? Surely she couldn't know. A year ago I would not have hesitated to answer her question with a no. But a year ago was before my neighbor Lisa was killed, before The Face.

Before my promise to God, made out of sheer desperation, to seek Him.

"Well —" I searched for the right words — "I've been going to church this year and . . . learning things. The people there certainly seem to think that God wants to lead us."

She studied me, no doubt wondering at my evasive answer. "I believe that too." Her words were quiet but firm. "And I don't mean to scare you or put you off, but I do think He's led me here today. To you."

I could find no response. Edwin studied the floor.

Emily shifted, crossing her ankles. "For twenty years, Annie, I've prayed for justice concerning my husband's and Peter's murders. Twenty long years. All this time Bill Bland has been a fugitive. Hard to believe that he could just disappear into thin air, but he has. Over the years the trail has grown cold. The case is still open, but the Shasta County Sheriff's Department hasn't been actively looking for him. Now we're approaching a major anniversary. I'd been praying for a way to put the case before the public again, and God answered my prayer. Most creatively, I must say. As I mentioned on the phone, *American Fugitive* wants to run the story of the murders — with an updated sketch of Bill Bland. That's where you come in."

Edwin raised his eyes to my face. I worked to keep my expression from sagging. I'd guessed right: they wanted me to create the adult age progression; specifically, a fugitive update. An update of twenty years. In my studies of forensic art in the past year, this kind of assignment was the one I'd hoped never to receive.

"Annie? You're awfully quiet."

I laced my fingers and squeezed. I would not relish disappointing this woman. Or Edwin. "Do you realize what's involved in a fugitive update?"

Emily lifted a shoulder. "I know you have to understand how the face ages. Which would require knowledge of facial anatomy and how it changes. But you've studied that, haven't you?"

"Yes. But I have to be honest with you, it's not the anatomy part that bothers me. It's the *inside* part."

Her eyebrows knit.

"I'd have to study the suspect, Emily. I'd

have to learn everything I could about him. His genetic background. His habits, his facial expressions, how he eats, how he moves. How he *thinks*. All these things determine how a face ages. For instance, his eating habits affect how much weight he'll gain. Certain facial expressions, like squinting, will affect how wrinkles appear."

Edwin nodded slowly. "I see. You said you *would* have to learn these things. As if . . . you won't?"

I tipped my head toward the ceiling. How to explain to these strangers that my stubborn, independent brain made me the worst possible candidate for such a task? My mind ran its own movie projector on a daily basis, envisioning in screaming color any stray thought that ventured its way. I could only imagine the insanity it would wreak upon me if I embarked on this assignment. The deeper I dug into understanding Bill Bland and his murderous brain, the more I would "see" every picture in my head. I'd play captive audience to his abandonment by his wife. To his heart-banging fear at his first stealing of the company's money. To the black and desperate moment of his decision to kill.

"You fear — how to put it — descending

into the mind of a murderer. Is that right?" The worry lines in Emily's forehead deepened. "I do imagine that would be a frightening proposition. But isn't this what you're training for?"

"Yes, but there are all kinds of assignments in forensic art. Drawing composites, aging children who have been missing, reconstructing skulls. I'm training for all of them, but it's just this one —"

"Please." Emily held up her hand. "Please just think about it. We don't need your answer right this moment. Although we do need it very soon." She pressed two fingers against her mouth. "What do I have to say to convince you?"

I sought diversion in details. "Why are *you* asking me to do this? Shouldn't someone from *American Fugitive* be choosing the artist?"

"Normally, no doubt." Edwin's hand lifted from the chair arm, then began drumming again. "But —"

"This is where God's answer to my prayers comes in." Emily leaned forward. "Sharon Dessinger, Peter's wife? She moved back east years ago. Her daughter, Stacey, lives in New York. Last Christmas Stacey finally began dating again — five years after a messy divorce. And who does she end up going out with? A man who writes for *American Fugitive.* Now you see why I cannot think of this as mere coincidence. Neither can Sharon. This show was her idea."

It *was* quite amazing. *American Fugitive* had a track record of success that would make even the most cool-minded criminal on the lam lose sleep. In the past ten years the series had seen hundreds of murderers, rapists, burglars, and con men brought to justice. If an on-target drawing of Bill Bland was televised on the show, he most likely would be caught.

Had God opened this door for Sharon and the Tarells?

"But why me? Why doesn't the show pick someone in New York?"

Emily smiled. "Because you're *here.* Right near the Shasta County Sheriff's Department, which handled the case. You've even worked with detectives in that office. They'll trust you with the whole file. You can go over it, read it, absorb it —"

She pulled back, mouth closing, as if realizing she'd used the wrong word.

"Plus —" she raised her chin — "you have easy access to the people you'd need to interview — people who knew Bill Bland.

Edwin would be a good place to start."

"I see." I looked from Emily to her son. "It does make sense that you have someone local — and I'm about the only forensic artist around. But I'm afraid I'm not qualified to take on such a major assignment yet."

Since my first case last summer of drawing The Face, when I wasn't even a forensic artist, I'd completed five other sketches of suspects in the Redding area, mostly for small-scale robberies. A grand total of six — a far cry from the minimum twenty-five needed to be certified even at Level I. And this bereaved widow and fatherless man wanted my work to be on a national television show?

"Annie." Emily's voice firmed. "You're qualified. You handled that case last summer like you'd been doing it for years."

That was a laugh. If she only knew half of what I went through.

"Well, I . . . thank you for your confidence." How lame my words sounded.

"Nothing to thank me for. You've earned it." She patted both palms against her thighs. "All right then. It doesn't seem there's any more that we can say. Edwin, do you have anything?"

He cleared his throat. "No. Well, yes." He cupped his hands, resting both elbows on the arm of the chair. "Let me be honest with you, Annie. I sense your hesitation. I just ask that you not start this unless you think you can do it successfully. My mother has been through enough, and I don't want her disappointed."

"Oh, Edwin." Emily frowned at him, then fixed me with a determined look. "You'll have to forgive my son; the executive in him is coming out. I'll be disappointed if you *don't* do this. Very disappointed. Because I know you can, Annie. And I know you're God's answer to my prayers. To put an end to this . . . purgatory of waiting. To finally see justice done." Her voice dropped. "And I'll tell you this plainly. If ever you'll be given a case that demands justice more loudly, I'll be surprised."

She held my gaze as I absorbed her words. Emily seemed to know she'd found the point of my weakness. In my darkest moments of pursuing The Face, only my strong desire for bringing Lisa Willit's killer to justice had kept me going. I couldn't let Dave and Erin Willit down. And every day I spotted them now in their yard across the street, every time Erin came over to see Kelly, I felt a satisfaction in the depth of my being. Despite the danger I'd encountered,

I'd made the right choice.

"One thing," I hedged. "You can't even know if Bill Bland is still alive."

"True." Edwin dipped his head.

His mother lifted a hand. "If he's not, I'd like to find that out. We'd still need your drawing to do that."

My drawing.

My heart panged. I so wanted to help these people. If I was in a position to bring an end to their purgatory, why shouldn't I? Focusing on the circular oak stairway across the great room, I thought of my own losses — Vic and our marriage; my father's sudden death; Lisa's murder; my son's rebellion and drugs.

"Emily, what would be the timeline for this assignment?"

She raised her brows. "I'll admit time is tight. Sharon received a late go-ahead for the show, and the drawing has to be done in a few weeks." She shook her head. "All the more reason, Annie, that you are the person for this job. Besides, you've got the talent to do it quickly, and more important, you've got the heart. Yes, I know about your way with people and your tenacity. I talked to Detective Ralph Chetterling at the Sheriff's Department before coming here. He assured me you'd accept the assignment.

And that you'd succeed."

Oh, really. How presumptuous of Chetterling!

But I could not dwell on that. Instead, I wondered at the man's confidence in me. How could I tell the Tarells no when he'd given me such rave reviews? Even if they were undeserved.

I stared at my feet, Sharon's and Edwin's request sucking at me like quicksand. I wanted to help. But I so feared the process of creating a fugitive update. How had Emily put it? *Descending into the mind of a murderer.* I did not welcome such a descent.

"Okay, tell you what." I spoke the words to the floor. "I'll . . . think about it and give you a call tonight or tomorrow. How's that?"

A tired smile creased Emily's face. "I suppose that's all we can ask. Thank you." She rose, Edwin doing the same. "Don't worry about your fears, Annie. If you take this on — *when* you take it on — I will pray for you. God has helped me through the last twenty years. He'll see you through this."

Descending into the mind . . .

A shiver snaked down my spine.

If I took on this assignment, I'd need all the prayers Emily Tarell could muster.

■ ■ ■ ■

THURSDAY, MAY 6

■ ■ ■ ■

CHAPTER 2

Three boxes of copied files. I slumped in my office chair and stared at them, lined up like sentinels upon the area rug.

At the moment I'd term my situation anything but an answer to someone's heartfelt prayers. This wasn't God's doing. It was all Ralph Chetterling's fault.

Yesterday, after a night of tossing and turning over my decision, I'd paid a visit to the Sheriff's Office in Redding. Just to talk to Chetterling. Ask him why on earth he'd been so confident about me to Emily Tarell. Well, now, and hadn't the detective acted like he'd expected my visit? He proved downright jovial, which was hardly the Chetterling I knew. The man stands six-foot-three, towering over my five-foot-five frame, with huge hands and small dark brown eyes. At one time he'd intimidated the daylights out of me. I've worked with him enough by now to get over most of that, but still, Chetterling is Chetterling: no nonsense, pulsing with authority.

"Annie, what's the matter with you?" He folded his arms and looked down his nose at me. "It never occurred to me you wouldn't want this assignment. One year's training as a forensic artist, and nothing less than *American Fugitive* lands in your lap?"

"Ralph, it's not the show that bothers me, it's the assignment! You know how sensitive to people I am. The last thing I want to do is get under the skin of some cold-blooded killer. The very thought gives me the creeps."

He shot me a look. "The last thing I'd expect from you — sensitive, caring Annie Kingston — is to turn down a request from someone who really needs you. How could you say no to Emily Tarell?"

I glared back at him. Clearly, I'd have to change my tactics. "For your information, I really would like to say yes. But I'm just not ready. I need more training."

He pulled his law-enforcement stance on me — hands on hips, legs spread apart. "Care to try again?"

I looked up at him, my shoulders slumping. He was almost as bad as my sister. But not quite. Even with all his bulk, Chetterling couldn't match Jenna's bullheaded bossiness. When I'd called her the previous night about my predicament, she'd done everything but crawl through the phone line and force my fingers to dial Emily Tarell's number on the spot.

The world was pitted against me. As I faced Chetterling, all remaining argument died in my throat.

"Oh, Ralph." I summoned my most plaintive expression. "I'm going to hate myself in the morning."

He smiled with slow satisfaction. "No, you won't. And I predict, when this case is all over, your career will never be the same."

Chetterling insisted that I call Emily Tarell from his office before I changed my mind. Emily responded with a simple, "I knew you'd say yes. I've been praying."

Then, with an air of victory he couldn't hide, Chetterling led me straightaway to Sheriff's Sergeant Justin Delft, who'd been one of the detectives called to the scene of the Tarell/Dessinger murders in 1984. Delft was ecstatic about the upcoming *American Fugitive* show. He wanted nothing more before he retired than to close the case that had plagued him for two decades. Delft went through the bureaucratic procedure of releasing the files of the case to me. We agreed that I would take a full day to read through everything before meeting with him for an interview.

So here I sat in my office, the three boxes of files mocking me. Why had I gotten myself into this?

I could not put off opening the first box any longer.

Pushing to my feet, I lugged the box marked #1 off the rug and onto the desk that had once been my father's. Only in recent months had I been able to think of it as mine. It looked the same as it had when my father used it. The rest of the room had changed considerably, however. Gone were the couch and end tables, the pictures on the wall of airplanes, and the tall wooden file cabinet. I'd replaced them with a drawing table, a pair of squat, three-drawer cabinets to hold my art supplies, and a montage of scenery photos. In case I ever again interviewed a victim in this office, as I'd done with Erin Willit, I could not hang pictures of people on the wall. Someone trying to recall the face of a suspect could be influenced by the features of others.

I opened the box. "Read them in order," Delft had told me, "starting with Emily and Edwin Tarell's statements. You'll get the best picture of what happened that way."

That's what I was afraid of.

But I had the perfect excuse to put off my reading for another minute or two. First I wanted a good look at Bill Bland. I sifted through the files until I found a picture of him blown up to a grainy eight-by-ten.

So this is the man.

I stared at the photo for a long time, pulling in every detail. He did look bland. His hair was medium thickness, parted on the left and cut above the ears. He wore black-framed glasses. His eyes, a sort of dull gray, were small and rounded. Was he near- or farsighted? If the former, his lenses would make his eyes appear smaller than normal.

"Doughy," Emily had described him, and she was right. Little definition to the jawline, a soft chin, although he did not appear overweight. He reminded me of an unfinished clay sculpture, the artist called away before its final shaping. His lips were fairly thin, with the slightest downturn at the edges. He had not smiled for the picture. His suit jacket was dark blue over a white shirt and solid dark maroon tie. About as conservative as one could imagine.

Bill Bland looked harmless. Even his photo exuded a reserved, quiet personality.

Yet the longer I gazed at it, the more I sensed a certain . . . essence. What was it?

Something about the way he looked at the camera, his chin raised a little too high, one eyebrow lifted ever so slightly.

Arrogance. That was it. A preoccupation with his own intelligence.

What do you look like today, Bill Bland? Why hasn't anyone been able to find you?

I turned the questions over in my mind, imagining the pull of two decades upon his skin and eyes, the deepening nasolabial furrows — "laugh lines" — from the nose to the outside of his lips . . .

Okay. Enough of this, Annie. Time to read.

I took a deep breath and pulled out the top file, marked *Emily Tarell.*

Within minutes I found myself immersed in Emily's description of her unsettling premonition that fateful night as the four men met in her husband's study. On cue, the ever-present movie projector in my brain whirred into gear, translating the flat words on paper into a vivid scene. I visualized Emily making a cup of tea, sitting down to drink it — waiting. How the shots had rung out. The fight she'd witnessed after stumbling into the study. Wailing over her husband's body. Retching . . .

Oh, Emily.

The torment of her emotions battered my

heart. I leaned back in my chair, eyes closed. Emily's story was too real, too raw. Different, certainly, from the circumstances Erin had faced when her mother was killed in their home, but all too reminiscent of the shock and fear.

It was a good thing ten months had passed since Lisa's murder. If it were any more recent, I wouldn't have been able to deal with the emotions this new case was sure to bring.

Five minutes passed before I forced myself to reach for the file on Edwin Tarell — the interview that would contain details of what had transpired in that study as the four men met. Slowly, I opened the folder.

"It's all my fault!"

Right at the top Detective Delft had recorded these words: *"It's all my fault; it's all my fault!"*

My eyes closed again. I pictured a much younger Edwin, crying those words.

Edwin told the detective that he, his dad, and Peter had met at his parents' house a half hour before Bill was scheduled to come over. Peter came directly from work. Edwin made a quick stop at his own town house and then headed to the home in which he'd grown up. The moment Bill appeared at the door, Edwin felt sure the man knew something was up. He could see how stiffly Bill moved, how both elbows hovered away from his sides.

"Bill has this weird tic of jutting his chin upward in two rapid jerks, then letting it sink," Edwin told the detective. "When he's nervous or stressed it gets worse."

Jutting his chin upward. I wrote that down in my notes. Would Bill still have that tic today? How might that affect how his features had aged?

I looked back to the file. Edwin had described to Delft every detail, including his own thoughts as he reacted to Bill Bland. In no time I again was sucked into the vortex of the story, the movie camera in my mind beginning to whir. Vividly, I pictured Bill Bland through Edwin's eyes,

standing in the foyer, his chin jutting and sinking. Bill still wears his suit. Edwin, his dad, and Peter have their jackets off, ties loosened, as they often do at work. But Bill never takes his jacket off. Edwin once teased him that he slept in it.

Bill's so precise about everything. So finicky.

"Come in, Bill." Edwin's dad does not even attempt a smile. He still can hardly believe the news Edwin brought to him and Peter the

previous week. Neither can Edwin. Not even when the proof in the books stares them right in the face.

"Thank you." Bill nods. So formal, like a stranger. Like he's already pulled back from them emotionally, knowing what he's about to do. Edwin will think of this only later, wonder why he didn't see what was coming, why he didn't know. Peter says nothing, slipping into the study behind Dad and Bill like some funeral home attendant.

Edwin's stomach flutters. Maybe he shouldn't have told them. Maybe he should have just confronted Bill on his own, made him give back the money.

But then what? Say nothing and let Bill keep working at the company he's stolen from? The company Edwin will own one day?

Bill hesitates, then lowers himself to the edge of an armchair. Peter takes the couch on Bill's left, perpendicular to the chair. Edwin wanders over to the fireplace, opposite Bill, and leans against the mantel. Out of habit his dad makes for the desk but stops in front of it, knuckles rapping against the wood.

No one speaks. Bill swallows, and his throat clicks.

Edwin's dad pushes away from the desk,

faces his chief financial officer. "I'll get right to the point, Bill. We know what you've been doing. We've seen the books, and there's no use denying it. We've spent the last week trailing the money — almost half a million. The trail led to an account you opened at the Huntington Bank three months ago. When I talked to the bank president — someone I happen to know — he only went so far as to confirm that you'd opened the account. He wouldn't show us the statements without a police warrant. Bill, we're willing to bet the money's there, and we've got plenty reason to go to the police right now. But before we do that we wanted to talk to you first, give you a chance to explain. Peter and Edwin are here as my witnesses. I'm asking you — is our company money in that account?"

Bill flicks his eyes at Edwin, then to the floor. His fingers fumble with the hem of his jacket. "Yes. Some of it."

Edwin's dad sags against the desk. Bill's uneven breathing fills the room.

"Why, Bill, why did you do it?" Peter's voice thickens.

Bill works his jaw. When he speaks, the words are barely audible. "I was trapped. Susan took everything in the divorce. I needed money fast to buy out her half of the house or I'd have to sell it — the last thing I could call mine. And I didn't know where I'd get the money to pay for child support and alimony. So I took a little. And then it was so easy, I just . . . kept taking it."

Disgust burns in Edwin's throat. The guy is a cheating, whiny weasel. A coward. Can't even look them in the eye. Edwin knew he would crumble the minute he was confronted. Bill lacks the imagination to be a good liar.

"I'd have lent you money. I'd have done anything to help you." Grief crosshatches Edwin's dad's face until Edwin can't bear to look at him.

Bill's right hand works up to his jacket buttons. "I'm . . . sorry."

Hours from then, when it is far too late, Edwin will remember the way Bill says those words. The way they squeeze out of his throat. Like he isn't only apologizing for what he's done but for what he's going to do.

Edwin's dad shakes his head. "We demand the money back immediately. And you're out of the company as of this minute. Even with that, Bill, we'll have to go to the police. This is just too big to let —"

That's when it happens — those few sec-

55

onds of stunning sequence that will last a lifetime. Edwin keeps his eyes on Bill as his dad speaks. Bill unbuttons his jacket. Reaches into an inside pocket as he pushes from the chair and pulls out something. Something black, metallic. Edwin's eyes see it, and his shocked brain scrambles to interpret, but it is slow, too slow. Bill raises the thing and points it at Peter.

Gun, it's a gun! Edwin's mind shrieks, but there's no time to do anything. An explosion rips the room. Peter never makes a sound. He just falls over on the couch.

Edwin's jaw drops open to yell, but his throat closes up. The world grinds into a strange, slow gear like it's tilting the wrong way on its axis. And then that gun starts to move through the air, rotate right toward Edwin. Bill is turning, turning, the barrel aiming at the table lamp, and then the wall, and then the mantel and then Edwin's chest. I'm dead, Edwin thinks, but then the gun keeps moving. Past him, to the end of the mantel, Bill's feet pivoting, turning that deadly weapon toward Edwin's dad.

"No!" The scream rips Edwin's throat like a jagged knife. His body shudders into motion, feet running, arms outstretched. He runs a *step and the gun turns; runs a step and the gun turns.*

Boom! Edwin's dad falls. Edwin sees this from the corner of his eye as he is launching toward Bill —

My office phone rang. I nearly jumped out of my skin.

Half focusing on the file before me, I hovered in two worlds. My mind rushed with Edwin to tackle Bill Bland while my hand slowly lifted from the desk. I blinked a couple of times, then picked up the receiver.

"Hello?"

"Annie. You sound like you just saw a ghost."

It was Jenna. "Oh, hi. Yeah. Maybe I did."

"What are you doing?"

I told her.

"Oh." She hesitated. "Is it as bad as you thought?"

"Worse. And I haven't even begun to learn about Bill Bland yet."

"Think positive thoughts, Annie. Think your name on *American Fugitive*."

"Think my body in the mental ward."

Jenna sighed. Which spoke volumes. Although seven years younger than I, my sister possessed two lifetimes' worth of extra gumption. And she'd used it too — to run my life whenever she considered I wasn't doing such a hot job of it. Which was often. I'd told Emily Tarell the truth — I *did* have Jenna to thank for pushing me into forensic art. Although I'd bolstered my dignity by pretending to have made the decision entirely on my own.

I'd come a long way in the self-confidence department during the last ten months. Even Jenna couldn't deny that. Still, it would be years before I caught up to her.

"So, Jenna, what's up?"

"First things first. You didn't know it was me calling, did you?"

"No."

"Uh-huh. Which means you still haven't gone out and bought new phones so you can hook up to caller ID. And I'll bet you haven't taken the time to make your phone number unlisted yet."

I winced. Great, here we went again. My know-it-all sister had caught me red-handed. "Um, no, but I really was planning on —"

"Annie, you've been *planning* on it for months. What are you waiting for?"

"Well, nothing's happening now; I haven't had a reporter bother me in months." Since last fall, to be exact.

"Doesn't matter. In the line of work you're in, I just don't think you should be listed. After all —"

"Okay, okay, I get your point. You're right, as always. I'll do it, okay?"

"Promise?"

"Promise."

Wonderful. I'd now lost all concentration on the Edwin Tarell file. "Did you call just to bug me about this, Jenna?"

She made a sound in her throat. "No, you ingrate. I just wanted you to know I have a heavy project to finish here so I may not be flying up this weekend."

Last summer Jenna had been laid off from her job in the marketing department of a Silicon Valley software company. After a month of floundering, she'd decided to do consulting on her own.

"You could work from here."

"I'd rather not."

"Why? You worried about flight time? In that plane of yours it takes less than an hour to get here."

"It's not that. It's just that there's . . . too much going on there. I need peace and quiet."

Oh. Now I got it. Translation: *your rebellious son really gets on my nerves, and I don't want to be around him right now.* This was understandable. Stephen got on my nerves too. In fact, if I managed to raise my first-born without killing him, I'd be most surprised.

"Okay, Jenna, I understand. But if you change your mind, just let me know."

Jenna had her own room, of course — the master suite — so it really didn't make a difference whether she came or not. Even though I was the one who lived in Grove Landing full time, I'd chosen the end suite upstairs so I could be next to Kelly's room.

"Sure. Thanks for understanding. And, Annie, I know you're going to be working on that case. If it gets too tough for you, call me, okay?"

I promised I would.

As I hung up the phone my eyes were already drifting back to the file.

Soon I was reading how Edwin tackled Bill Bland and fought to knock the gun out of his hand. How his mother had run into the study as they were fighting. I couldn't help shifting for a moment to Emily's emotions as Edwin described running after Bland. How terrible for her to be left with the bodies of two men as Edwin disappeared into the dusk. How she must have despaired, having lost first a son the previous year, and now her husband. For all she knew at that moment, the second son would also be killed — or kill in revenge and end up in prison.

I looked back to the detective's notes of Edwin's story as he gunned his car in pursuit of Bland.

"I wasn't completely aware of what I was doing," Edwin admits. His mind seems to hover on some other plane as he drives around and around, searching vainly for Bill. He can't even tell the detective how long he was gone. He does remember some of the places he looked — the offices of Tarell Plastics; Bill's house; the apartment where his estranged wife, Susan, and his baby now live; parking lots. Edwin rushes from one location to another, not even stopping to tell a bewildered Susan why he's come wild-eyed and banging on her door.

He doesn't see one trace of Bill, not one hint of where the traitor could be.

At some point Edwin comes to his senses, remembering his mother at the house, the two bodies on the floor. Detectives will be there by now, asking questions. His mother will need him.

Edwin races back to his parents' home only to be hit with another shock. In her stunned state, his mom has spent all that time tending to his dad's body — and hasn't called 911. *What if Bill Bland has fled the town by now? Edwin runs to the phone to report the crime. "Hurry!" he pleads to the maddeningly calm voice on the other end. "You have to find him before it's too late!"*

Sergeant Delft's report of Edwin's first interview ended there.

I leaned my head back against my chair, staring at the high-beamed ceiling. Wondering about Edwin Tarell's emotions as year after year passed and his father's murderer remained free. Did he ever wish he'd found Bill Bland that night? That he'd killed the man himself?

Wouldn't that thought cross my mind, if I were in his shoes?

I stood and stretched, trying to clear my head a little before turning to the next file. Perhaps that more technical one — Sergeant Delft's report of the crime scene — wouldn't whir my mental projector into such high gear. Arching my shoulders, I gazed out my office window, my thoughts drifting to Bill Bland. There were so many questions that needed answering before I could understand this man. Why had he shown up at the Tarell house that night in the first place? Why hadn't he just skipped town without resorting to murder? What inherent personality weakness would push a seemingly nonviolent person over the edge like that?

Where had he gone when he fled the Tarell house?

And where on earth had he been for twenty years?

FRIDAY, MAY 7

Friday Maze

CHAPTER 3

The air in Sergeant Delft's office seemed to hum with a low-charged electricity. I hesitated in the doorway, wondering at the sensation. Was it from my own nervousness in pursuing this case? For the second night in a row I hadn't slept well. After reading the case files, I'd been plagued with disjointed dreams about the murders, playing in my head like worn-out film.

But no. What I sensed did not emanate from me. The charge in this room was an expectation. And it bristled from Sergeant Delft.

He invited me to sit down in a straight-backed wooden chair, then plunked his body with toned precision in a matching one behind his battered desk.

Justin Delft was a broad-shouldered man who reminded me of a Marine drill sergeant, right down to the crew cut hair and permanent frown. According to Detective

Chetterling, Delft prided himself on his long record of success with the Shasta County Sheriff's Department. For over thirty years his life and identity had been his work. Only one thing marred his career: his failure to capture Bill Bland. Now, seven months before his retirement, he'd been given a final chance. Serendipity had raised her captivating head in the form of a nationally televised show that had brought many criminals to justice.

Apprehension thrummed through me as I took my seat. For all my reading the previous day, I felt no closer to understanding Bill Bland. I fervently hoped my interviews, starting with Sergeant Delft, would provide answers to my nagging questions. Delft's obvious anticipation only heightened the stakes. Twenty years of this man's frustration. Not to mention twenty years of deprived justice for the Tarells and Sharon Dessinger. And the success of the *American Fugitive* show now rested on one thing: my fugitive update of Bill Bland.

"You read the files?" Sergeant Delft sat stiff spined, his gaze piercing.

"Yes. It took me most of yesterday." I opened my notebook. "I made notes here to ask you about. As I mentioned when you gave me the files, I need to understand everything I can about Bill Bland so I can age him accurately."

"Yes. Understood. Fire away."

"Okay." For a moment I wondered where to begin. "First, the crime scene. I went over everything you found, but I'd like to hear your overall . . . feeling about it."

"It was trashed, that's how I felt about it. Mrs. Tarell and her son couldn't have done a better job of messing it up if they'd tried." Delft narrowed his eyes at the wall behind me, as if reliving the moment. "The bodies had been moved. The murder weapon was gone. 'Course that wasn't their fault. Mrs. Tarell, in her shock, had felt compelled to straighten the room. People do that sometimes, you know, executing what control of the situation they can find. A form of self-preservation. She'd covered her husband with a throw blanket from the couch — not his head, but the rest of his body, like he was merely sleeping. Denial, you understand. She'd cleaned up her own vomit. She was even cleaning up blood when we arrived."

I winced. "What specifically had she straightened?"

"Things Edwin had thrown. Worse, the chair where Bill Bland sat. Edwin and Bill crashed into it when they fought. I asked

Mrs. Tarell to put it back the way she'd found it. She'd also reset the pillows on the couch where Mr. Dessinger had been."

"And the blood?"

"All the blood spray from Peter Dessinger was intact. I'm sure you read that in the notes — how it was on the back of the couch and on the floor behind the couch, extending out quite a few feet. This was all consistent with Edwin's account of where Bill Bland stood when he pulled the trigger. We determined this by following the trajectory of the bullet. But Mrs. Tarell saw to her husband before covering him with the blanket. As I recall, some of his blood seeped onto it, so we included the blanket with the items we took from the room as evidence. Before covering him she'd wiped the blood from his chest, rearranged his shirt. We had a time pulling her away from the body."

"And —" I consulted my notes — "as best you can figure it was about forty minutes before Edwin came back and called 911?"

"Yes. I remember these details like it was yesterday. The meeting started at eight o'clock. Within ten minutes Dessinger and Tarell were dead. Approximately five minutes after that, Edwin ran out. The call came in at 8:57 P.M."

"I'm really surprised Emily Tarell didn't call 911 in all that time."

Delft raised his shoulder. "Well, no doubt it was a terrible mistake. Who knows, we might have caught Bland if that many minutes hadn't been wasted. But all Mrs. Tarell could do at the time was cope. If you'd seen her, you'd understand. She was completely beside herself. She'd lost a son, you know, a little over a year before that. Now her husband was dead, and her only other son was likely either to kill or be killed. That house is five miles outside of Redding — which is why it's in our jurisdiction rather than the police — but we were there within minutes of Edwin's call."

Defensiveness edged the sergeant's final comment. Clearly, he did not doubt he and his men had done all they could, under the circumstances.

I nodded. "You mentioned the gun. A . . ." I tried to remember the make. It was the same type my sister owned, only bigger. I knew very little of guns, although after my experience with The Face, I'd vowed to learn to shoot someday.

"From the bullets we could tell it was a four-inch Smith & Wesson thirty-eight special. Common weapon, easy to buy and learn to use."

"Did Bland get it legally?"

"Apparently not."

I thought about that. How would a man like Bill Bland know where to buy an illegal handgun? "Did anyone else around him, like the Tarells or the Dessingers or other friends, own a gun like that? Maybe he stole it?"

"Not that we know about. And we did pursue it. But in the end we didn't make it a priority to look for the source of the weapon. We had to spend all our manpower — and then some — looking for Bland himself."

I made a note. "Okay. I need to turn now to Bill Bland. Mostly I need to understand why he did this. I'm confused on numerous points. First, it seems to me from Edwin's statements that Bland came to the Tarells' house knowing he would kill. He was carrying the gun, and he certainly didn't hesitate to whip it out the minute he confessed to the embezzlement."

Sergeant Delft leaned forward, placing his forearms on the desk. "Actually no. I don't think he went to that meeting *knowing* he would kill. He did go with plans to kill if, in his criminal eyes, it became necessary. His 'plan of necessity,' as we could call it, also included withdrawing all the stolen money from the bank account before the meeting — in case he had to flee. And apparently figuring out an escape route."

I considered this. "Then what made the murders necessary?"

"You said it yourself. He shot those two men right after he was confronted with his embezzlement."

"But why? If he thought he was about to be caught for stealing, why didn't he run *before* the meeting?"

A slow exhale seeped from Delft's throat. "*That,* Ms. Kingston, is the sixty-four-thousand-dollar question. To understand the answer, you must understand Bill Bland's mind. And when you understand Bill Bland's mind, you will see what a truly chilling foe we are up against."

A frisson nibbled my shoulders. "I'm listening."

Delft leaned back in his chair. "On the surface, Bill Bland was a quiet, mild-mannered number cruncher. But underneath that persona lay a combination of weaknesses that would break him apart and prove fatal. Like a double fault line."

What had Edwin said? *The man my father*

hired was not the man I came to know. "Edwin referred to him as a control freak."

"Right. Edwin can tell you more about that. I assume you'll be talking to him again."

"Oh yes. I plan to interview him next."

"Good. Talk to Bill's ex-wife too. Her contact information is in the files. Susan and Edwin were the ones who saw the other side of Bland. Yes, he was calm and quiet, but only as long as he was in control. When he felt pushed, stressed, when he felt control slipping away, it would so upset him that he would change. He would do anything to regain control of the situation. Where he would typically plan things out well, he could become impulsive, make stupid choices. Where he was typically mild mannered and predictable, he would become angry and unpredictable. As Susan said to me, 'It's like Bill was two different people.' "

Two different people. The thought made me uneasy. I wrote down the words and circled them.

"Another thing you might remember from the files, Bland had one hobby — reading. Remember what he read?"

"Yes. Murder mysteries."

He nodded. "Exclusively. Bland owned

every Agatha Christie ever printed. And many of the well-known and not-so-well-known mystery novelists since then. Susan told us Bland would read every night after work for about an hour, no matter what time he got home. And the folks at Tarell Plastics worked late. On weekends he might read a complete novel. Mysteries were the one thing he'd consistently spend his money on. No library books for him; he wanted to *own* 'em. When we went through his house, I was amazed. They were lined up, shelf after shelf, alphabetized by author. Then even the ones by the same author were in order according to title."

I wrote in my notebook. "So you think he was gathering data as he read? About murder and detective work?"

Sergeant Delft shrugged. "I think he read for pleasure. But you're right — all that information sifted into his brain. So when he found himself in potential trouble, he turned to what he'd been steeping himself in all along: how to commit a murder and vanish into thin air."

I bit my lip, thinking. "So back to my question. Why didn't he run before the meeting?"

"All right. It comes down to this." Delft

cupped his jaw with one hand. "We know that Edwin Tarell went into Bland's office around noon that day to tell him about the meeting at eight o'clock. Now this was highly unusual for Bland, being summoned to his boss's house like that. He probably figured something was up. We also know that around three hours later he went to the bank and withdrew all the stolen money remaining in the account. This was unfortunate for Don Tarell. If Don had gone to the police first, that account could have been frozen.

"So it's clear that Bland was prepared to flee with the money, if he had to. But you see, Bland didn't know for certain what the meeting was about. He'd already lost his wife and baby son. If he was caught stealing, he'd also lose his job and career. And he'd end up in jail. In light of all that, if he was caught, there was little to keep him from fleeing. But what if he *hadn't* been caught? Disappearing would only raise questions, and most likely ensure that he *would be* found out. Plus, if he ran, he'd never get to see his son for visitations — an important thing to Bland. He wasn't going to throw what was left of his life away and take up a life on the run unless absolutely certain he had no other choice. So what does he do? He comes to the meeting with money stashed in his car, just in case. With a gun. Just in case. Then once he discovered he was caught and had no way out, he acted on the option he'd already made possible: he pulled the gun."

"Why not just run at that point?"

Delft lifted a hand. "How far would he get — the front door? If not Don Tarell or Peter Dessinger, Edwin surely would have chased him down."

Of course he would. I rubbed a thumb back and forth over my pen. How could Bill Bland have such a complete lack of conscience? "Edwin saved his own life, didn't he? And his mother's."

"No doubt. Bland would have killed them all to escape. That was his most crucial need — time. In fact, time is the other main reason he didn't skip town before the meeting, because then he'd only have had a couple hours to run. But think about four dead bodies in a house at night. No one's going to miss them until the next day, when the three men fail to show for work. That would give Bland over twelve hours to run. And you can get quite a distance in that time."

Clammy fingers traced the back of my neck. Bill Bland was willing to kill four people just to make an escape. *This* was the man whose head I needed to crawl inside. The man whose skin I needed to feel on my face. How and when would he smile? Grimace? What wrinkles would move when he did? I shifted in my chair. The more I got to know of this man, the more of a monster he became.

Why had I gotten myself into this?

I looked back to Sergeant Delft. "I studied that one blow-up photo of him in the files —"

"You're aware that the driver's license photo of him was more recent?"

"Yes. I'll probably use that for my update. Anyway, studying his face, I saw what looked like arrogance."

"Oh, sure. How can you not be arrogant when the world is all about you?"

The comment hit home. There lay the key to Bill Bland: everything was about *him.* Regardless of the cost to others.

I wrote down the words, then stared at the floor. How in the world could a person fall to such coldness? "But he loved his wife, right? He was a good father?"

Delft shrugged. "Define 'good.' He didn't

run around on his wife, as far as we know. Provided for them well. But he had that driving need to control, and that surfaced again and again."

I shook my head. "It's just hard to picture that normal-looking face being capable of such a horrific act."

"Oh, but that's the danger of living in this world, isn't it, Ms. Kingston?" Delft's eyes locked with mine. "I'll tell you something. A few months ago I watched a Larry King show about Gary Ridgway, that Green River serial killer up in Washington. They know he killed at least forty-eight women. Prostitutes, most of them. 'Why?' a detective asked him. Answer: 'Because I didn't want to pay for sex. And I was having trouble with my wife.' " Delft lifted both hands. "That was it. Because he wanted free sex, forty-eight people had to die."

The thought made me shiver. "Gary Ridgway was a family man too, wasn't he?"

"Sure. A loving husband and father. No one would have guessed, least of all his family. *No one.* Even the detectives said Ridgway was quiet, polite, hardly ever cussed. The kind of guy you'd sit down with at a bar and have a friendly conversation." Delft leaned forward, both hands flattened against his desk. "People want to think evil looks monstrous, Ms. Kingston. It doesn't. Evil is the guy next door."

I closed my eyes, feeling the impact of the words. *The guy next door.* That was as good a description of Bland as any. The man you'd talk to over your fence. The man you'd overlook in a crowd.

A man who led a secret life no one would ever suspect.

I glanced at my watch. "Thank you for your time, Sergeant. I need to be going so I can pick up my kids from school." I pushed back my chair and rose.

He stood too, arching his shoulders in a quick, decisive motion. "No problem, I'm glad to give you as much time as you need. Far as I'm concerned, you're doing *me* the favor."

He ushered me to his door, but stopped at the threshold. "I suppose you know we're keeping a tight lid on this television show. Surprising a fugitive is crucial, especially in this case. So we absolutely don't want the local media to hear about it. Bill Bland's probably on the other side of the country, but city news can be followed from anywhere."

Of course I knew this. I'd talked to the

American Fugitive producer that morning about my assignment, and he also warned me about the importance of surprise. But the way Sergeant Delft put it . . .

I hugged my notebook to my chest. " 'Especially in this case'?"

Delft surveyed me for a moment. "Like I said, Bland needs to feel he's in control. He lost that control for a while twenty years ago, but no doubt thinks he's gotten it back after evading the law all this time. So what's he going to do when that control's shattered again? I'm hoping he's not watching television when the show airs. I'm hoping your update is right on target, and leads pour in immediately, so we can send in law enforcement to surround him before he knows what hit him."

Right on target. Just a little pressure, Annie. "You think he'll hole up and fight? Kill someone?"

The sergeant narrowed his eyes. "I think Bill Bland will do *anything* to save his own skin, Ms. Kingston. Last time he was willing to take down four people. People that he knew and worked with. So you tell me. After twenty years on the run — just who, and how many, do you think he'd be willing to take down now?"

CHAPTER 4

Policeman.

He clicked off the Internet.

His eyes fastened on the uniform. The man stood across the store, talking to Al, the owner. Who was it? A glare on his office window smudged the man's face.

He got up. Pretended to stretch his legs. Stared.

Officer Ted Dallings. Local cop. Reminded him of Zackary Bright in *Twitch.*

Dallings laughed. So did Al.

Friendly conversation.

His muscles relaxed.

He sat back down at his computer. One eye on the cop, he reconnected to the Net. Local news site in Redding. He read the headlines. There'd been nothing early this morning, but sometimes updates filtered in during the day.

Still nothing.

Off the Internet. He erased the history of the visited site.

"Hey, you getting ready to call it a day?"

He turned. Two-chinned Billy. Jovial. Clerk at the store. "Soon."

Did Dallings leave? He flicked a look through his window.

"Well, I'm headin' out. Hey, you want to try that new restaurant with me for lunch tomorrow?"

"I could."

"Heck, man, I know ya could. But do you want to? Wouldn't wanna twist your arm."

Nobody twists my arm.

"I choose to go with you, Billy."

The man shook his head and grinned. "You 'choose to go,' huh. Well, now, and ain't you made my day."

Yes. He could do that to people.

CHAPTER 5

"Stephen, I told you no."

Being around my son was such a joy these days. We'd argued ever since I picked him up from school. By the time we reached home I nearly shook with anger.

"Why?"

"How many times do I have to tell you?" I pulled my car into the garage and turned off the engine. "I can't trust you or your friends."

"You don't *know* my friends."

"That's part of the problem. I vaguely know their names. I vaguely see them hanging around when I pick you up from school. And frankly from what I see —"

"*Don't* tell me you don't like the looks of them!" Stephen grabbed his backpack, shoved himself out of the car, and slammed the door. "You don't know anything about them so how can you possibly judge?" His last sentence was loud enough to pierce through the closed car windows.

I took in his scowl, almost perpetual these days, and the coldness in his dark eyes. His hair, spiked straight up with gel. The low-crotched jeans and oversized T-shirt. The way my son looked, people probably judged him as a troublemaker. With a sigh I opened my door.

"I'm tired of hearing you two fight." Kelly made a *tsk*ing sound as she slid out of the backseat. "That's all you ever do anymore."

"Well, it's not *my* fault." Stephen jerked his heavy backpack onto his shoulders. "If she'd only let me do something once in a while."

Kelly shook her head and disappeared through the door into the kitchen.

I pulled myself from the SUV, gathering my purse and keys. If my son were more trustworthy I would leave them in the car for convenience. But lately I trusted him very little. It seemed entirely within pos-sibility that he'd sneak off with the car again at night. Or even steal money from my purse. Seemed to me a twenty-dollar bill had been missing lately, on more than one occasion.

"Stephen, I give you as much freedom as

I can, under the circumstances. And I'd let you do more, if you acted more responsibly. But what am I supposed to do when your grades are practically all *D*s? When you steal my car to go joyriding with your friends in Redding? When you come home smelling of pot?"

He sneered at me. "Oh, Mom, you wouldn't know what pot smelled like if —"

"Can it, Stephen!" I shot up a hand, my spine stiffening. "I am *not* going to have this conversation for the tenth time. No, you cannot use my car tonight to go out with your friends."

His face reddened. "I'm *sixteen* years old! I've got my *license!*"

"Just because you have it doesn't mean you can use it. Especially with *my* car."

"Then buy me my own."

I threw him a disgusted look and made for the door.

"So what am I supposed to do?" He flung the words at my back. "Stay out here in the country all weekend? Play video games by myself?"

We weren't exactly in the country. But, given the problems I'd had with Stephen in the past year, I was thankful we'd moved from the San Francisco Bay Area to Grove

Landing, about fifteen minutes' drive outside Redding. In the Bay Area, Stephen could easily slip out of the house at night to meet up with friends. Out here, surrounded by forest, he couldn't pull off such nighttime forays as easily.

I turned around. "What you're *supposed* to do, Stephen, is bring your grades up. Stop doing drugs. Start acting in a way that makes me trust you. And bring home friends that don't look like scrunge off the streets."

Even as the last sentence left my mouth, I regretted it. Voicing my sentiments of Stephen's buddies would only alienate my son all the more.

Stephen stopped in his tracks, cold hatred flowing from him like dry ice. "Fine, Mom." His voice was low, hard. "You don't like my friends, you don't like me. And I don't like you. And I *really* don't like living here. So why don't you let me go live with Dad, huh? You'd be a lot happier without me around."

At the dreaded words, the fight drained out of me. For months I'd seen this coming. I knew once the intent was spoken it would hang between my son and me like pecked and rotting fruit on a tree. I leaned against the door, one hand on the knob, my mind thrashing for a response. The truth was too much for Stephen to bear, although deep inside he surely recognized it. His father would never consent to taking him. Vic's young wife had made it painfully clear she would not raise someone else's child. *Especially mine.* As if I'd ever done anything to her.

"Stephen. I wouldn't be happier with you gone, and you know that. I just wish we could . . . get along."

He glared at me, lips pressed. "Well, that's *nice* of you."

Before I could say another word, he pushed my hand off the knob and jerked the door open. He stomped through the kitchen and great room as I trailed into the house. As I lay my purse on the counter, I heard him clump down the stairs to his basement-level bedroom.

Kelly stood at the pantry, backpack at her feet. I watched her pull out an open bag of chips and start munching. She regarded me with semi-indignation, apparently still ticked over Stephen's and my thousandth argument. I pulled out a chair at the table and sank into it. My son's anger was hard enough. Kelly's irritation on top of that was too much.

Vic, why did you leave me all alone to raise two kids?

"Mom?" Kelly walked over to peer at my face. "Are you okay?"

"Yeah. Fine." I tried to smile, but it came out lopsided.

"Stephen's a jerk sometimes." She plunked the bag of chips on the table.

I made no reply.

"Is Aunt Jenna coming up this weekend?" Kelly sat in a chair to my right, turning to face me. Clearly she was trying to take my mind off Stephen.

"No. She's got to finish a consulting project."

"Oh." She crossed her ankles and wiggled a foot. "Erin's supposed to spend the night tonight. Remember?"

I nodded. "That's fine."

Sudden rap music clamored through the heater vents. Stephen had turned on his stereo — to a volume equaling the squall of his mood. I repressed a sigh. I *hated* that music.

"But if you two plan to spend the day together tomorrow, maybe in the later afternoon you can go over to Erin's house. I have to go into Redding for an appointment."

Kelly shook a strand of long brown hair away from her face. "For what?"

I hesitated. A part of me still cringed

whenever I talked to Kelly about my new career in forensic art. The residue of last summer, when I'd drawn my first composite, still coated our memories.

"I have to interview a man for that drawing I'm doing for *American Fugitive*."

She grinned, surprising me. "That is just *so* cool, Mom, you working for that show. Erin thinks so too."

"Erin? Kelly, you haven't told anyone else, have you? You promised you wouldn't tell anybody. Remember, it's really important that this show stay a secret until it airs."

"Um-hum, okay. But will your name be on TV, like, you know, at the end with the credits?"

If only that was the worst of my worries. "Probably, but I'm not positive."

"Well, the producer called you yesterday, right? Didn't you ask him?"

The blissful innocence of the young. I leaned over and drew a knuckle down her cheek. "No, I didn't."

Stephen's music throbbed.

"They must be paying you a lot." Kelly's brown eyes shone.

I raised my hands in a shrug.

"Well, aren't they?"

I regarded my beautiful daughter. "It's enough."

In truth it wasn't. A million dollars wouldn't be enough. I just couldn't shake my anxiety about this case. Besides, I'd hardly embarked on my new career for the money. I didn't need an income. With the stocks and cash Jenna and I had inherited from our father, a successful criminal defense attorney, neither of us ever needed to work again.

A slight frown knit Kelly's brow. "What's wrong? You don't seem very happy about doing the drawing."

Uh-oh. Kelly was sensitive. She could pick up on my moods in a heartbeat.

"This isn't going to be dangerous, is it?" she pressed. "I mean, it'll just be like the other drawings you did this year, not like . . . like when Erin's mom . . ."

"Of course not."

She held my gaze as if not quite sure whether to believe me.

"Really, Kelly, it's not dangerous. Don't worry about it."

"Okay. But just don't —"

The doorbell rang.

Kelly's head swiveled toward the great room. "That's Erin." She pushed from her chair and trotted out of the kitchen.

I listened to her footsteps across the

hardwood floor, to the happy greetings of the two friends. Normally, Erin carpooled home with us, but today she'd left school early for a dentist appointment. Just as well — she missed the argument between me and Stephen. Now, Erin launched into immediate conversation with Kelly about their school day, and had Kelly heard that Tom and Selena were going out?

Going out. The girls were only in eighth grade. I couldn't get used to that term being used by junior highers.

"Hello, Erin." I entered the great room to give her a hug. She looked cute in a pink shirt that set off her light skin tone and pale blonde hair.

"Hi." She clung to me for a second, as she tended to do. As always, my heart gave a little lurch. We spoke of her mother's absence rarely, but the thought was ever between us.

"Oh, I like that song." She jutted her chin toward Stephen's lair.

"Well, I don't. I'm going to make him turn it down. I've got work to do."

My work called me with the fateful beguiling of the ancient Sirens. I needed to strand myself in the office, read the notes from my interview with Sergeant Delft. And I needed to review some of the interviews with Edwin Tarell to prepare for my meeting with him tomorrow.

The girls bounded up the wide curving staircase, headed for Kelly's room. Erin toted a lavender overnight bag. I forced my feet toward the steps to the lower level. Stephen's music pounded my ears the moment I opened the stairwell door. I headed down to the rec room, teeth gritted. The raspy voice and heavy base malleted through my chest.

Stephen sat hunched over his computer, typing with fury. No doubt pouring out his ills online to his friends. The sliding door leading to our large back deck stood open, letting in a slight breeze. And flies. He'd neglected to close the screen. I walked over and slid it shut, barely noticing the beauty of the forest beyond our yard. The noise made it impossible to think.

"Stephen —" I slapped off the stereo. Instant peace assaulted me.

"Hey!" His head snapped up, dark brows nearly colliding in their frown. "Why do you come down and do things like you own the place?"

"Because I *do*."

He flexed his jaw.

"Look, you can turn your stereo back on, just keep it down. I'm trying to work —"

A phone rang distantly one floor above — a different musical tone from our home line. My personal business number, in the office. Probably a call about the case.

"Oh, drat."

I scurried across the rec room and up the stairs. Before I was halfway up, Stephen's music jolted on. The phone rang again. "Turn that stereo down!" The music lowered a few decibels as I hurried into the great room and closed the door behind me. The girls' voices filtered down from above, then were drowned out by Kelly's favorite punk rock band. Wonderful. Her bedroom was right above my office.

The phone rang for the fourth time as I snatched up the receiver. "Annie Kingston."

"Hello, Ms. Kingston. It's been awhile since we talked. This is Adam Bendershil from the *Record Searchlight*."

Oh no, don't tell me . . . Adam Bendershil was the crime reporter from our local Redding newspaper. I leaned over the desk, trying to convince myself that this was just a coincidence.

CHAPTER 6

"I understand you're drawing an updated face of Bill Bland for *American Fugitive*." Adam got right to the point. "I wanted to ask you a few questions."

Kelly's stereo clamored and Stephen's throbbed. I pushed away from my desk, trying to form an evasive answer, but I could hardly think.

"Just a minute, okay? It's, uh, kind of noisy here." I left my office and crossed the great room. Stepped outside onto the front porch. Across the street, Erin's dad was weeding the flower bed by his sidewalk. He did not look up.

"Ms. Kingston?"

"I'm here."

What do I tell him? Should I just deny everything?

"Good. I understand the kind of drawing you're doing is called a fugitive update, is that correct?"

"How do you know about this?"

A pause. "I talk to people in law enforcement all the time. That's my job."

"But who told you about *this?*"

"I can't divulge my source. Sorry."

"Adam. You can't print this story. Do you have any idea how it could hurt the case?"

"I don't see how it could hurt at all."

Kelly's window cranked open above me, her music spilling out onto the street. At the sound, Dave looked around from his weeding.

"Oh, really. Well, just imagine the public reading your article. And just imagine that somehow Bill Bland hears about it. How nice for him — advance warning so he can disappear from whatever life he's set up."

Dave raised a gloved hand in my direction. I waved back distractedly.

"I don't see how that would happen, Ms. Kingston. You think Bland is still hanging around Redding after all this time?"

"No. But as you very well know, news is online these days. I do think somebody on the run might be checking out the crime stories in the area where he killed two people — especially with an important anniversary coming up."

"Wow. You give the guy that much credit? Most murderers don't think that much."

"Most murderers don't manage to outrun the law for two decades."

Silence.

"Ms. Kingston, I'm going to run this story, with or without you. That's my job. I'd appreciate you helping to make the facts as accurate as possible."

As a courtroom artist for ten years, I'd worked alongside many reporters. I knew all about their job. I also knew that they'd cross many a line to get a story before some competitor.

"Please don't run it, Adam. At least not now. Don't you understand it could tip off the killer? I know that's a remote chance, but why take any chance at all with the high stakes here? Look, I'll talk to you all you want after the show airs."

"Good, we'll talk then too. But I'm *not* pulling this story. It's breaking news now."

Anger flushed through me. I paced a few steps, thrusting a hand in my hair. "Let me make this very clear. You run this story now and you *won't* talk to me after the show. In fact, I won't discuss a case with you ever again."

"Ms. Kingston, it can't be that bad. All I want —"

"All you want is to put your own desire

for a story over the needs of other people. People who've grieved about these terrible murders and worked on this case for twenty years. And I won't be a part of that." My voice rose. "As far as you're concerned, I'm not working on any such case. In fact, I have absolutely *no* idea what you're talking about!"

I yanked the phone away from my ear and punched off the line.

My daughter's music still ragged at my ears.

"Kelly!" I yelled toward her open window. "Kel-*leee!*"

"What?" Her face appeared above me, creased with irritation.

"Turn that music off! *Now.*"

"Sheesh. Okay." She disappeared. The noise stopped.

I leaned against a log pillar, phone dangling from my hand. Had the reporter called Delft yet? Oh, the sergeant would not be happy. When he found the leak in the department, he'd probably call for the person's head on a platter.

How about Emily and Edwin Tarell? Had Adam called them? I did not want to be the one to tell them this news had leaked. They were counting on the *American Fugitive* show so much.

"Hey, neighbor."

I raised my head to see Dave Willit standing on my sidewalk, dirt-caked gloves on his hands. He looked at me as if not sure whether to bother me or not, green eyes half squinted. Sweat trickled from his blond hair down his temple. I felt my cheeks flush. How could I have yelled at Kelly like that in front of him? And been so loud on the phone? He'd probably heard every word I said.

Ten months after his wife's death, I still didn't feel quite comfortable around Dave, whether around the neighborhood or at church. Although he continued to assure me I had no reason to feel guilty about what happened — in fact, he seemed to have nothing but praises for me — I couldn't entirely shake my sense of culpability. Or maybe his now being a single father and my being a single mother set up a propriety alert within me. I didn't want people to jump to any conclusions about our relationship. Our daughters were best friends, that was all.

Propriety alert. Now there was a phrase.

"Hi, Dave. You must have knocked off work early." Dave owned commercial real estate in Redding and worked from an office in his home.

"Yeah, well. It's Friday." He glanced at Kelly's window. "Sounds like our girls are getting obnoxious."

"Oh no, they're fine." What to do with my free hand? I hooked a finger into a belt loop on my jeans. "I'm sorry, I shouldn't have yelled like that. It's just . . . I . . . this was not a good conversation —" I indicated the phone — "and the music is a little much."

"Would you rather they come over to our house for the night? I'm home, so it makes no difference to me."

"No, really, it's okay." I smiled at him. "The girls are the best thing going on in this house right now."

Oh, great, Annie, what a lead line.

He pulled off a glove and wiped sweat from his face. I had the sense he was stalling, wondering whether or not to ask questions. "Is it Stephen? I mean, a few times Erin has mentioned that he's . . ."

"Still giving me trouble?" I set the phone down on the porch, cradled my elbows. "Yeah, he is. And I'm afraid I'm not very good at handling it."

He pulled in a deep breath. "Remember last summer I told you I'd be willing to help with him in whatever way I can? It's a hard age in a boy's life."

100

Especially without a father around. I knew that's what Dave was thinking. And he was oh, so right. But who was I to ask for *his* help? He was trying to raise a teenage girl alone while dealing with his own grief. Every time I laid eyes on Dave I saw the pain etched into his face. He'd loved Lisa with his heart and soul. Their life together had looked perfect. Before meeting them, I'd seen only the dark side of marriage, thanks to my cheating father and equally unfaithful husband.

"Thanks, Dave. But I really don't know what you —"

"You help so much with Erin, Annie. You have her over all the time, and you're always watching out for her. Sometimes I feel like I owe you the world, and there's no way I can pay you back. So *anything* I can do to help with Stephen, believe me, I'd love to do it. Maybe I can take him out sometime, do something with him."

I stared at him. Owe *me* the world? I couldn't think of a single word in response. "Okay. I thank you. Very much."

How stilted that sounded. I gave him a self-conscious smile.

The phone rang. I narrowed my eyes at it, knowing I would not answer. *Shouldn't I*

101

explain all this to Dave? What if he thought the caller was a friend of Stephen's? What if he did something crazy like suggest he take Stephen out right now, tonight? I knew what my son's response would be, given his current mood. Erin's dad? The boring Christian man Stephen saw every Sunday when I dragged him to church? No *way.*

"It's probably just the reporter who called before." I folded my arms. "He wants information that I can't give him about the case for *American Fugitive.* I'm assuming Erin told you about that, since I know Kelly told her. But people aren't really supposed to know. And the reporter's not supposed to be doing an article before the show airs, but you know how they are. No doubt this will be front-page news in tomorrow's paper. And what if the worst-case scenario happens —"

Good grief, I was running on. I looked away in embarassment.

Dave shook his head. "I remember all the reporters' calls last July. The last thing I wanted to do was talk to them. They just seem to have no sense of . . . propriety."

I almost laughed. He'd used that word.

"Yeah, I know." I raised my shoulders. "Well, guess I better get inside. I've got work to do on the case."

"And I need to get back to my flowers."

"They're beautiful, by the way. As always."

"Thanks."

As I started to open my front door, phone in hand, Dave called my name. I turned back to see him at the curb.

"This case you're working on? Growing up in Redding, I remember when it all happened. Seemed like it was about our only news for a long time." He hesitated.

I let the silence hang between us, waiting.

"The guy's . . . really a cold-blooded murderer, Annie. Not like the last few drawings you've done of petty robbers and car thieves. This one's more like . . ."

"I know." I didn't want him to have to finish his sentence.

Dave took his time pulling his gloves back on. "Just tell me you'll be careful."

My throat tightened at his concern. "You know I will."

He nodded.

I watched him start across the street, then I turned back toward my house. Stephen's rap music thrashed my ears the moment I opened the door.

■ ■ ■ ■

SATURDAY, MAY 8

■ ■ ■ ■

CHAPTER 7

American Fugitive to Air Redding Murder

The front-page headline mocked me from the sidewalk as I retrieved our morning paper. I scooped it up and hurried back inside the house. Fortunately the kids weren't awake yet. Like a moth drawn to flame, I could not keep myself from reading the article. And I wanted no interruptions, no teenagers' presence requiring me to pretend everything was fine.

Unfolding the paper across the kitchen table, I sank into a chair and read.

On June 2 *American Fugitive* will feature the 1984 Redding double homicide of businessman Don Tarell and his associate Peter Dessinger. Local forensic artist Annie Kingston, known for her composite last summer in the Lisa Willit murder case, will do the "fugitive update" drawing of suspect Bill Bland, who has been on the run from the law for the past twenty years.

Neither the Shasta County Sheriff's Department nor Kingston would comment on the show. Calls to the homes of Edwin Tarell, son of one of the victims, and his mother, Emily Tarell, were not returned. The producer of *American Fugitive,* Michael Erwin, would not affirm or deny they are covering the case, saying only that their episodes "depend on surprise" in the apprehending of featured suspects.

"No kidding." I pressed my fist against the paper, wishing it was Bendershil's head. "Thanks for spoiling it."

Don Tarell was founder and CEO of Tarell Plastics, a —

The phone rang. I eyed the receiver warily. Was this another reporter?

A second ring. Steeling myself, I picked up the phone. "Hello?"

"Annie. It's Emily Tarell."

I let out a silent breath of relief. "Emily, please know I had nothing to do with the news story. The reporter called me yesterday, and I tried my best to talk him out —"

"I know, Annie." Her tone mixed frustration and resolve. "I just called to say thank you for not telling him anything. I realize this could be a lot of publicity for you, yet you backed off for the good of the show. I'm grateful."

"You don't have to thank me. I didn't *want* to talk to him."

"Exactly. Give yourself credit for your integrity."

Integrity? The guy just made me mad.

"I called Sharon back east this morning to tell her about the article. She got in touch with her daughter's boyfriend, who writes for the show. He said not to worry. The show's not going to be cancelled or anything because of this. And it certainly isn't the first time local news has divulged information on one of their segments. Of course they don't like it when that happens, but all we can do is hope Bill Bland doesn't hear about it. Even if he did and ran from whatever new identity he's created, it's still quite possible for leads to put law enforcement on his trail. Knowing where Bill has been for the past few years, and what name he's been using would be a good place to start."

"Emily, thank you for telling me this." I imagined Sergeant Delft had already been in touch with the *American Fugitive* producer over this issue. Talk about not wanting to lose control. Even with these consolations, I doubted the man would feel pacified. "Believe me, I'm going to do everything I can to make my drawing right — for your sake. You so deserve to see an end to all this."

"I know you will, dear. I know you will."

Clicking off the line, I turned back to the newspaper article. It continued on an inside page, recapping the crime and speaking of Edwin and Emily, both of whom still lived in Redding.

Edwin. I had an appointment to interview him at three-thirty.

I leaned back in my chair, picturing his face, thinking over some of the follow-up statements he'd made to Sergeant Delft all those years ago. Evidently, Edwin came to rely on Delft heavily during those first few days following the murders, often showing up at the sergeant's office to tell him "one more thing that might help." With the weight of such a case on his shoulders, Delft would have been very pressed for time. Yet he met with Edwin again and again, just letting the young man talk, taking notes of

Edwin's ramblings in case a clue lay buried somewhere.

One scene that Edwin recounted particularly haunted me — the time at which the shock had worn off enough for him to realize his father was gone forever. My own mother had died when I was sixteen. To this day, I remembered so well that moment the reality of her death hit me full in the face. It was like being slashed deep inside, the pain so great that it tore all breath away. As I read Edwin's description of his own emotions, tears had filled my eyes.

I gazed out the kitchen window, remembering Edwin's words. Of its own accord, my mental projector clicked on, bringing the scene to life. I could feel Edwin's grief as he returned to his own town house a few hours after the shootings. Could hear the silence as he

slips inside, hands trembling. He scurries from room to room, turning on every light. In his heart he knows Bill Bland is long gone, but his erratic heartbeat forces him to search every corner for the man. No set of walls will feel safe anymore; no lock will put him at ease. If tragedy unfolded in his father's house — and from the hand of a trusted employee

111

— it can happen anywhere. Nothing will be the same again. Ever.

Edwin finds himself sitting on his bed. He doesn't know how he got there. One shoe is off. He is staring at the dresser against the far wall, looking through it until it blurs. He visualizes the similar wood on the desk in his father's study. Sees his father's knuckles rapping on that desk. Rap rap, rap rap. The sound repeats until it cycles with the beat of his own heart like some inner circadian rhythm.

Rap rap.

Only then does Edwin notice it. The blood on his shirtsleeves. Spatters and streaks on the white cuffs.

The last drops of his father's life.

His chest grows hot, and his throat closes. He touches a spot with a fingertip, then presses it between thumb and forefinger until his hand cramps. I couldn't save him, I couldn't save him, I couldn't save him. *Anger swells within Edwin. His wrists begin to prickle as if the blood is biting him, and he shoves to his feet, tearing at the buttons, yanking off the shirt. He throws it onto his bedroom floor. It taunts him, screaming at him from the carpet. He grabs it again, runs into the kitchen and drops it into his trash compactor. When he kicks the compactor door closed, he can still hear the shirt's cries.*

They will drive him crazy.

With a curse he opens the compactor door and seizes the entire bag of its contents. Then out he races into his attached garage, where he flings the bag into a garbage container and clamps down the lid. Suddenly he remembers what day it is. Tomorrow morning the truck will be around to pick up garbage. Edwin hits the button on the wall to open his garage door, then drags the rubber container outside.

He scuttles back into the garage, closes the door, hurries to the light of his kitchen. The shirt is far enough away now. He cannot hear its cries —

"Hey, Mom."

I jerked my head around and stared at my daughter, unfocused. Erin appeared behind her, leaning against one of the tall log support beams that separate our kitchen from the great room.

My daughter frowned. "What's wrong?"

"Oh." With one hand I folded the newspaper, turned it over. "Nothing. I was just . . . daydreaming. What are you doing up so early?"

She shrugged. "Dunno. We were hungry."

With that, her head disappeared behind the refrigerator door. Erin gave me a half-asleep smile. "Morning."

"Hi. Your orange juice is in there." I indicated the refrigerator with my chin. Neither of my kids liked orange juice, but I always kept a bottle for Erin.

"Thanks."

I poured myself some coffee and drank it while chatting with the girls, trying all the while to push away my nagging thoughts about the news article and my upcoming interview with Edwin Tarell. But something about the girls' presence only made me feel the weight of my responsibility all the more. Their slim young bodies clad in pajamas, their shiny hair and smooth skin, pulled at my mother's heart in ways I couldn't quite define. Perhaps my love for them reminded me how much I had lost in my own mother's death. How much Edwin had lost. And Emily.

The girls rummaged around the kitchen, pulled out two kinds of cold cereal from the pantry, then decided they wanted pancakes.

"Have at it." I lifted a hand toward the box of mix that Kelly placed on the counter.

"Oh, Mom, can't you do it?"

"Sure I *can*. But so can you."

I made my exit then, carrying the newspaper and my mug of coffee. "Just clean up when you're done."

Three hours later, it was almost noon. I'd looked over the case files some more and was fully prepared for my interview with Edwin. I'd argued — again — with Stephen, who got up in a particularly foul mood. And I'd talked on the phone with Jenna. Whined was more like it. First about Stephen and how miserable he made me, then about the case.

Regarding my son, Jenna empathized completely. She knew how difficult he could be. As for the Bill Bland assignment, she'd now heard me give her a dozen reasons why I shouldn't have accepted it. Being Jenna, she shot every one of them down.

"Annie, knock it off. You've got to stop thinking of all the things that could go wrong. Think instead of what can go *right.* Imagine how you're gonna feel if they catch that guy. *When* they catch that guy."

The house phone rang while I was on my business line with Jenna. I vaguely heard Stephen answer it from the TV room. A moment later he stuck his head in my office.

"Mom, I gotta talk to you. Right now."

"Just a minute, Stephen, I'm on the phone." As if he couldn't notice.

"Mom, now. Please!"

Only Stephen could make that word sound more like a curse. My son was wearing me down on the grindstone of motherhood, and the weekend had just begun. I couldn't argue with him anymore. Sighing, I told Jenna I needed to go and hung up the phone.

"Can I go to the school baseball game tonight with Jeff?" The receiver still dangled from Stephen's hand, apparently with Jeff waiting at the other end.

Jeff. One of those kids I didn't like the looks of. A shaved head, ear piercings, and a permanent slouch.

"If you let me take you and pick you up."

"Jeff's got a car."

"So do I. I'll take you."

He flexed his jaw, started to say something, then stopped. "Okay, fine. But Jeff'll bring me home."

That was even worse. No telling what they would do between the game and home. *If* they stayed at the game at all.

"No. I'll come get you."

Stephen's face reddened, his eyes narrowing. "Come *on,* Mom! What is *wrong* with you? You never let me do anything. It's just a baseball game!"

"It's not the baseball game I'm worried about, Stephen, it's —"

The doorbell rang. I ignored it. Kelly would answer.

"— what you might be doing *outside* of the game."

"What are you talking about? I'm not going to be doing anything!"

"Stephen, look, I don't —"

"Mom!" Kelly's voice floated from the upper level. "Are you going to answer the door?"

With a sigh, I pushed away from my desk and crossed the room to yell up to her. "Can't you answer it?"

"We're trying on clothes and we're not all dressed."

I closed my eyes. "Stephen, let me get the door."

"But I have to know —"

"No, you don't have to know right now. You can call Jeff back."

My footfalls echoed off the hardwood floor, bouncing against the rich wood wainscoting of the great room. I reached the front door and opened it to a beautiful, sunny May afternoon — and an empty porch. I stepped outside, looking right and left. A small blue car was driving down the cul-de-sac, away from my home. Had its

117

driver been here and left that fast?

I dropped my gaze. Only then did I notice the long white box lying at my feet. Tied with a red ribbon. It looked like the kind of box that would contain long-stemmed roses.

Surely not. No one had ever sent me roses. Including Vic, during our entire marriage.

I bent down, tilting my head to read the handwriting on a small envelope taped to the box. It was addressed to Ms. Annie Kingston.

Ms.? If someone was sending me roses, the title sounded so formal.

I reached out for the box, then stopped to first close the front door. No need for Stephen to come barreling to the threshold, intent on his own agenda, and gawk impatiently at me while I discovered what lay inside.

Could someone *really* be sending me flowers? My heart fluttered at the thought.

Carefully, I picked up the box. Roses were delicate. I wouldn't want to lose the smallest leaf. I carried it the length of the porch, then sat in one of the wicker chairs I'd recently bought. I laid the box on my knees.

Which to open first, the card or the box? I hesitated, then pulled off the envelope and opened its flap. Slid my fingers into it.

Nothing.

I pressed the sides of the envelope, ballooning it open, and peered inside. Not even a tiny slip of paper.

Strange.

Setting the envelope aside, I began working at the red bow. Pulling out the loops, untying the knot. When it gave way I slid the ribbon from the box and dropped it to my feet. I placed my fingers on either side of the cover and gave it a gentle tug. It resisted at first, then lifted with a little *shushing* sound. At the slight jostle something sounded from within — almost like a crackling.

What was that? Flowers didn't crackle.

Apprehension drizzled through my veins. This wasn't right. I didn't know anyone who would send me roses, particularly without a signed card. And that sound . . .

I shook the box gently.

A dry whisper-clatter, like the rustling of skeletal fragments.

Visions of brittle bones twitched through my head. What would they do upon my opening the box? Pull together, unite themselves with mummified flesh into a grasping hand . . .

For heaven's sake, Annie. Enough.

Firming my mouth, I took off the cover

with one swift motion and threw it aside. Looked into the box.

A dozen long-stemmed roses. Completely dead. Withered leaves, dessicated flowers. The buds were so blackened, I could hardly tell they used to be red.

A chill dusted my shoulders. What kind of trick was this? Who could have done it? Surely not a woman. The joke was too sick, too defiling of something a female considered sacred. It had to be a man. Someone I knew? The projector in my head clicked on, flashing an imagined close-up of

a man's hands laying the roses into the box. One by one. Carefully, watching out for the thorns. Brown/black on white, the crumbling leaves scraping each other and the cardboard . . .

I blinked the scene away.

Then I saw the single, lace-edged paper — a note card that matched the envelope. Stuck between the thorny stems, with half-hidden small block letters in red ink. Using thumb and forefinger I pulled it out. Held it up to read.

SOME THINGS ARE BETTER LEFT
ALONE.
LIKE THIS CASE.
STAY WELL, ANNIE. AND ALIVE.

I gasped, then flicked the card aside like a match burning my fingers. I jumped to my feet, the box spilling from my lap. It turned on its side, the contents hissing against my porch like snakes.

Who did this? Was he still close? Was he watching me now?

My thoughts tangled, then hurled me back to last summer, to The Face. For a minute I couldn't move. What should I do? I wanted to run in the house and hide. To deny, *deny* this was happening again, that I'd gotten myself into another dangerous assignment, and now I would pay.

I swiveled toward the front door — and smacked into a figure blocking my way.

CHAPTER 8

He scrutinized her face.

Rounded cheeks. Hazel eyes. Brown hair to her shoulders, wispy bangs. Lips slightly turned up at the corners. Not beautiful. But . . . appealing. Something about her beckoned.

His narrowed eyes cut back to hers. Yes. There. Softness in those windows to the soul. Caring.

This was good. Very good. Traits he could bend for his purposes.

Leaning back in his chair, he folded his arms, chin raised. Stared at her picture on the computer screen. *I will come to know you, Annie Kingston. I will read every article written about you and your "heroism." But something tells me you don't feel like much of a hero, do you? You're just . . . pliable. Your heart pangs for the underdog.*

This, too, he would use.

She was Valery Ness in *Doom's Night.* The

122

unwitting pawn. He was Mel Platson. Mastermind.

He checked the clock in his small home office. The one room where family was not allowed. Time mocked him. Too many hours gone since he'd seen the dreaded news story. Good thing he'd diligently watched. Few had his foresight. Now tenacity and planning would save his life. Again.

He clicked on to the next article.

The clock ticked.

He had less than twenty-four hours.

CHAPTER 9

"Ah!"

I jerked backward on the porch, fists rising. In a split second my mind flew me to last summer, to my enemy's hands,

pulling me across the room of a strange house, around the couch, and into the kitchen. He shoves me up against the cabinets, my head bouncing back to hit hard. Folding his arms, he looks at me, death in his eyes, biceps pumping. The questions spit from his mouth, questions he needs answered before he kills me —

"Mom, what's the matter with you!" Stephen dropped the phone, sending it spinning toward the steps, and threw up both arms.

I took in my son's form, his startled expression, and my knees went weak. "Oh.

124

Oh." My heart kicked against my ribs like a horse in a fiery stall. I brought up both palms in trembling apology. "I'm sorry. So sorry. I thought . . ."

"What's that?" Stephen looked beyond me, frowning at the white box, the scattered dead roses. He brushed me aside, drawn toward them, one side of his mouth curling in morbid fascination.

"No, Stephen!" I pushed in front of him. "Don't touch them."

He looked over my head, eyes narrowed. "What is it?"

My mind scrambled for some vapid explanation. "It's . . . something somebody sent me."

He stared at me. "Dead flowers?"

I tried to laugh. It sounded more like a half strangle.

Stephen's expression firmed, and in it I saw the remnants of his fear from last summer. "Why would somebody —" he dragged out the words — "send you *dead* flowers?"

My tongue slid over my lips. "Look, Stephen, please. I don't want the girls to know about this. They could come out any minute."

He absorbed my words. "This is about the case you're working on, isn't it."

"I . . . Yes."

The off-the-hook signal emanated from the phone. Stephen sidled over to pick it up, clearly distracted. "I was going to call Jeff. Tell him you'd let him bring me home from the game tonight." The words sounded distant, as though he made small talk to put off his burning questions. And my answers.

"So. Mom." He scrunched his mouth and glared at the flowers. "Are you in trouble again?"

"I don't know. But I think I'd better call the Sheriff's Department. They'll want to take a look at that." I indicated the roses with a tilt of my head. "And we don't need your fingerprints on them."

Fear tire-treaded his features. Almost immediately his face reassembled itself. He gave an exaggerated shrug. "Probably just some nut who read the paper. Jeff told me there was an article in there about you."

I managed a tight smile. "Probably." I pointed to the phone. "Go put that away for now, okay? And get me a pair of gloves under the kitchen sink. I need to put these dead things back into the box. Then I'll stick it in my office, out of sight. I don't want to have to explain this to Kelly right now. It will only scare her."

"Yeah, okay." He headed for the front

door, looking over his shoulder at me. His puckered forehead betrayed the truth: he felt more concern for his mother than he'd ever let me know.

Dear God, please help me deal with this. Please help us all.

The next half hour whirled by as I attended to one need after another, doggedly focusing on details. It was the only way to keep my anxiety level down.

First I gathered the crackly flowers into their box, adding the card and envelope. I managed to take the package into the office and shut the door without being seen by the girls. Then I called upstairs to Kelly until she and Erin materialized out of the bedroom, wearing an interesting assortment of clothes. I raised an eyebrow at their getups but said nothing. "Time to go over to Erin's house now. Kelly, don't forget to take stuff to stay overnight."

Naturally my son seized the opportunity of my distracted state to ask again about Jeff bringing him home from the ball game. I'd lost the energy to argue. "Fine." I waved a dismissive hand. "And can he come get you too? Looks like I'm going to be busy."

Stephen ogled me, then caught himself. "Sure."

He beat a hasty retreat downstairs before

I came to my senses.

Guilt somersaulted through my head. In self-defense I turned to rationalization. *He'll be fine, Annie, you've got enough to deal with right now.*

That thought propelled me back into the office to call the Sheriff's Department. I told my story, requesting Detective Chetterling. With our history in working on cases, I naturally turned to him over Sergeant Delft. Thank goodness Chetterling was on duty. Within minutes of my call he phoned from his car, saying he'd be on his way.

Only then did I remember my meeting with Edwin Tarell. I sank into my office chair. *What should I do?* By the time I gave my statement to Chetterling, no way would I make the appointment on time. Even if I did, how could I keep my mind focused?

A bigger question loomed. Why should I go at all? Wasn't my grim present enough to convince me to pull out of this case?

Breathing a prayer, I flipped through the files stacked on my desk until I found the folder containing all the contact information. I dialed Edwin's number like a robot. How much should I tell him? If I pulled out of the assignment, he'd surely want to know why. But if I did pull out, what would happen to the *American Fugitive* segment? With this tight a deadline, I doubted they'd find another artist to do the fugitive update in time. The show would have to be put off — who knew for how long?

Vaguely, I heard a hello then realized Edwin had said it more than once. My tongue felt tied in knots.

"Hi. Edwin. This is Annie Kingston."

"Oh yes." The anticipation in his tone sank through me like lead. A large part of me still did not want to let him and his mother down.

"I'm afraid I'm going to have to cancel our meeting for today. Something . . . has happened."

"Oh, no. Not with your children, I hope."

"No, my children are fine. But I received a . . . threatening package today. About our case. I don't quite know what to do about it yet. Somebody from the Sheriff's Department is on his way over, and I don't know how long that will take."

A second of stunned silence passed. "Annie. Please. Tell me what happened."

Briefly, I told him. When I finished, he said nothing. I could picture his shocked expression, his mind filtering through possibilities.

"Bland sent you *dead roses?* And *threatened* you? What exactly did the note say?"

"Basically to keep away from the case. But, actually, we can't be completely sure Bland sent the package."

"Who else would send it? There isn't a person in town who doesn't want to see that man caught."

"I don't know." My throat tightened. I didn't want to think that it was Bland. Surely Stephen was right. "It could just be some prankster."

"Maybe." Edwin didn't sound very convinced.

"You . . . don't think so?"

Our breathing intermingled on the line. "It could be, Annie. I want to tell you that's all it is. But I know Bill Bland. I know what he's capable of. Now I'm feeling terrible — like I should have foreseen this. I saw the two sides of Bland before, but still never thought he'd kill my father. Now you get this threat. I can't stand back and let anything happen to you, too. I'd never forgive myself."

"Edwin, I'm not blaming you for this."

"I know, but . . . look. You've done the right thing by calling the Sheriff's Department. Surely they can trace where this package came from. If it did come from Bland,

130

the good news is, this just might lead us to him all the more quickly. But then you could be in real danger in the meantime."

Please, God, no. "Even if Bland did send the package, that doesn't mean he's *here*. He could have read the newspaper article online from anywhere and ordered those . . . things. Although I can't imagine from what store."

"True. But this could merely be step one in some wild scheme of his." Edwin fell silent for a moment. "It just doesn't make sense, though. That package has to be easy to trace, and Bland's smarter than that."

"What if it isn't traceable?"

He hesitated. "Well, that would definitely leave us with too many questions. But let's worry about that if the time comes."

I stared at the boxes of files, picturing the murderous man they represented.

"Annie, I'm so sorry this happened. It must have scared you terribly. Particularly after what you went through last year."

"Well. I have had better days."

A car door slammed outside. I swiveled in my chair to see Ralph Chetterling heading toward my front walk. "Edwin, the detective's here. I need to go."

"Okay, good. Look, while they're tracing

this package, why don't you come on over and talk to me whenever you're done with the detective? Because if it turns out to just be a prankster, we both know there's little time to waste on the drawing."

"Uh, okay. Let me see how it goes, then I'll give you a call."

"Right. And Annie. Does my mom know about this package?"

"No, it just came. And I haven't talked to her."

"That's good. Would you perhaps not tell her? She's been through enough, and now she's really placed her hopes on this show. If she knew this has happened, she'd be terribly upset and fearful for you."

"I know she would. I won't tell her."

"Thank you. Take care now, Annie. And call me as soon as you can."

I hung up the phone and headed for the front door, my mind on a fast track. The previous circumstances that had brought the detective to our house had been nothing but threatening. I'd have to give the girls a diffusing reason for Chetterling's presence.

In other words, I'd need to lie.

"Girls, you ready to go yet?" I called upstairs.

"Coming!" Kelly and Erin spilled out of the bedroom, laughing. They bounded down the steps, each carrying an overnight bag, verbally jousting in half whispers. My heart panged at their innocence. I could not imagine putting them through any more trauma.

"All right, out you go." I grabbed Kelly for a hug. "See you tomorrow."

The doorbell rang. Kelly frowned at it. "Now who's here?" She trotted over to open the door. At the sight of Chetterling, she stepped back, her smile fading like an eclipsed moon.

"Hi, Ralph, come in." My words practically floated on their forced lightness. "Kelly, say hi. The detective is here to talk about that drawing I'm doing for *American Fugitive*."

"Hello." Kelly threw me an uneasy glance.

"Hey there, girls." Chetterling stepped inside, his stocky frame an authoritative presence. The coiled spring of tension in my chest loosened a little. If anyone could help me see this situation clearly, it would be Ralph.

"Hi." Erin's lips curved in a split-second smile. "Come on, Kelly, let's go."

The girls scurried outside and down the porch steps.

The detective turned to watch them. "They don't seem to like me much."

"That's not true." I shut the door. "Just too many memories, I'm afraid."

He nodded, then gazed at me, probing. "How are you?"

My shoulders raised. "I'm not sure. Scared. Mad. Thinking maybe I'd better pull out of this assignment."

"Can't say I blame you for feeling any of those things."

"Yeah. So. Let me show you my little present."

In my office, Chetterling perused the florist box and its contents with gloved hands. He said he'd take the package to the lab for fingerprinting. I told him every detail I could think of — the time it arrived, the blue car I'd seen driving away.

"You know we'll do everything we can to find who did this." He stood near my desk, gazing across the room at my drawing table and materials. "At first guess I'd have to agree with Stephen — it's probably some nut who read the morning paper. With all the publicity from the Willit case, just about anybody could figure out where you live."

I searched his face. Did he really believe that?

"I can't tell you how sorry we are that the information about the TV show got out, Annie. We have no idea who leaked it. Delft is

134

fit to be tied."

"I know." My arms crossed, hugging my chest. "Ralph, what if Bill Bland sent this box?"

He pushed his lower lip up, puckering his chin. "Then we'll trace the payment to his whereabouts and catch him. Believe me, I'd love that. But it doesn't seem likely. First, this would be quite a careless move for him, don't you think, after all these years? Second, I can't imagine he'd bring the box himself or that he's even anywhere near this area. Which would beg the question: What florist fills phone requests for *dead* flowers?"

Mentally, I cataloged what I'd learned of Bill Bland. Exacting. Arrogant. Controlling. Compulsive reader of murder mysteries.

Complete lack of conscience.

Two personalities.

Would a desperate Bland, intent on regaining control, have become this reckless?

If it meant catching him soon, I almost wished he had.

CHAPTER 10

Chetterling encouraged me to keep my appointment with Edwin, assuring that the Sheriff's Department would get to work immediately on tracing my package. In spite of my fears, I knew he was right. Besides, if I didn't go, what would I do — sit around the house alone and allow my fears to mount? Better to stay busy, keep focused on the case for now. Kelly was safe at Erin's; Stephen was off to his ball game. No using my children as an excuse.

"Annie, I promise you," Chetterling said as he left, "we'll call as soon as we know anything. If you go out, keep your cell phone on."

I'd phoned Edwin and told him I was on my way.

Edwin Tarell's meandering ranchstyle home was backed up to an upscale golf course in Redding. A tasteful mixture of stucco and beige stone, it sported elegance befitting a successful businessman. One of the doors to the three-car garage was up, revealing the white Mercedes Edwin had driven to my house a few days ago. Lush, multicolored flowers lined the front walk. Either Edwin employed a gardener, or he spent a lot of his free time on the lawn.

I knew a little of Edwin's personal life from updated information in the case files. He was forty-five — four years older than I. He'd been married and divorced twice. Neither marriage had produced children. From what I gathered, Tarell Plastics had faced a few rocky years when he first took over the company. Delft had noted a conversation with Emily in which she'd admitted her disappointment in Edwin's decision to run the company himself. Perhaps she felt he was too young, too inexperienced. Whatever her reasons, in the end Edwin proved his abilities. Today Tarell Plastics ran strong and employed over one hundred people. Edwin was a respected man in Redding. He was a member of the rotary club, the chamber of commerce, and other local organizations.

Still, I found the grief over his father and the two broken marriages to be most telling. I knew what it felt like to look successful on the outside — and feel like a failure within.

Edwin invited me in with a wan smile, taking my hand in both of his. "You all right?" He wore a pair of pressed light-colored jeans and a designer knit shirt. I caught the slightest whiff of aftershave.

"Fine, thank you." I told him about Chetterling's reaction to the package. "My cell phone's on in case he finds something right away."

"Good, good." His brown eyes lingered on mine. "So, do come in."

He led me into a big family room with overstuffed sofa and chairs, and a flat-screen TV even larger than ours.

"Wow. You watch baseball games on that?"

He smiled. "And football and basketball. Even soccer, from time to time."

Edwin offered me something to drink. I declined. We settled in two matching chairs, his facing the television. His usual seat, I guessed. His fingers lightly rubbed the fabric on the arm. "If that package is a hoax, do you have any idea who'd do something like that to you?"

"None at all."

He nodded. "I just wondered if it could be somebody connected to your past cases. Perhaps someone not happy that one of your composites led to an arrest."

I hadn't considered that.

"Well." He thumped his chair. "Let's not worry about that until we have to. On with the case at hand. I'm happy to give you whatever information you want to know." Edwin shook his head. "I can't tell you how many times in the past I've been assured they were getting close to finding Bland. Especially in the first couple years. Some woman saw him here, some man claimed he lived there. Tips came in from all over. Every time the Sheriff's Department told me they might be getting close, I'd break out in a sweat. I couldn't sleep through the night. Then time would pass . . . and nothing. I'd fall back into normalcy." He gave a little snort. "If you could call my life normal."

The comment struck me. How to respond to such vulnerability? For a moment I busied myself with opening my leather-bound notebook and pulling out a pen, writing Edwin's name on the top of the paper. "Okay. Edwin, what I need from you are further insights into Bill Bland. I've had a number of questions answered by Sergeant Delft. But I'm going to ask you some specific questions to help me fill in the blanks. Tell me for starters — was there anything unusual in the way Bland walked?"

He raised his eyebrows. "Walked? Is that important?"

"Well, maybe it doesn't directly help me in drawing the face. But indirectly it might help me understand him more as a person."

"I see." Edwin rubbed his jaw. "Bland was quiet when he moved. He was almost uncanny sometimes. You'd swear he'd purposely snuck up on you in a room."

Could Bland have been playing some kind of game? Would this lover of mysteries try to slink around just to see if he could do it?

I jotted a note. "What kind of clothes would he wear when he wasn't working?"

"Khaki pants, belted, and a tucked-in button-down shirt. Never jeans or a T-shirt."

"Sergeant Delft said he loved his wife and baby. Would you agree with that?"

"Yes. They were all the family he had. I never heard him talk about parents or cousins."

"Okay. Remember when you first talked to the detective on the scene about . . . that night. You mentioned Bill had a habit of jutting his chin up, then letting it fall. You also mentioned he was precise and finicky."

"Oh, he was finicky, all right. And that thing with his chin — yeah."

"Can you show me what that gesture

140

looked like?"

"He did something with his mouth first, like this." Edwin drew his chin up, causing an indentation beneath his lower lip and increasing the downward furrows at the sides of his mouth. Two vertical puckers appeared in his chin.

"Could you hold that for me a moment?" Quickly I sketched the expression, wondering how this habitual movement might have affected Bland's facial structure after so many years. "Okay. Go ahead."

Edwin jerked his head up, allowed it to sink slowly, then repeated the pattern.

I wrote in my notebook. "How often did he do this? Like in one day."

"I don't know, maybe three times in a day, that I noticed. More if he was stressed."

"Was he stressed a lot?"

"I'd say so. He was nervous when my father first hired him. Then he'd look nervous whenever we had a meeting about accounts. Especially those last few months. Of course, now we know why. Plus he got really stressed out over Susan leaving him."

"Did he ever show anger?"

"Yes, but only when he was extremely pushed. Most of the time he'd just turn silent, like stone. For, I don't know, maybe the first year I knew him, this was the only way I saw him handle anger. I used to admire him for that. Being able to keep it all inside. But then I began seeing a different side of him. One time we argued in the office over some mistake he'd made. I'm telling you, in seconds he went from that cold statue of control to red-faced and yelling. I couldn't believe it. It's like he'd flipped some switch. And when he got that way he'd lose all sense of logic. Say stupid things, make some impulsive decision. He almost hit me once." Edwin glanced away, as if looking down the corridor of the past. "I should have realized, you know. I should have seen what he was capable of doing. There was so much going on beneath the surface of that man. *Especially* when I discovered he was stealing money, I should have known."

"No one else did either," I said gently.

He looked back to me, his chest filling with air. "But I'm the one who's still alive."

I gave him a pained smile. If only I could do something to take away his guilt. "I'm so sorry, Edwin. So sorry things turned out the way they did."

He nodded.

I looked back to my notebook, taking a minute to refocus. "Okay. You said most of the time Bland was the controlled person, right?"

"Yes."

"I'd like to concentrate on that for a minute. Can you tell me about a time when he was mad but stayed in that cold kind of anger?"

He focused on the blank television screen. "There was one time about two months before the Christmas party — the last one he attended. I think on this day he must have found out something about his wife. Maybe even caught her with the other man. He went home for lunch, see — unusual for him. And when he came back to the office, he was . . . well, nearly robotic."

Robotic. I envisioned Bill Bland's features, stiffened like papier-mâché. "What happened?"

Edwin clasped his hands. "I saw him walking past my office. He stared straight ahead, his chin up — and staying that way. His cheeks seemed kind of red. I can't explain it, but something about the way he strode by made me follow him to see if he was all right."

As Edwin told me his story, the film reel in my head began to turn. I pictured him easing down to Bill's office, sticking his

143

head inside . . .

"Are you okay?"

Bill stares out the window, hands in his pockets, feet apart, elbows shoved forward at an odd angle. Like he's standing firm in a high wind. He turns and looks at Edwin, and his face looks like death. No red in his cheeks now, just ghostly white.

"Of course I'm all right." Each word falls like a popcorn seed on a bare floor. "Thank you for asking."

The hands stay in his pockets. Edwin can see the pull of the fabric, like he's digging fingers into his thighs.

Edwin places a palm against the door frame, frowning. His mind catalogs potential problems with the company. Something wrong with the accounts? Negative profit for the quarter? It does not occur to him to consider Bland's private life.

Bland shoots him a look of cool venom. "Is there something I can do for you?"

"No, I just . . . you don't look right, that's all."

"I told you. I am fine." Bland walks to his desk. One hand emerges from his pocket. He reaches out with his forefinger to tap a thin stack of paper into precise alignment. Tap,

tap. His hand is trembling. The top pages don't move far enough. Tap, tap, tap. Bland doesn't stop until he's satisfied.

"Okay, then —" Edwin tries to return to business — "remember those numbers on Corville Industries you were putting together for —"

"Edwin." Bland nearly spits his name. "I have not forgotten. Do I ever forget what people want from me? Do. I. Ever. Forget?"

"No, I just —"

"Good. You will have them in the morning. Which, if you have not forgotten, is when you wanted them."

Anger knocks through Edwin's veins. How dare this guy treat him like this? He is the boss's son. Edwin straightens, takes a step into the office. "I don't know what your problem is, Bland, but you better watch yourself."

"I do watch myself, Edwin. All the time. And I am watching myself now like you would never imagine. So lay off, all right?"

With exaggerated calm, Bland pulls out his desk chair and sits down. He slides a folder toward himself, opens it. His right hand, like some remote appendage, picks up a pen and holds it midair. He grips it until his knuckles blanch.

"Good day, Edwin." His eyes do not raise from the file.

Edwin stalks away, feeling like an obnoxious kid who's been put in his place . . .

His voice faded, and we sat in silence for a moment.

I set down my pen. "You didn't like Bill Bland."

"Not after that. And now . . ." He snorted. "If I saw him on the street, I'd shoot him in a heartbeat. But the terrible mistake I made back then was I never told my father. At the time, I didn't know what I could say. 'Wow, Dad, Bill was really mad. It was kind of creepy.' I figured my father would just brush it off. He always thought the best of everybody."

I watched Edwin's fingers return to the arms of his chair and begin to rub. What had Bill Bland learned that day at lunch that upset him so? That his wife wanted a divorce? *Had* he caught her with the other man? In that scenario, I couldn't blame him for working so hard to hold himself together. It would be amazing that he'd returned to work that day at all.

"Edwin, Sergeant Delft talked to me about Bland's motivation. But I'd like to hear from you. Why do you think he resorted to murder? Why would a quiet man, a white-collar criminal, fall into violence?"

"Hard to figure, isn't it. Yet it happens all the time. How many people out there who kill ever thought they'd do it?" Edwin considered the empty television screen. "Ever hear of Mark Hoffman?"

"No."

"About five years after my father was killed, I read a book about him. It . . . helped me think through some things. Hoffman was a master forger back in the eighties. Real brilliant guy. He wrote over eight hundred documents, supposedly from famous people like Daniel Boone and the founders of our country. Not to mention his forgeries that included scandalous 'information' about Joseph Smith. You know, the guy who started the Mormon church? Hoffman made a fortune selling these documents."

"And he reminds you of Bland?"

Edwin nodded. "For more than one reason. He looked like Bland in a way. A nerdy-looking guy. He could make himself seem like a country bumpkin when he needed to fool someone into buying a document. And I do mean fool. Even the FBI and the Library of Congress declared his forgeries authentic. Shows how smart he was. He spent his spare time reading and studying — like Bland and his mystery novels. And Hoffman learned how to forge perfectly. He'd go to libraries and cut blank pages from the backs of books that were as old as the document he wanted to create. He learned how to make ink using the old formula. And it had weird stuff in it, too, like wasp larvae or something like that. But he went even further. Hoffman knew that the documents would be closely examined because of their potential worth. So he figured out how to beat the carbon-14 test. He took some of that old paper from books and burned it, then scraped the ashes, which would contain the right age carbon, into the ink." Edwin shook his head. "Brilliant."

"Then how did they catch him?"

"That's my point." Edwin's voice snagged. "Hoffman was a smart, cagey, white-collar criminal. Just like Bill Bland. But guess what happened when he was backed into a corner? When he got really desperate? He turned stupid and took crazy risks. And he killed two people."

The words sank into my chest. I held Edwin's gaze.

"Just like Bland, Hoffman planned it. He

sent a pipe bomb to one of the Mormon church officials who'd been involved in buying the forgery about Joseph Smith and blew him apart. The same day he sent a second one to another official, but it killed the guy's wife instead. And, like Bland, he planned to kill more, but things went wrong. The third bomb blew up in his own car. He didn't die, but he was injured pretty badly. Talk about stupid."

I turned the information over in my mind. "So what do you think made Hoffman change like that?"

Edwin sighed. "I don't think he changed, that's just it. I think he carried out what he was capable of all along. Same as Bland, he was caught in a downward spiral. In Hoffman's case, this wallflower guy made lots of money selling his forgeries, and he started living it up, drawing attention to himself. After a while he was spending more than he'd earned, and he fell into serious debt. The debt put pressure on him to promise more documents than he could forge in time. Then his debtors came after him and were going to expose him for all the money he owed. And of course there was speculation about all these important documents he continued to 'find.' Basically, what it came down to was, he was going to be caught. And that, he couldn't allow. He was already a criminal. He already lacked morality. Mix that with desperation, and you get a very dangerous person. Just like Bland."

Edwin's words crawled through me, slime-trailing comparisons of the two criminals. What about the dead roses? If Bland feared getting caught because of the *American Fugitive* show, wouldn't he resort to desperate measures like that? What would keep him from harming me and anyone else whom he viewed as a threat?

No. I would not tread that path right now.

With controlled movements, I closed my notebook and put the pen back in my purse. "Edwin, thank you very much. You've helped me a lot."

"Sure." He rose, giving me a little smile. "I'm glad you could come."

He walked me to the door with an air of reluctance. He stopped in his entryway, hands in the pockets of his jeans. "Look, Annie, I have mixed feelings here. I want you to do that drawing. And I think Chetterling's probably right — your package was a prank, and they'll soon trace it. But if they can't trace it . . . *if* there's the slightest possibility that Bland could have sent it, I don't want you putting yourself in danger."

I hugged my notebook to my chest. "Thanks. You know I'd hate to let you and your mom down. I wouldn't make that decision lightly. And I shiver to think how I'd need to do it. I mean, in order for Bland to know, we'd have to make public that I'd been scared off the case. The newspaper would have to print the story."

Edwin frowned. "I still say the whole thing sounds crazy. Bland can't possibly expect to keep the show from airing forever. They'll just get another artist for a future show."

"But he'd be buying escape time, wouldn't he." I thought of my conversation with Delft. "Like he did twenty years ago."

"Yes." Edwin's voice fell. "That he would."

In a somber mood, we walked out to the front porch. "Call me as soon as you know anything." Edwin gave me a little smile. "I'm betting we're worried over nothing."

Sliding into my car, I placed my purse on the passenger seat. Edwin stood on his porch and waved as I drove off. When I was halfway down the street, my cell phone rang. *Oh, great.* It seemed too soon for any news on the package. Was this Stephen? Had he already managed to get himself in trouble with his friends? I pulled the phone from my purse and checked the incoming number.

Detective Chetterling.

Holding my breath, I clicked on the line.

CHAPTER 11

My heart beat a little too hard as I pulled into the parking lot of the Sheriff Department's North Station. "Annie," Chetterling had said on the phone, "we've run down a lead on that gift of yours. Can you get over here right away? Got someone coming in I think you'll want to see."

Lacking the time to explain, the detective left me with many questions. One thing I did know: he was going out on a limb in allowing me to be present during any questioning.

Chetterling met me outside the door of Delft's office, the sergeant at his side. "You're just in time."

My eyes widened at the sight of both men. "Did you find somebody that links to Bland?"

Delft held up a hand. "We don't know all the connections yet. But we'll soon find out. We're going to let you watch the interview through a one-way glass. You'll be able to hear everything in the interrogation room. The walls are thin."

They led me to an inside window of a small room containing a table and three chairs. A young man in faded jeans and denim shirt with rolled-up sleeves perched in one of those chairs like a trapped jack-in-the box, eyes darting around the room as if searching for a hand to turn the crank. His hands gripped the seat, both legs jiggling. He jumped when the door opened. Chetterling and Delft introduced themselves and sat down. The young man managed a meek hi.

Chetterling recited the Miranda rights and ensured that the young man understood them. "All right. You are Sam Borisun of 2853 Declan Way. You are twenty-six. And you work in the Roses by Redding florist shop, correct?"

I glanced at a video camera mounted in the room's upper corner. Chetterling's introduction was probably for the benefit of a rolling tape.

"Yeah."

"And you understand you're here to tell us about the, uh, flowers you delivered to a Ms. Annie Kingston on Barrister Court?"

"I didn't do anything, really." The words

tripped over themselves. "I mean, I delivered the package, but I don't know any more than that."

"Okay. First tell me about the florist shop. Who is the owner and what hours do you work?"

Stuart Welsher owned the shop, Sam replied, along with a second store on the other side of Redding. Welsher went back and forth between shops during the week, leaving Sam in charge at his location every Saturday.

"And these shops deliver normal flowers, right? Live, pretty ones."

"Yeah." Sam's legs continued to bounce. "Most of the time. But last summer I came up with the idea for the dead ones."

Last summer. Surely there was no correlation to Lisa Willit's murder. All the same, my skin pebbled.

"I was trying to get sales up, you know? Mr. Welsher was trying this and that. But I'd read about it being started somewhere, maybe like in New York. How one guy delivered dead flowers as a joke, like when a guy had been jilted by a girl and wanted to get back at her. Anyway, the idea caught on, and now lots of florists send dead flowers. Some people order them for gag gifts when a person turns forty. Or lots of people like them around Halloween. At first Mr. Welsher thought it was a terrible idea, but then I showed him all the circumstances it could be used for, and how I'd market it and tell all my friends. So he let me try."

Chetterling nodded. "How are your dead flowers advertised?"

"We have a sign in the florist shop. And we included it in our ad in the yellow pages of the new phone book. Also it's on our Web site."

Delft and Chetterling exchanged a glance. *Web site.* Anyone in the country could have found the service.

"Okay." Chetterling flattened his large fingers against the edge of the table. "You took the order for Ms. Kingston's flowers, right?"

"Yeah."

"How? And at what time?"

"It came by phone." Sam popped his knuckles. "I think it was about ten forty-five."

"Was anyone else in the shop?"

"Bettina Gregory. She works weekends."

"Would she have heard your side of the conversation?"

"Yeah, she was standing right there."

"All right. The person on the phone. Was it a man or woman?"

"A man. With a raspy voice."

"Raspy?"

Sam shrugged. "He said he was losing his voice but hoped I could understand him. I said I heard him just fine."

"Okay. What happened then?"

I closed my eyes, praying that what we heard in the next few minutes would convince me — convince us all — that the delivery had been nothing more than a sick hoax. Sam's voice whirred through my head, flashing the scene of him standing at the florist counter with the phone to his ear . . .

"I'd like to play a joke on somebody," says the caller. "You got any dead roses around, like you advertised?"

"Sure do."

"Can you deliver them today?"

"Right now if you want."

"Good." The man states the recipient's name and address. "You can include a note, right? Here's what I want to say."

Sam grabs a pen as the man speaks the words slowly. "Got it." He reads the words aloud, just to be sure. "Sounds kind of sinister. You sure that's okay? What does the second line mean anyway — 'Like this case'?"

The man grates a chuckle. "If I told you, it wouldn't be a secret, now would it? I want her to have to figure this out."

This is nothing new. The clients who order dead flowers tend to have warped senses of humor, like Sam. Utmost stealth is a part of their game. "Yeah, okay. As long as she gets the joke. I don't want her mad at us or anything."

"She won't be mad. She's such a prankster, she'll love it. But make her work at figuring this out. Use an envelope without your shop address, can you do that? And leave the box on her porch, ring her doorbell, then leave in a hurry."

"Okay."

"It's not as if the flowers are going to die, right?"

"Right." Sam laughs, and the caller emits a sound like metal scraping over rock.

"So." Sam readies his pen. "I'll need a credit card."

"Don't believe in them."

"Then how would you like to —"

"Look outside your shop, to your right as you walk out. See that pot with the red flowers? Check underneath it. You'll find twenty-five dollars. I believe that covers the cost, as *you advertised."*

"Uh, yeah." Man, this guy really has his scam down. "Hold on a minute, okay?"

He covers the mouthpiece and asks Bettina to check outside under the potted geraniums. She returns with a twenty and a five-dollar bill. No envelope. Sam twists his mouth at her in an ain't-people-strange expression.

"Okay, we have your money." He opens the cash register and places the bills inside. "You're all set."

"Good. Oh, and one last thing. Just as a favor between you and me."

"Shoot."

"She's going to track this thing down like a real detective. So if she finds you, tell her something for me. But you have to say it exactly. You ready?"

Sam picks up his pen again. "Ready."

"Good. First, say this: 'Fourteen moves in twenty years drives a man to desperation.' " He pauses. "Got that?"

"Wait." Sam finishes writing the sentence, his mouth moving with the syllables. "Yeah." He repeats the words.

"Here's the second part, very important. This is kind of like that game Clue. Tell her: 'It happened in the study. Don stood by the desk.

Peter fell over on the couch.' "

Sam writes once more, flicking a bemused look at Bettina. Wait till she gets a load of this. "Okay, let me read it back to you."

The man listens. "Yes. You have done well."

Sam laughs at his formality. This guy is really nuts. "Thanks. And, uh, anytime you want to send dead roses again, you know where to come . . ."

Sam Borisun's voice faded, and the scene shimmered away. I found myself staring at the young man, my fingers sinking dent marks in the strap of my purse. Detective Chetterling sat with arms crossed, his jaw working. Delft's features were a hardened mask slapped on to keep a poker face from slipping.

My thoughts tossed like leaves in the wind.

"Don stood by the desk. Peter fell over on the couch . . ."

Details of the murders that no one who'd simply read the newspapers would know.

"Fourteen moves in twenty years drives a man to desperation."

Was this Bland, feeling desperate? I

wanted to deny it. Surely there were a number of people in the Sheriff's Department who'd worked on the case. Any one of them would know the details the caller had stated. But why would someone in the department want me off this assignment? Why would anyone take the great risk of getting caught?

After a pale-looking Sam Borisun was allowed to leave, Chetterling and Delft quickly spoke with two deputies, giving them certain information from Sam to check out. Afterward, the three of us met in the sergeant's office.

"What do you think?" I paced about, too nervous to accept the seat offered me.

Chetterling deflected to Delft. "Does it sound like Bland to you?"

"It's looking pretty suspicious." Delft perched in his chair, back straight. "There aren't too many people around here who'd remember the details he mentioned. In fact, I'm the only one who worked on that crime scene crazy enough to stick around this department for twenty years. Other than me, there's you two. And the Tarells, but they're as anxious to find Bill Bland as we are."

Air seeped from my mouth. "Do you think

he's *here?* In the area?"

"I don't know." Delft tapped a thumb against his desk. "I wouldn't put it past him. If he thinks we're closing in on him — and with the TV show we have a good chance of doing just that — he's liable to concoct any kind of scheme. But he also could have paid someone to drop off the money. I can't imagine who, because I don't know anyone in the area he's friendly with. But we'll check with people who live and work around that flower shop. If we get lucky, somebody saw someone dropping off the money. And may remember the make of the car."

Delft blinked at a new thought, then picked up his telephone and punched in three numbers. "Wonder when Bland could have first seen that article?"

We waited while he was connected to the *Record Searchlight* office. After identifying himself and his question, he was forwarded to the Web master for the newspaper. In a few minutes Delft had his answer: articles were posted online at about 2:30 a.m.

We discussed the possibilities. Bland's call to the florist shop came in about 10:45 A.M. Sometime previously, he or his messenger dropped off the money, most likely before the shop opened at 9:00. If Bland had checked his computer in the middle of the night, the most time possible between reading the article and placing the money would have been about eight hours. Driving eight hours from the south would place his home somewhere between San Francisco and the Los Angeles area. In eight hours from the north he could have come from nearly anywhere in Oregon or just over the Oregon border into Washington. From the east, he could have started near the far side of Nevada.

Sergeant Delft reached for a piece of paper and scratched a note. "We need to start checking all the motels in a couple hours' radius."

I brought a hand to my forehead. This was all happening too fast. What was I going to do?

Chetterling touched me on the shoulder. "Do you want out of this assignment, Annie? Another artist could step in, someone far away from here. On the East Coast."

I pressed my knuckles against my chin. "But there's no time to find anyone else on *this* schedule. The show would have to be postponed. That would just give Bill Bland all the longer to be on the streets. Maybe even *these* streets." I looked from one man to the other, feeling my throat tighten. "Right now I don't know what to say. I want out, sure. But I also want that man behind bars. Now he's threatened me, so how can I rest until he's caught?"

Chetterling put his hands on his hips. "Look, we'll be on the alert, in case Bland is in the area. We don't have all the manpower I wish we had, or I'd be putting an unmarked car out front of your house right now. But I'm going to have deputies drive by your house often, all right? You stay home tonight and keep your doors locked. And call us if anything at all looks suspicious. Is Jenna up here this weekend?"

"No."

"Can you call her to come up? Either that, or you go stay with someone."

I stared at the floor, shoulders caving. How I dreaded the night, the coming days. I could not believe this was happening again. "I'll call her."

"Annie." Delft spoke with quiet urgency. "I understand you're upset about all this. With good reason. But there *is* a positive side. Bland's leaving more trails for us to follow. For the first time in years we've got something to run down. And if he happens to be in this area, we could find him before the television show even airs." He paused. "If you pull out of the case, I'll understand. But consider this: if Bland's here, we need that update more than ever." He looked me in the eye.

"In fact, we need it *now.*"

CHAPTER 12

"Jenna. Sorry to bother you when you're working." I gripped the kitchen phone, peering anxiously through the front window. As I'd driven home, righteous anger had settled over me like toxic fallout dust. I'd told Bill Bland off in my mind. Told him he wasn't going to stop me from putting him behind bars — *now*. Told him his own stupidity would trip him up before he got anywhere near me.

Once I walked into my house, my defiance lasted all of two seconds. I turned off the alarm, silencing its high-pitched squeal. Then stood in my kitchen. Alone. The house felt empty. Too quiet. Scary. Instinctively, I'd reached for the phone.

"What's the matter, Annie? You don't sound good."

"I'm not."

"Oh, no. Is it Stephen? The case?"

"The case, big time. Well, Stephen too.

But I can't think about him right now." I cringed. What a horrible thing for a mother to say.

"Okay. Take a deep breath. Now what happened?"

Sometimes it was easy to forget Jenna was younger than I. She possessed everything I did not: self-confidence, beauty, grace. I could picture her heart-shaped face as she talked to me in her kitchen, the thick auburn hair she often pushed behind her ears. Her large and rich brown eyes, full of concern, her brow knitted.

"I'm in trouble again."

The story spilled from my mouth. The dead roses, the note. Bill Bland's possible presence in the area. My ambivalence about what to do. I could hear Jenna's little gasps with each new piece of information.

"Oh, Annie." Her voice squeezed. This was not good. She was supposed to be the fearless one. "Why are you telling me this now? Why didn't you call when you got those flowers?"

"Because you were busy. And I had no time. I had to phone Chetterling right away, and then the interview, and after that —"

"You could have taken a minute."

"I know. Sorry."

"You idgit. Don't *do* this to me again!"

She exhaled in frustration. "All right. Okay. I'm flying the plane up there tonight. I'll stay with you until . . . until this is all over."

"But what about your consulting project?"

"It . . . doesn't matter. I'll work on it up there." Irritation edged her words. "Don't think you can tell me all this and then expect me to stay away."

"I . . . didn't expect that. I *want* you to come."

"Then stop trying to talk me out of it."

Ragged relief widened my throat. The world had not turned upside down just yet. I stood in my kitchen, in my house with its alarm. The kids were okay. And Jenna and I were arguing.

"Sorry, I'm just —"

"And stop saying you're sorry. This is not — Annie, look. *Who* ended up taking on that killer last year? *All by herself?* You are not helpless and this situation is not beyond you. You've come a long way since last summer, and this isn't the time to fall into your I-can't-handle-it routine."

Wait a minute, where did she get *that?* "Okay, okay. Do I sound like I'm falling apart to you?"

She ignored the questions. "On the other hand, if you go out and do something crazy,

168

like you did last time, I will shoot you myself, do you hear? Don't you do a thing until I get there."

Jenna at her best. Working herself up over *my* life.

"I hear." I drifted over toward the sink. "Jenna, do you think I should stop working on the case?"

"I don't know. You're not that far from getting ready to draw, are you?"

"Well, I still have to talk to Bland's ex-wife. I was going to interview Emily Tarell, too, but really I don't know how much she can add."

"Okay, so you interview the ex —"

"And then I have to look over all my notes and make sense of them. Really get a handle on how Bland thinks and acts, and how that might affect his appearance."

"So you're only talking about a couple of days, right? Three at the most? As scary as this is, Annie, it's not much time, especially when you consider your drawing might help catch Bland. Besides, if you pull out, it would be too late to tell the newspaper tonight. So Bland wouldn't even know about it until Monday morning."

I shook my head. "I can't believe it, Jenna. You're actually encouraging me to get into something dangerous?"

169

"*Get* into it? What are you talking about? You're already *in* it! The question is, what's the safest thing to do now?"

Get Bland off the streets. The knowledge punched me in the chest, clear and cold. The safest thing to do — for me and the rest of society — was get Bland off the streets. And my updated drawing was the one thing that could best ensure this happened.

"Okay, Jenna, just . . . get here. We can talk about it more then."

"I'm on my way. Are the doors locked? The alarm on?"

I flicked a look at the ceiling. Caught again. "Yes and yes, Miss Know-it-all."

I hung up the phone and walked to the keypad to activate our alarm. Its light flicked from green to yellow, signaling it was activated to the lowest level. All doors and lower windows were monitored, but I could walk around inside the house without tripping the laser beam sensors.

An hour and a half later, I heard the distant drone of a plane nearing the Grove Landing private runway. Soon the *chut-chut* of my sister's Cessna 210 told me she was taxiing down our wide street. I ran to open the hangar door.

As soon as Jenna was settled inside, we discussed my situation at length. I told her I was scared to death and would just as soon hide in bed with the covers over my head. Me too, Jenna said, but then what? Even if Bland were to hear that I was no longer on the case, would he stop threatening me? Or was he warped enough to continue, just because I'd dared to help apprehend him at all?

"Okay." I slumped on the TV-room couch with my feet tucked under me, rubbing my aching head. "I think you're right. I need to continue this thing and get it done. I can try interviewing Bland's ex on the phone tomorrow. Then get right on to drawing. In a few days I can be finished. And I have to admit, with an update of Bland circulating, I'll feel better protected than I do now."

Before my sister could say one more thing, I pushed from the couch. "I'm going to call Chetterling. Tell him I'm still in."

I made the call from my office.

"Great!" Chetterling responded. "You're a real trooper. I knew you'd make this decision."

"Oh, really."

He emitted a low chuckle. "Annie Kingston, sometimes I think I know you better than you know yourself."

Something about his words. They wrapped around me in a new way. "How . . . frightening."

We paused for a moment that seemed almost awkward.

"Ralph, one thing." My gaze rested on my drawing table as I thought of the work before me. "When the update is done, how are you going to use it? I mean, *American Fugitive* is paying me for it, and what if they don't want it displayed before the show airs?"

"I'm not so sure they'd mind. After all, their whole reason for the show is to catch the bad guys. Still, I don't think we'll post it publicly. We'll use it internally. It'll help us know who to look for as we check hotels in the area. And our deputies on the street will have it."

"Okay. Sounds good." My voice fell as I imagined what could lie ahead.

"Annie? Don't waste time second-guessing your decision now. Just get to work. And we *will* catch him. I promise you that."

I hung up the phone, thinking Emily and Edwin Tarell had heard the same promises for twenty years.

■ ■ ■ ■

Sunday, May 9

■ ■ ■ ■

CHAPTER 13

Church. The gathering of the saints.

His mouth twisted.

While his family went to church with the rest, he performed his own type of gathering.

The box and its crucial contents. Shirt in a plastic bag. Camouflage clothes. Backpack. Rarely used pair of contacts. Wire cutters. Extra license plate. Lock pick. Backup fake ID. Night-vision binocular goggles.

He stopped to caress the sweet gadget. It weighed barely over a pound, including the headgear. Afforded forty degrees width of sight, and distance viewing of one hundred twenty yards on a cloudy night. A handy flip-up raised the goggles from his eyes. Carefully, he wiped the lenses, checked for dust, then wiped again.

Blake Cremmer had used a pair of these in *Last Second on Earth.* Effectively.

Next a blond wig, and a black one, and five hundred dollars in cash.

The gun.

His fingers ran down its sleek barrel. He would not think now of the situation that would force him to use it.

He checked his watch. Almost eleven. Church was in full swing, the preacher spilling his platitudes about hope and peace.

Time for battle.

All the items went into the trunk of his car. He positioned himself behind the wheel and drove away, steel-minded, focused. Refusing to look back. He *would* return to all that held him here. Safe and sound.

But he would not be the same man.

CHAPTER 14

The dead roses and threatening note were designed to make me drop my fugitive update assignment like a sizzling pan. Instead, as I entered church Sunday morning, I faced the grim reality that I'd been drawn right into the flame.

I couldn't help looking over my shoulder. True, Bill Bland might be far away. He might have sent a messenger to drop off that money. But so far the Sheriff's Department had found no leads as to who left the twenty-five dollars. No one in the area saw anything. And so my overactive brain flashed scene after scene of Bland's shadowy figure sneaking to that florist shop in the middle of the night. Now I couldn't shake the feeling that he was close, watching me. Somehow certain of his ability to hide in plain sight. Had he changed his appearance over the years? With what I'd learned of the man so far, I wouldn't have thought so. I'd expect him to alter little to nothing of himself, even dressing the same.

Was I wrong?

Following Kelly's lead, I drifted into the pew where Erin and Dave sat. Normally I would allow Kelly to sit with them while Stephen and I settled a few rows behind. I hadn't wanted people to see me hanging near Dave and jump to any conclusions. But this morning I gave social etiquette no thought.

Neither did I dwell on the fears plaguing me about Stephen. Jeff had dropped him off the previous night a good hour beyond his curfew. Stephen acted even more belligerent than normal, and I couldn't help but notice his enlarged pupils. My head knew what this meant, but my heart refused to absorb the truth. After the day's events I already strained against the quicksand of anxiety, and any movement toward my son's rebellion would have pulled me under.

I lowered myself into the church pew, glancing left and right, searching men's faces. Kelly and Erin sat between me and Dave, giggling over who knows what. Stephen glowered on my left. If only Jenna had come, but she never went to church.

"Hi." Dave smiled at me over the girls' heads.

"Hi."

I could not hide my distraction. A crease flickered across Dave's forehead, but he smoothed it away. He would not ask me what was wrong in front of the kids.

The service began, and we stood to sing. Since starting to attend church last summer, I'd learned many of the praise choruses. When I didn't know a song, I could follow the words that were projected on a giant screen. This morning I could not begin to focus on them. Instead, my mind took up its own mocking chant.

Here I am again, God. Here I am again.

My father had been an open cynic of Christianity, and though I would not belittle anyone's faith as he had, his heavy-handed attitude had left its fingerprints on my soul. But after Lisa's murder I'd witnessed the strength that Dave and others who loved her possessed through clinging to God and His promises. Gerri Carson, who volunteered with the Shasta County Sheriff Department's chaplaincy program, had also made a deep impression as she prayed for me and answered my unending questions about God's forgiveness of sins.

The biggest reason for my attendance in church, however, lay in my brink-of-death promise to God. I'd faced a danger I knew

I could not survive without help. *Save my life,* I'd cried to Him, *and I'll seek You.*

Annie Kingston, despite all her shortcomings, does have one redeeming trait. She keeps her promises.

Promises. The faces of Emily and Edwin Tarell filled my mind. Because of my commitment to help them, I faced this new danger. Because of that commitment, I now cried once more to the heavens.

Help me again, God, and this time I'll find You.

"Mom, you're not singing." Kelly elbowed me. Kelly, my beautiful daughter, who'd loved church since the first morning we came. Now *she* was a prize for God.

"Sorry." For her sake, I sang along. On the other side of me, Stephen stood silent, arms folded. Resentment undulated off his shoulders like heat from asphalt.

A male voice some rows behind me began singing loudly, off-key. The sound made my spine tingle. Was it Bill Bland this close, mocking me? Ridiculous as that seemed, my heart stumbled. Of its own accord my head began to turn toward the source.

Please, God, no. He'll have seen my children . . .

I came to my senses. How tactless I would

seem, craning my neck to see some poor man who sang badly. I forced myself to face forward.

The singing ended. I sat with the rest of the congregation and tried to listen. But thoughts of Bill Bland continued to grind my personal projector into motion, pictures of Don Tarell's and Peter Dessinger's murders flashing through my head in vivid sequence.

Don Tarell's knuckles rapping against his desk . . .

Flash —

Edwin Tarell's eyes widening at the sight of the gun . . .

Flash —

A slow-motion bullet hits Peter Dessinger below his hairline, pushing his head back, spraying blood and tissue through the air . . .

"This week I'm going to continue my two-part sermon on 'The Reality of Redemption.' " Pastor Storrel's voice cut through my gruesome thoughts.

"Turn with me please to Isaiah chapter one, and we'll read verse eighteen again. 'Come now, let us reason together,' says the Lord. 'Though your sins are like scarlet, they will be as white as snow; though they are red like crimson, they shall be like wool.' "

Flash —

The scarlet stain of blood on Don Tarell's shirt . . .

"We spent most of last week on that first phrase, 'Come now, let us reason together.' " Pastor Storrel moved away from the podium, relying on the small microphone clipped to his lapel. "We talked about the awesome promise of these words. That the *Lord of all,* the *God of the universe,* would humble Himself to approach mankind and say, 'Come.' That He would offer 'let us reason together,' as one friend or spouse might say to another."

Flash —

Emily kneeling beside her spouse, watching his life drain away . . .

Pinpricks marched up the back of my

neck. The more intense the images, the more I sensed Bill Bland's presence. Could he possibly be here? Watching me?

I forced the scenes from my head.

"That the God who hung the sun and moon would say these words to *you* and *you* —" Pastor pointed to various sections of the congregation — " 'Come, let us reason together.' People, if you ever doubted your worth, if you ever doubted what you mean to God, that phrase alone should set you straight. You mean enough to God for Him to beg just to talk to you."

Talk to you . . .

Edwin Tarell had phoned last night, wanting to hear how the dead roses had been traced. He was appalled to learn the trail went no further than the florist shop, and that we believed Bland could be in the area. "Annie, then *please* tell me you'll drop the assignment. I don't want anything to happen to you. Do it for me. I just couldn't handle the guilt over one more person's — lack of safety."

". . . not done with that verse yet," Pastor Storrel's voice sliced into my thoughts, "but turn with me for a moment over to Jeremiah 2:22."

I dragged my mind back to the sermon.

Something told me I would need the pastor's words in the coming days. I looked to Kelly and we exchanged a smile. I patted her arm — a touch to ground myself.

"Here's the verse. 'Although you wash yourself with soda and use an abundance of soap, the stain of your guilt is still before me,' declares the Sovereign Lord." The pastor looked up. "Now that word 'soda' sounds kind of strange to us. We're not talking about a soft drink. The word could be translated as 'lye.' What God is saying here is: It doesn't matter how clean you are on the outside. It doesn't matter what you do or where you go, for that matter, or any of your surrounding circumstances . . ."

Where you go.

Bill Bland had run for two decades. He'd escaped justice, but he hadn't escaped the stain of his sins. Surely he'd paid for them every day. Had it been worth it? Running, hiding, ever on the defensive? If I were Bill Bland, wouldn't I get tired of it all? Wouldn't I just want to stop fighting and turn myself in? Twenty years, and what did he have to show for it?

". . . and what are you left with? Sin that stains your soul, on the inside, and separates you from God. That is the circumstance we are all in, folks. But thank God He doesn't end it there, with Jeremiah 2:22. No. Instead, He gives us the divine invitation of Isaiah 1:18. 'Come, let us reason together. Let me wash away your sins; let me take that scarlet stain and make it white as snow.' " Pastor Storrel leaned toward the congregation. "Now I know there are some here today who've resisted that invitation. Who've run from God for years. Let me ask you, in light of all He has to give, *why* do you keep running?"

The question fisted around my heart. The pastor seemed to be looking into my own thoughts. I changed my position on the pew. Why *did* I keep running?

Now wait a minute, I hadn't really run from God. I was in church, wasn't I? I'd learned a lot about Him in the last ten months — about how He sent Jesus Christ to die on the cross, and how through that death all people could be forgiven of their sins if they would only accept the gift of salvation . . .

So why hadn't I done that myself?

I shifted in my seat again. Checked the floor to make sure my purse was still there, as if it may have magically vanished. Because I wasn't ready, that's why. Because even if I accepted this sermon, accepted God's promise to wash away sins and make

185

me like new, it would be no time at all before those stains were right back in place. In a way, it would be like Bill Bland turning himself in. We both could say, *Now it's over, no more resistance.* But he'd have to be accountable for his actions from then on. So would I.

Resisting may be a disheartening job, but at least I was my own boss.

"There's no need to continue carrying the burden of your sins, folks. No need at all. Not when God has provided you a way out. And don't think you're sitting on the fence about this. There *is* no sitting on the fence when it comes to Christ. If you're not saying *yes* to Him, you're saying *no.* 'No to your gift of redemption; no, I don't need You in my life; no, I'll take my chances with eternity.' And each no, you see, puts a new stain on your soul. So I ask you: Is it worth it?"

No to your gift of redemption.

I did not want to think about this.

My heart knocked around in my chest during the closing hymn. I could feel the flush of my face as I meted out a smile to Dave and Erin, as I quickly herded my kids out of the suffocating sanctuary.

"Why do we come here, Mom?" Stephen

kicked at a nonexistent stone as we crossed the parking lot. "You don't even like it."

"Yes, I do." My tone could have cut steel.

"No, you don't."

"Knock it off, Stephen."

We headed for the car to go home. A home, by the way, that I couldn't be sure was safe anymore. *Well, thanks, God. I come to church to seek peace in the midst of all I face. Couldn't You just give me that? Instead You make me feel guilty.*

"Let me drive home, Mom." Stephen swiped at the keys in my hand.

"Fine." I climbed into the passenger seat, ignoring Kelly's questioning looks.

I am not running like Bill Bland, God. I am not.

CHAPTER 15

"Mom, are you sure you're all right?"

Kelly slumped on one of the couches before our fireplace, curling a strand of hair around a finger, her forehead creased. "I know there was something wrong with you after church. Erin and her dad saw it too."

Regret washed through me. Kelly had not forgotten the dangers I'd faced the previous year. I really needed to hide my emotions better. Not for the world would I upset my sweet daughter. Sinking down beside her, I put an arm around her shoulders.

"I'm fine. Really. It's just that this case I'm working on is beginning to get to me."

"Why?"

I stared at the glass coffee table, searching for an answer that would not be a lie. "I've had to find out a lot of information about this man who killed two people. Soon I'll be holed up in my office, doing the drawing. I'm just feeling a lot of pressure right

188

now. That television show depends on me getting everything right. Just imagine if I didn't do a good job, and as a result, the man isn't found. I'd feel really bad."

She twirled her hair. "But how would you know if you didn't do a good job? I mean, you could draw him perfectly, but still he's hiding so well that he can't be found. That wouldn't be your fault."

How right she was. Kelly knew all too well my tendency to take on blame.

"Erin guessed that you're worried about the drawing." Kelly gave me a wan smile. "She said to tell you she's praying for you. And I will too. Okay?"

I pulled back to study her face. "Thanks. I . . . didn't know you prayed."

She shrugged. "I didn't until we started going to church. But in our Sunday school class, they talk a lot about telling God your problems. You know, like letting Him kind of get you through the day."

My lovely girl. So open with her emotions. I brushed her cheek with my knuckles. "Does it help?"

"Yeah." She looked at me askance. "Don't you pray? I mean, now that we go to church and all."

I felt a twinge of discomfort. "Sure I do."

So what if it wasn't very often?

Kelly leaned her head against my shoulder. "You should go talk to Erin's dad and tell him you're okay. Erin could tell he was concerned, you know? And she doesn't want him to like feel bad or anything."

How ironic, this circle of protection. I worried about Kelly; she worried about Erin, who worried about Dave. Who worried about me.

Me.

I could hardly take hold of that thought. Surely only Dave's strong faith in God made him so caring, after everything that had happened last year. I wondered if that niggling part of me would ever believe that he didn't blame me.

"Okay. I promise I will. But first I've got to make a phone call in the office. I'm trying to get hold of this last person I need to interview."

Her fears allayed, Kelly scampered off to Erin's house. I walked to the stairway that led downstairs and opened the door. The computerized cries of dying men and machine guns plagued my ears. My son was playing a video game. Killing people for fun.

With a shiver deep enough to surprise me, I turned toward the office to call Bland's ex-wife, Susan Effington.

From the files Sergeant Delft gave me, I

knew quite a bit about Susan. She'd married the man for whom she'd left Bill Bland within three months of Bland's disappearance. Gary Effington was an insurance broker who'd been transferred from Redding to Washington State shortly after the Tarell/Dessinger murders. He and Susan lived in the suburbs of Seattle and had two children. Susan's first child with Bland, a boy named Nick, made the third in total. Nick was now twenty-one years old and about to graduate from college. Gary Effington was the only dad he had ever known, and Nick had not been told his biological father's sordid tale. Delft informed me that both he and *American Fugitive* had contacted Susan regarding the show. She was willing to be interviewed only if her identity was completely concealed, and she did not want the show to include her current name or her son's name.

At the time of the murder investigation, Susan provided the detectives with photos of her husband, none of them high quality, and one picture of Bland's father, whom Bill was said to favor. I was grateful for that one photo of the senior Mr. Bland, as both he and his wife were now deceased.

I settled at my desk, pen and paper before

me, my questions jotted and ready. I'd pulled out Bland's driver's license picture so I could look at him while Susan and I talked. If she was home.

Fortunately, I soon learned, it was raining in Seattle, which had kept Susan and her family home on this Sunday afternoon instead of going on a planned outing. When I explained to her that time on my assignment had suddenly become urgent, she agreed to talk.

I wanted to put her at ease from the beginning, distance her from any guilt she may feel. "I know that you were as surprised as anyone about what your ex-husband did."

"More like shocked about the murders, yes." Susan's voice had a chilly, thin ring to it. "But I will tell you the truth — not about the stealing."

"No?"

"About three months before the murders, we had a major fight. I'd already moved out, and he came over to see Nick. I wanted him to leave, but he insisted on staying. We started arguing. And he shouted these words that would haunt me later: 'All this money you're costing me — you have no idea! You wouldn't believe what you've made me do!' I didn't think much about this at the time. But once I heard about all the money missing, I remembered those words." She paused. "Still never would I have thought . . . I just couldn't believe it."

My brain flashed the scene as Susan told me the details of Bill Bland standing in her kitchen, shoulders hunched, yelling. I stared at his picture, envisioning the redness of his face, his lips pulled back.

"Edwin Tarell told me that most of the time Bill's anger was one of cold control. He only saw Bill lose it a couple of times."

"That's true. I'd never seen Bill raise his voice until we started having trouble."

Started having trouble. I couldn't help but wince at her way of putting it. As much as I didn't like Bland, he had a right to be upset about their marriage falling apart. After all, she'd walked out on him for someone else. Like Vic had done to me. Worse, Susan had taken Bland's only child away.

"Susan, can you tell me about any facial expressions or habits he had?"

"He had this thing with his chin, where he'd kind of jerk it up."

"I've heard about that. Any others?"

"I . . . don't think so."

"Okay." I checked my list of questions. "What were his eating habits like?"

"He liked sugar. Loved cookies and cakes.

He must have had a fairly high metabolism, though, because he wasn't overweight. Just his face was a little pudgy-looking. But that was the way his dad looked too."

"There were strong similarities between them, right?"

"Yes, a lot. And they ate the same. Bill often said he got his sweet tooth from his father."

"It looks like his dad was heavier than Bill."

"A little heavier, but not much."

I made note of that. "By the way, Bill's eyes. Was he nearsighted or farsighted?"

"Uh, near."

"How strong were his lenses? Or, let me ask it another way. Did his eyes look substantially bigger when he wasn't wearing glasses?"

"Well, some, I guess. But not that much. Oh, I should probably say that I think he'd still be wearing glasses today. Instead of contacts, I mean."

An important point. "Why?"

"He'd tried contacts, but he never liked them. His eyes were too sensitive. He'd only tried hard contacts and today everyone wears soft, so maybe . . . But I don't think so."

"Because you think his eyes would still be

too sensitive?"

"Because I think he'd still be Bill. He wasn't someone to change unless forced to. He was very set in his ways to be so young. I would tease him sometimes about being as narrow-minded as an old man."

I gazed across the room, turning her words over in my mind. This information fit with everything else I'd heard.

"Susan, I need to know more about Bill's personality. From what I could see on his photo, I detected a sense of arrogance. Would you agree with that? Also, both Sergeant Delft and Edwin Tarell have said that Bill always needed to be in control. And that when he felt that control slipping away, he would completely change. Can you tell me more about all this?"

"I'll try. It's very hard to explain." She sighed. "Okay. First, you have to understand three important things. One, it's true that Bill wanted to be in control. Two, he was an intricate planner. Three, as you sensed, he was arrogant. Now these things sometimes worked against each other. For example, sometimes his arrogance superseded his ability to control. He owned all these mystery novels, have you heard that? They were all perfectly alphabetized. He was so finicky about it — that's part of the control

195

issue. But as he read a novel, he'd always lose his place. He refused to 'mar' the book by turning down a corner of a page, and he never used a bookmark because he insisted he was smart enough to remember where he was reading. Then of course, he wouldn't remember. He'd do this over and over again. I even went out and bought him a special bookmark. He never used it.

"Here's another example of how these three traits came into play. For my birthday after Nick was born, Bill planned a great surprise party. He hatched this incredible scheme that involved me getting a phone call, and then this and that happening, until I was forced to end up at this restaurant, where my family and friends were waiting. Everything went off to perfection, and Bill was very pleased with himself. He had remembered to line up a babysitter for Nick. But he had to talk to her quickly, and he forgot one little detail: with my being called to the party, who was going to pick up Nick from day care and get him home? The babysitter was too young to drive. So there she was, waiting at our house for someone to bring the baby; meanwhile, day care was calling my office, wondering why I was so late. When Bill realized he'd messed up on this, his arrogance couldn't handle it.

He became furious and ended up blaming *me*."

I was writing as fast as I could. "Do you think that arrogant look in Bill's expression would be more obvious today?"

"After not being caught for twenty years?" Cynicism coated Susan's words. "Yes. I believe that whatever bad traits he had in the past will now only be magnified. He'll be more arrogant, more controlling. Perhaps somehow that will lead to his downfall. No doubt today he's overlooking the fact that the reason he's had to hide all these years is because he made some major mistakes. Understand that to Bill's mind, he is always right. And he's always smarter. That kind of thinking ultimately led to the death of two people. To Bill, he simply did what he had to do."

Did what he had to do.

The changeling soul of Bill Bland was forming before me, the parts of him joining together like muddied water droplets. Water always did seek the lowest level.

I bent over my notes, scribbling, concentration forced upon the words themselves, not the meaning — or the threat it might pose to me. "Okay. Thank you for all that explanation. Now — besides arrogant, could you list other words to describe Bill? Name everything you can think of."

I heard her slow intake of breath. "Where to begin? I suppose with meticulous. Also he was set in his ways. Sorry, that's more than one word."

"Doesn't matter, you're doing great." My pen poised over the paper.

"Humorless. Exacting. Precise." She chuckled. "Oh, wow, this is getting easier. Controlling. Mystery buff. Introvert. Fairly intelligent. Tight. Oh, was he tight with money."

I perused his photo, thinking of wrinkles that would have appeared in two decades. "Was he stressed much of the time? Did he frown a lot?"

"He didn't used to. You see, he was also very logical. He reined in his emotions — except for when he lost it. So most of the time his face looked expressionless, because he wouldn't want it any other way. Because then he would seem out of control, which wasn't an option with him, do you understand?"

Like Mark Hoffman. An intelligent, white-collar criminal who had everything under control. Until he snapped.

"Yes. But you said he 'didn't used to.' "

"That's because when we separated, he had a harder time controlling his emotions.

He started to frown more. And he'd get sort of narrow-eyed. That was a new expression for him."

Crucial points. I looked at Bland's picture again, imagining lines across the forehead, around the eyes.

"How about the sun? Did Bill stay outside much and get tan?"

Susan laughed. "Hardly. He was white even in the summer. Definitely an indoor man."

"All right. And finally, just to be sure. Have you discovered any photos that you didn't know you had? Pictures of Bill or his parents?"

"No, I'm sorry. I wish I hadn't thrown them away. But of course, that was long ago, after he'd disappeared, and I was so . . . ashamed."

Because people would know her as the woman married to a murderer? Or because she realized that her leaving Bland had been the catalyst for his downfall?

I couldn't help but wonder: what if Susan hadn't walked out on him? Maybe Bland never would have stolen the money . . . never would have killed . . .

"Did Bill have any medical condition that would affect his aging? Something, for example, that may cause him to gain or lose weight, or lose his hair early?"

"Not that I know of. Bill was always healthy. I can't even remember seeing him with a cold."

Nothing in the case files had suggested a medical condition, either.

"Okay, Susan, almost done. Is there anything else you'd like to tell me? Something that you think would make a difference as to how Bill would look today?"

"You know, something tells me he won't look all that different. If I saw him, I bet I'd know him in a heartbeat. Bill just wasn't someone who would seek change. In fact, I wouldn't be surprised if he's still working as an accountant. Unless he's ended up in a bookstore, stocking the mystery section."

Interesting thought. Perhaps I would need to draw two personas of Bland, one dressed as a white-collar employee, the other dressed more casually.

One final look at my listed questions told me I'd heard all I needed. I thanked Susan for her help, requesting that I be allowed to call her again if something else came to mind. She told me I could.

"Annie? Do you . . . think they'll find him?"

Her voice edged with anxiety.

"Well, I'd say with the show they'll have

the best chance they've ever had." I lay down my pen, forming my next question carefully. "Would it be better for you if he wasn't found?"

She hesitated. "In a way. That is, of course he should be. But if he is, there'll probably be news coverage. And I want to protect my son. I *don't* want Nick to find out about his real father. What if some snoopy reporter tracks me down and calls the house? It will be *awful*. I told the *American Fugitive* people I'd cooperate with an interview. But I lie awake these nights, worrying what will happen."

Her words tugged at my heart. I thought of my own children — how I'd wished I could protect them from the hurtful truth about their father when he walked out on us all. Susan's situation was so much worse.

"How hard this must be for you. I can see why you may not have cooperated at all."

"It was my citizen's duty." She made a little sound in her throat. "But as for my mother's duty? I hope the show doesn't work. There. I said it out loud. Gary and I both hope —"

"It's okay, Susan. I really do understand. And I hope if Bill is caught, you'll be left alone, completely. If I can do anything to help about that, I will."

"Thank you. Very much."

A moment later I hung up the phone and sat staring at my notes, trepidation ballooning in my chest. My interviews were complete. Now came my descent into Bill Bland's mind. I would review the information I'd learned about him. List the important details. Read them again and again; let them wash over me, through me, until I could see him, feel him.

Reach out and touch him.

■ ■ ■ ■

MONDAY, MAY 10–
TUESDAY, MAY 11

■ ■ ■ ■

CHAPTER 16

My drawing table and supplies were laid out and ready. Sunday night I'd busied myself with this task, putting off the review of my notes with much rationalizing. No point in starting in until I had a full day to devote to it. Besides, the kids were around and dinner needed preparing. And Kelly had made me promise I'd talk to Dave. Which, even without studying my notes, I did not find time to do.

It was now eight-thirty in the morning. Jenna had taken the kids to school and would return after shopping for groceries. We'd gotten a little scarce in the food department the last few days. Dave and I carpooled to school, and usually he drove in the mornings. But since Jenna had errands she wanted to finish early, she'd offered to take the girls and Stephen in. She did not want to leave me alone for long.

I sat in my office chair, tired eyes fixed on

my work area across the room. I'd chosen a lightly tinted paper to draw on, one that appeared similar to Bland's skin tone. The paper was eleven-inches-by-fourteen, the typical size I used in composites. I would do the drawing in color, starting with light lines in graphite pencil, then layering on skin tones in pastels, and finally colored pencils. It would be in horizontal format, which would easily fill a television screen without being cropped and would include the neck and shoulders, so the head would not appear to float.

All the logistics were firmly in my head. All I had to do was . . . *do* it.

What if you don't get it right? That question had haunted me most of the night. What if my drawing was way off-base, and Bland could not be found? How would I ever rest easily again, knowing he lurked out there somewhere? This man who had killed two people, who'd threatened me, could not be assumed predictable — now or later.

Please, God. Help me.

In the past year I'd studied age progressions and had done well in my classes. I *knew* facial features; goodness knows I'd drawn faces for a decade in the courtroom. I could almost hear Jenna's no-nonsense voice: *Annie, you can do this. Now buckle up and get to it.*

With a deep breath, I opened my file of notes. To its right I placed a yellow pad, ready to list each detail as I reread the information. I needed to let myself sink into Bland's story, become one with him. Then I could apply what I knew of his uniqueness to the scientific concepts of aging.

Above the yellow pad I placed Bland's driver's license photo. Bland's eyes seemed to bore into mine. I pulled my gaze away.

Okay. First, I would tackle Sergeant Delft's interview. I began reviewing my notes, writing down key words. Then I went on to my talk with Edwin Tarell, and finally to Susan. As I read and jotted, I forced my visual brain to stay on hold until I had all the words in front of me. Then I began to study them — these pieces that formed the abstract puzzle of Bill Bland:

low integrity — resorted to stealing when
   backed against the wall
cunning
managed to buy illegal gun
arrogant
plans elaborately, but makes stupid mistakes
quiet, mild mannered

murder-mystery buff
neatnik — alphabetized books by author
   and title
fairly intelligent
few friends
moved quietly, could sneak up on people
dressed in preppy clothes for casual,
   always a suit at work
fiercely in love with wife and baby
only child, parents deceased
meant to kill all four people in Tarell
   house
nothing left to lose —

My mental projector smacked on. I closed
my eyes and let the scene come. I saw Bill

*sitting in his office, staring at a wall devoid of
pictures, blank and empty like his heart. His
feet plant themselves apart, his fingers press
into his desk. One thought circles like a
vulture, circling down, down until he can feel
the cold of its shadow: nothing to lose, nothing to lose. His wife and baby are beyond his
reach, soon will move out of state. He has no
sibling, no parents to disappoint. Control of
his life — gone. Control of his finances —
gone.*

   If they've found out about the money he took

— his reputation, his freedom, everything will be gone.

Emotions surge through him, clammy waves trailing fear that clings to his soul like sea-weed. With every ounce of willpower he fights the waves, forcing them to still . . . be still. Until the calmness within him is so profound, so eerie, that it prickles the back of his neck.

Now he can think.

Plan.

He's lost too much. Nothing more — noth-ing more — will be taken away.

He stares at the wall, mulling, remembering bits and pieces of crime stories . . .

He needs a way to disappear fast in case the missing money is discovered.

And if he's surrounded by people who want to lay hold of him, he'd better have the means of forcing his way out.

The scene shimmered away.

I sat motionless, eyes closed, straddling the tenuous threshold of Bill Bland's world and my own. When I could pull myself back, I inhaled slowly, flexed my shoulders. Then turned my attention back to my words of description. I listed the rest of his traits. The jerking up of his chin. His tendency to stay out of the sun. His sensitivity to hard contacts. The later habit of narrowing his eyes . . .

Finally done I picked up Bland's driver's license photo and studied it until my head hurt. *Bill Bland, what would you look like today?*

He would now be fifty-four. In the driver's license picture, taken when he was thirty-three, he had no beginning wrinkles as someone his age might, due to the pudginess of his face and his habitual placid expression. But during the thirties, the transverse frontal, or frown lines, deepen, as do the upward, curved lines at the inside corners of the eyebrows. Lateral orbital lines, or crow's-feet, and the furrows between nose and mouth also become more pronounced. My sense told me all these wrinkles would have appeared with a vengeance by the time Bland turned forty, weighted as he must have been by the stress of his life on the run. During a person's forties, more lines can appear, such as the inferior orbital grooves, running from near the inside corners of the eyes out toward the cheeks. Lips can thin, and the oromental grooves — lines pulling down the outside of the mouth — may begin to show. The jawline can become less firm. Bland already lacked a strong jawline, so this could have become even more pronounced. Excess skin above the eyelids can develop. Bland's upper eyelids at the time of his driver's license photo showed no hereditary extra skin. Even so, by now he would be showing some of this.

Bland's habit of jerking up his chin would make a difference in his wrinkle structure. Edwin Tarell's mimic of the movement had included pulling his mouth upward until a deep groove appeared beneath the lower lip and tucks appeared in the chin. With Bland's facial structure, this habit, added to his tendency not to smile, would increase the oromental grooves and probably the mentolabial groove — the downward curve beneath the center of the lips.

One disappointing factor: Bland's ears didn't stick out, weren't too big or too small. A person's ears can stay the same for years, only perhaps beginning to appear bigger during one's sixties. An unusual shape can be very helpful in drawing a composite or age progression.

Bland's hair could be somewhat thinner, his hairline a little receded.

He would probably still wear glasses instead of contacts. I agreed with Susan that he was unlikely to change or try new things. I even sensed that the frames of his glasses would be a similar black, despite the more modern variations of today.

How would you be dressed, Bill Bland?

If I made two drawings, one of him dressed in the white-collar, accountant style, and the other showing a more casual look, I would not have to draw the face twice. I could do it once, high on the paper, then, using overlays of matte acetate sheets, create the different clothing looks beneath it.

But now I sensed that concept was off-base. It seemed to me, given Bland's need to feel in control and his meticulous nature, that he would have held on to all he could of his past habits. I could picture him in the same type of job, wearing suits without taking off the jacket, as he'd done before.

I leaned my head back against the chair, closing my eyes. Beginning to envision Bland as he would look today. And I could *feel* the inside of him — the cold calculations as he assessed a situation of possible danger. The fierce determination to protect all that he had —

Did he love his wife and son?

Fiercely.

Yes. Fiercely enough that he would hold on to his past habits. Try to restructure his life with stability. He'd want a family to control. He'd probably remarried and had children.

Children from whom he would ferociously guard the knowledge of who he is.

A sand castle of a new life, meticulously constructed on shifting earth. Granules heaped, shaped, cut into turrets and fortresses, trenched into moats. Rooms molded, walls packed tightly into place, far back from threat of the sea. But a new tide had risen and now came rolling, rolling, bearing down on Bland's castle with relentless force. What would Bill, the ersatz king, do to protect his threatened domain? Raise destructive barriers? Charge the waves in a murderous frenzy?

A chill coiled itself around the length of my spine and hung there, flicking its tongue.

My phone rang, the sound sinking teeth into my nerves. I jumped, then slowly turned my head toward it. I can't say for certain how I knew, other than the uncanny timing. But I did. Deep within, my consciousness intertwining with this deceptive man's, I sensed who would be on the line.

A second ring. A third.

Fourth.

Mentally, I scurried to sweep up broken bits of courage. Just before the message machine clicked on, I picked up the receiver.

CHAPTER 17

The phone may as well have been barbed wire against my ear. I couldn't find the voice to say hello.

I heard the breathing first. The labored seep of air from a tightened throat. Funny, how I was struck with the sensation that he was almost as nervous as I. As if I could feel his desperation to shield himself, his new life, from me, the interloper.

"Annie Kingston?"

My name scratched like an ancient phonograph. *Raspy,* Sam Borisun had called it. The sound of a man intent on masking his voice.

"Y–Yes."

A hesitation followed, and in that moment I felt our minds connect. Perhaps from my reticence in speaking, he realized I'd known it was him. This would throw him like a rogue wave on the seashore. His modus operandi for years had been separation, stealth.

He would not know how to handle my ability to sense him.

"I am not happy with you, Ms. Kingston. You have been working on the case even after receiving my suggestion that you stop."

I could not answer.

"Do you know where your daughter is?"

A block of ice sank in my gut. I felt all blood drain from my face. *"What?"*

"She was wearing a purple top this morning. And jeans." The voice scraped its evil into my ear. "Her hair is a lovely brown."

Air pooled in my lungs. I could not land on one specific thought, my mind spinning like dust in a whirlwind. My fingers clenched the phone.

"Ms. Kingston? You *don't* want to pursue this case. Do you?"

A strangling sound escaped me. "Where's Kelly? Are you saying you have her? Where *is* she?"

"Think about it. You *don't* want to do this."

The line clicked.

"No! Wait! Come back, come *back!*" I hunched over, screaming into the phone, tears flooding my eyes.

Silence.

"No, God, no, God, please." I threw down the receiver, dug fingertips into the sides of my head. *No, no, not Kelly. Anything but Kelly.*

Time warped. The next thing I knew I'd punched in the number of the Sheriff's Department, demanding that the receptionist let me talk to Detective Chetterling — *now.*

"Ma'am, he's out in the field. I can have him call you —"

"Sergeant Delft then. *Hurry!*"

Delft had barely answered when I spilled my story, the words hiccuped and barren.

"We'll send somebody out to the school right now." His response was clipped but empathetic. "Hang on a minute while I put this call out."

I waited for what seemed an eternity.

"Okay, a car's on its way. Annie, don't worry too much yet, your daughter is probably fine. He's just trying to get you, that's all."

"But he knew what she was wearing!"

"Yes. He may have been watching the school. But that's *good* news; that means he's close, and we'll get him."

How could he say that? Nothing about this was good news.

"Listen to me, Annie. Wouldn't the school have called if Kelly didn't show up?"

My chaotic mind stalled enough for this

one rational thought. "I think so." I drooped in my office chair, forcing myself to concentrate. "Look, if she's there, I don't want to scare her! She doesn't know any of this is going on. Imagine if she finds out a deputy sheriff is looking for her at school —"

"Okay, wait."

Silence again. I nearly hung up the phone. *Why did I do this? Why didn't I just call the school to see if Kelly's in class?*

The line rattled. "Okay, I checked. A plainclothes detective is almost at the school now. It's Ralph Chetterling, Annie. He was in the area."

Chetterling. *Thank You, God.*

Fresh fear balled up my chest. "I'm going to the school. I have to see Kelly right now!" *If she's even there.*

"No, Annie." Delft's tone was cadenced to soothe. "Don't you want to stay near the phone, hear what Chetterling has to report? You'll know in just a few minutes."

Was Delft a parent? Couldn't he understand the need, the *ache,* to see my daughter with my own eyes, to hug her and feel the *life* of her?

"Besides, think about it. If you go rushing to the school to see Kelly for yourself, she'll know something's really wrong."

217

That logic stopped all argument. I pressed my mouth closed . . . and tried to breathe.

"Listen now, while we're waiting to hear your daughter's okay." Delft was determined to keep me on the line. "We're going to put other cars in the area. We'll do some checking to see if anyone's seen a suspicious vehicle around the school. We will get this guy, Annie. We *will*."

Noise filtered through the great room from the kitchen. An opened and closed door. Jenna was home. I placed my hand over the receiver and yelled her name.

She materialized in the doorway, eyes wide. "What?"

I hissed the news to her — while listening for any word from Sergeant Delft. The information paled Jenna's tanned face. She sagged against the door frame. "She's going to be all right." Words uttered because they *had* to be so.

I nodded.

Then I saw the resolution return, the mettle that makes Jenna who she is. She straightened, her lips firming. A blaze crept into her cheeks. She pointed at me, as if to say *I'll be right back,* then disappeared.

"Annie, you there?" Sergeant Delft's voice pulled my attention back to the phone.

"Yes."

"Okay, we're just waiting."

Jenna returned with her purse, setting it down with firm purpose. She reached inside and drew out a handgun. Inspected it with precision. The gun had been my father's. Jenna had found it on the closet shelf when she'd taken over the master bedroom last year. She'd already known how to shoot. Then after the events of last summer she'd applied for a license to carry a concealed weapon, and it had rested in her purse ever since.

Satisfied with her inspection, she returned the gun to her handbag.

"*This* one —" her whisper was pure vehemence — "I'll kill myself."

I shivered.

She worried the leather of her purse strap. "How would Bland know what car to look for?"

The question cut through me. She was right. With all those parents letting kids off, he'd have to know the car. Have to know what Kelly looked like, since Erin was with her. "Oh, Jenna, how *would* he know?"

Her expression gave the answer she would not say. Bland had been watching our home.

Maybe he was right here in Grove Landing, watching them leave the house this morning. Maybe he was never at school.

No. He knew Kelly wore jeans. She'd have gotten into the car from the garage. He couldn't have seen her pants.

Maybe he guessed?

Bland would never guess.

I pressed a palm to my temple. My head was going to drive me crazy.

"Annie!" Delft's voice sounded in my ear.

"I'm here."

"Just heard from Chetterling. Kelly's in her math class, right where she should be. He even had the principal walk him past the classroom and peek through the glass on the door just to make sure."

"Oh. *Oh.*" Relief surged like dizzying heat through my body, wilting every muscle. I dropped the receiver on the desk.

"What, what?" Jenna snatched up the phone, demanding that the words be repeated. "Oh, thank God!" Her chin sank toward her chest.

Silence. I sat and cried while Sergeant Delft talked to my sister.

"You better believe we want you to come right now," Jenna barked. "And by the way, why weren't these phones tapped after what happened Saturday? You might have been able to trace that call."

I laced and unlaced my fingers as my sister

berated the Sheriff's Department, listening to my own heartbeat as tears dropped off my chin. My breath caught in little sobs that soon mingled with the sickened laughter of a mother's worst nightmare chased away.

Jenna hung up the phone and faced me across the desk, hands on her hips. Her features softened. "You okay?"

I nodded.

"Oh, Annie." She moved around the desk, and I stood for her embrace. Wonderful Jenna. What would I have done if she hadn't flown up?

She stepped back. "Chetterling and Delft are coming right now. Meantime they'll have some deputies keeping an eye out at the school. They'll watch to see Kelly get safely into your car when you pick her up."

I wiped my face. "How am I ever going to keep this from her? One look at me, and she'll know. She's so sensitive."

"Maybe you don't keep it from her."

"But I hate for her to know! To be scared."

Jenna spread her hands. "Annie, isn't it better for her to know? As uncomfortable as it is, at least she'll be aware to look around her, pay attention. She *deserves* to know that she and her family are being threatened."

"I know, but . . ." I laid a hand over my

eyes. "I just . . . can't go through this again."

"Yes, you can." Jenna's tone was quiet but firm. "Only because you have to. We'll get through this together."

I expelled a shaky half-laugh. "Yeah, you and your gun."

"Well, and where's yours?"

"You know I hate guns."

"Who said anything about *liking* them? You just need to know how to use one."

"Well, I don't."

She shook her head at me. "And after your scare last year. What happened to 'Yes, Jenna, I promise I'll take some shooting lessons, I promise, I promise'?"

"I just . . . I never got around to it."

She huffed. "I swear, Annie, sometimes I just want to shake you."

"Later, okay?" New tears bit my eyes.

Her peeved expression crumbled. "Oh, of course later." She hugged me again, holding on until I stopped crying. When I drew away, I was still sniffing. "This is all your fault, you know. You're the one who wanted me to get into forensic art."

"*Art,* yes. Danger with crazy criminals, no."

"Well, it's not like I asked for this."

"I know."

I raked a hand through my hair. The drive from Redding took about fifteen minutes. I wanted Chetterling and Delft to come *now*. "And what's all this talk about the Sheriff's Department not watching out for me? They've been doing all they can, given their manpower; you know they're always short-handed. Good grief, were you giving it to Delft."

"He deserved it. You wait till he gets here; I'll give him more."

I didn't doubt it.

CHAPTER 18

Detective Chetterling arrived first. I spotted him through the great room windows and hurried to open the front door. When I saw his face, so etched with concern, I threw my arms around him. He hesitated, then grasped me in a tight hug, patting the back of my head as if I were a child.

Suddenly embarrassed, I eased away.

"You okay?" He still had his hands on my shoulders.

"Yes. Now that I know Kelly's okay."

As we stepped into the great room I shot my sister a look, warning her to go easy on this man. It wasn't *his* fault Bill Bland was taking such desperate chances.

A few minutes later Delft arrived. The four of us plunked down on the great room furniture, words of desperation and anger spilling from my mouth.

"Let me tell you all something right now. That phone call isn't going to stop me. I'm still going to do the drawing and I'm going to do it *now*. Bland thinks he can scare me. Well, he has. But he's crossed a line. It's one thing to threaten me, but now he's threatened my *daughter*." Tears prickled my eyes. "There's no way I will sit back and let this guy stay on the streets. I will not rest until I know he's put away for good."

Jenna shot me a look of fierce pride. Fine. If she wanted to infer courage from my speech, she could go right ahead. But in truth I felt none at all. I just wanted my children safe.

"Okay, Annie." Sergeant Delft flexed his shoulders. "We certainly support you in that. As we said before, we'll be happy to have your drawing just as soon as we can get it. Now let me tell *you* something." His words fell even more sternly. The nearness of his twenty-year quarry had clearly raised his hackles. "With all these gambles, Bland is bound to slip up soon. And we'll be there when he does. You hear? We *will* be there."

My sister made a little noise in her throat. She didn't appear to be buying it. "So exactly what are you going to do for us right now, while Annie is finishing the drawing? She needs protection, and so do the kids. I think you should have somebody watching her at all times. If this drawing's so all-fired important to you, you'll *find* the resources."

"Jenna." I ducked my head.

"Don't *Jenna* me, Annie. After all you've done for them the past year?"

"Wait." Chetterling held up a hand. He looked to Jenna. "I understand your feelings. Your sister *has* done a lot for our department, and we value her highly. We've never had the kind of manpower it would take to run three shifts of men for watching someone twenty-four hours a day. All the same, I am going to stick my neck out and *make* this happen for Annie."

"I'll take a shift," Delft put in.

"Good, thanks. Let me think a minute." Chetterling rubbed his jaw. "Okay. Annie, you said you're going to do the drawing as soon as you can. I'm sure it'll help to have some peace of mind while you work. How much time is it going to take to finish?"

I closed my eyes, calculating. "I think by end of the afternoon tomorrow. Sooner, if I work late tonight."

"Great. So here's what we'll do. For the next twenty-four hours, while you work, we will have an unmarked sheriff's car watch your house. It will follow you when you take the kids to and from school. I'll get somebody on you soon. Delft, you can take over around dinnertime. And I'll probably end up doing the all-night duty. It's not going to be anything fancy, no SWAT team hiding behind tinted windows in some big van parked across the street. But you will have a deputy intent on watching you and your property."

I hardly knew what to say. What Chetterling had said was true — the Sheriff's Department didn't have the resources for such a thing. Especially when they'd need every person available to look for Bland. No one but Chetterling would have offered this to me. "Thank you." I licked my lips. "But one thing. With a car following me around, even if it is unmarked, the kids will have to know what's happening, right?"

"Not necessarily. It can be parked across the street and down a ways. And when you're on the road and at school, we can stay at a distance. However, the subject of what to tell your kids is an important one."

"Do you think I should?"

Chetterling bounced one heel off the floor. "That's up to you. But I would say yes, tell them. They're old enough to handle it. You know how kids are. If they sense something's going on and you deny it, they're still going to be frightened. But they won't know what to do about it. I'd rather they understand the need to be extra careful right now. No walking down the street, or off school grounds. Your whole family should be on high alert until this thing is over."

I nodded, sensing Chetterling's experience as a parent. As much as we'd worked together, I knew little of his personal life. Only that he'd been divorced for a long time and he'd raised a niece after his sister, the girl's mother, had been killed in a car accident.

"You have a gun in the house?" Delft made eye contact with Jenna.

"Yes. A two-inch barrel Chief Special. And I know how to use it."

"Fine. That's a good firearm." He looked to me. "Annie? You know how to use it?"

I winced, avoiding the I-told-you-so expression on my sister's face. "No. I don't know anything about guns. I *hate* guns."

"I understand, but it's time you learned." Chetterling placed his palms on his thighs. "Delft's right, that Smith & Wesson is a good, safe firearm. It's a little smaller than others. Holds five bullets instead of six. It's called a double-action revolver, meaning you don't have to cock it to discharge it. In fact when it is cocked, it's got a hair trigger, and you can too easily shoot someone by mistake."

Jenna nodded. "I never cock it."

Chetterling kept his eyes fixed on me. "I know right now you've got to work on your drawing. But when this is all over, you borrow your sister's gun, and I'll take you out to the firing range and teach you how to use it. Once you get used to a firearm, you won't be so scared of it. You'll see that it's just a tool like anything else."

A tool? A screwdriver was a tool. A gun was a killing machine. My mind whisked back to the previous summer, and I shuddered.

Chetterling gave me a half-smile. "Enough of that for now. Let's get back to your children. I will be alerting the school principals that there is a safety issue with Kelly and Stephen. That way, they can watch the kids on the inside. When you take them to school, don't leave until you see them disappear into the building. And, again, we'll have a car watching too."

"Okay, except . . . we carpool with Erin Willit. Is that a problem?"

"It's okay if Erin rides with you. But I'd think for right now you'd want to be the one driving back and forth rather than letting another parent do it."

"Yes, I —"

"I'll do it, Annie," Jenna said. "We'll have to talk to Dave, let him know what's happening. But if you stay up half the night working, you shouldn't have to worry about getting up early to get the kids to school. I'll just make sure the alarm's on when we leave."

"Another thing." Chetterling looked to my sister. "You mentioned to Sergeant Delft about a phone tap. We can't really do a phone tap like you see in the movies, but I do think it's a good idea to put in a recorder and a trace." He turned to Delft. "What do you think, Justin?"

"Agreed. Now that Bland's getting sloppy, this might be the way to catch him."

My shoulders slumped. A phone tap — in *my* house. Or a trace, or whatever. Wouldn't that still mean every call would be monitored? Not that I lived some wild existence, but the thought of strangers listening to my conversations was less than pleasant.

Delft noticed my body language. "Of course, it will only be with your permission."

As much as I didn't like the idea, what choice did I have? "I have two lines. One for business, and the house line. It's the

230

house number Bland called."

"Then that's the one we'd put a trace on."

"What exactly would it entail?"

The sergeant shifted on the couch. "For the recorder all we need to do is put a suction cup on your phone — say the one in your office — and set up a recording device. Just make sure when a call comes in that you answer from that location. Then if it's Bland calling, you push a button on the recorder. It's that simple."

"And the phone trace?"

"We don't even have to come into your house to set that up. We could have it in place probably by the end of the afternoon. We'd need to get back to the office and fax our report with a case number to the special agent at the phone company. He'll put the trace on the line from his end. That doesn't mean calls are monitored, understand. It does mean that every call you receive will be traced to its origin. We'll get the actual phone number. So if you receive a call from Bland, first, you'd want to record it. Second, as soon as you hang up, you'd want to call us immediately so we can send a car to the location of origin. Better yet, if your sister's home, have her call us with a cell phone while you keep Bland on the line. That'll give us all the more lead time to get to him."

"Okay, that's fine." I spread my hands. "Do it."

"All right." Chetterling stood. "We'll send a technician with the recorder back here as soon as possible."

Jenna and I walked the men to the door.

"Oh." Delft stopped on his way out. "Two things. First, I called the producer of *American Fugitive.* Told him we have reason to believe Bland's in the area. The show's being filmed now, except for the part when they display your update and give Bland's statistics. The host will mention that Bland has recently been around Redding."

"Good. Thanks for telling me."

"Second, I've still got guys knocking on doors around the Roses by Redding flower shop. I'll let you know if we hear anything."

"Thank you so much." Delft didn't have to keep me informed. I was grateful for his thoughtfulness.

"You bet."

The sergeant strode down my front walk, a man on a mission. Chetterling hung back, one hand on the door frame. "The technician can answer any more questions you might have about the phone. Just remember you need to tell your kids not to answer any calls for now."

"Can he be out of here before school gets out?" I clasped my arms, chilled. "This is going to be hard with Stephen. He won't be able to keep quiet about everything. Can't you just see him, telling all his friends, 'Hey, man, the Sheriff's got a trace on our phone.'"

Chetterling lowered his chin. "How's he doing, by the way?"

"Not good."

"More trouble with drugs?"

"I . . . think so."

The detective pulled in a breath. "You know my offer from last year still stands. If you ever need any help . . ."

"Thanks." I gave him a grateful smile. "So much. I just hope I don't have to take you up on it."

"Yeah." He straightened, pulling the all-business mask over his expression. "All right. You know where I am. And I'll have that car on you this afternoon. He'll follow you from here to the school. Okay?"

"Okay."

The detective clumped down my porch steps. Jenna closed and bolted the door.

I slumped against the wall. "I'm going to have to tell the kids, aren't I. Maybe not about the phone trace, but about everything else."

"Yeah. I'm afraid so, Annie."

I surveyed my feet, wishing for the millionth time I wasn't a single mother. When I felt so overwhelmed like this, I just wanted to strangle Vic.

"Go on now." Jenna would not let me descend into depression. "You've got work to do."

My feet dragged as I crossed the great room. Somehow I would have to regain my concentration.

And somehow I would have to greet Kelly after school without collapsing into sobs.

CHAPTER 19

Little good my plans for working that afternoon did me. I couldn't concentrate. Mostly I sat at my desk, staring at Bland's picture — the features I'd come to hate. When I could focus my thoughts, I saw him as he would be today. I visualized the droopier eyelids and mouth, the less defined jawline. But my mental projector constantly kicked into gear, flashing scenes of him stalking the school, watching Kelly as she got out of the SUV.

To think that he'd been that close to her.

More than once I shoved his photo away, disgusted, only to pull it back. I hated his face; I couldn't get enough of his face. At least until I completed the update. Then I'd just as soon never look at it again.

When I wasn't bound up in Bland, I worried about whether or not to tell the kids what was happening. Practicality said I should. As Chetterling noted, Kelly and

Stephen needed to be extra careful in the next few days. And they surely wouldn't comply if I didn't give them a reason. Especially Stephen.

Anxiety voted I shouldn't tell them. Stephen would hide his fear, whispering the news in morbid fascination to his friends. Kelly would hide nothing. She just plain wouldn't sleep at night. Nor would she keep it from Erin. And really, she couldn't. Right now I wouldn't allow Kelly to so much as walk across the street alone to Erin's house, nor even allow the girls to walk back together. How would I explain that to Erin — without the truth?

And if Erin knew, Dave would have to know. I bent over the desk, feeling almost physically sick at the thought. *How* could I put the two of them through fear again, after what they'd endured? Ten months after seeing her mother murdered in their home, Erin was just beginning to heal. How far back psychologically might this push her? What would it do to Dave?

What a horrible neighbor I'd turned out to be. Worse than someone in a Stephen King novel.

Face it, Annie, you'll never get over your guilt about Lisa's death.

Then again, why should you?

The technician from the Sheriff's Department arrived, recording device in hand. I hung back, hitting my knuckles against my chin, as Jenna and I watched him perform his duty. Afterward he explained the details and what we should do if a call from Bland came. In quick sequence my mental projector flashed scenes of my hearing Bland's voice, punching on the recorder, then of Delft and Chetterling, leaning over the tape, listening intently to the rasp of Bland's words, my hitched breathing . . .

By the time the technician left, my nerves zinged with the sense of privacy defiled.

I could not wait to see Bill Bland in jail.

At three o'clock, Jenna and I headed out the door to pick up the kids. We spoke little in the car, except that she read my mind. Naturally.

"You still haven't decided how much to tell them, have you?"

"No."

"When are you going to figure it out?"

"When I see them."

"Oh." She pondered my answer. "How will you know then?"

"I won't. It's just that I'll be out of time. So I'll have to decide."

"I see."

Smart as Jenna was, she didn't know everything. She wasn't a mom. She could not understand what I was going through.

Students spilled out the doors as I pulled into the parking lot at the middle school. Even knowing that Kelly was all right, even seeing the unmarked sheriff's car tail us from home, I could not keep my eyes from darting about, searching for a sign of Bland. If I saw the man, I would know him. Something told me I'd *feel* him first.

My cell phone was on, with direct access to our watchful deputy if I noticed anything amiss.

"There she is!" A ball of fire rolled up my throat, tears springing to my eyes. What had ever made me think I could hide my emotions from my daughter?

I hit the button to pop the trunk, then aimed an eagle-eye stare at the girls as they chattered their way toward the car.

"You okay?" Jenna sat forward, hands on the dashboard, watching the girls with equal intent.

Strange, how emotions can morph. Within a second my raw relief skidded into anger. This was *my* daughter. And her friend, who'd been through so much. Nobody, and I mean *nobody*, was going to threaten these girls. "Yeah." The words ran low and determined. "I'm fine."

Through sheer willpower I stayed in the car instead of jumping out to bear-hug Kelly as she and Erin threw their backpacks into the trunk. Erin opened one rear car door and Kelly, the other. My daughter slid into the backseat with a "Hi, Mom," took one look at my face, and hesitated.

"What's the matter?"

I managed a shrug. "We'll talk when we get home, okay?"

Kelly looked at me askance. "Am I in trouble?"

"Should you be?"

Erin pulled down one side of her mouth, glancing from me to Kelly.

"No."

"Good. Then you're not."

Erin flicked a look at the ceiling. "Parents."

At the high school, Stephen scuffed out the door with his usual troop of baggy-pantsed, slumping friends. The sun shone on his scalp just right, lighting a patch of skin beneath his spiked hair. He reached the car, noticed his aunt in the front seat, and scowled.

"Well, greetings to you too," Jenna muttered, but all I wanted to do was hug my son. I didn't care at that moment that he was self-centered and negative and bent on his own destruction. At least he was safe.

On the way home I checked the rearview mirror countless times. The unmarked car kept a fair distance, but never did I lose sight of it. When we reached home, Jenna stood outside the garage, watching Erin walk across the street and into her house. Kelly frowned, eyeing her aunt, then threw a questioning look at me.

God, please help me tell them.

Before Stephen could disappear into his cave, I asked him and Kelly to sit down in the great room. Jenna pointed to herself, and I motioned her over as well. We were all in this together.

I did not relate the details. Stephen knew about the roses, but I saw no reason to mention them to Kelly. Nor did I speak of the unmarked car that would watch us for twenty-four hours. I said only that the man whose picture I was drawing wanted me to stop. Badly. That with the help of my drawing, he would soon be caught. (Which I could only pray was true.) And in the meantime we would have to be extra careful. I told them about the recorder on the home phone, that they should let me answer any calls. I left wide spaces between the lines, but Kelly read right through them.

"He's threatened you, hasn't he?"

I took a deep breath. I could not lie to her. "Yes."

She absorbed my answer. "Have you seen him?"

"No."

She bit the inside of her lip. "How long until you get the drawing done?"

"I'm hoping by dinner tomorrow."

Stephen sat low on his spine, jigging a leg up and down, arms crossed. Trying his best to look nonchalant. He gave me a penetrating stare, saying without words, *I'll bet there's more than what you're telling us, because you didn't even mention the roses to Kelly.* "I needed to go over to Jeff's house tonight. He was supposed to come get me."

Right. "Out on a Monday night? Whatever for?"

"We have this science project. We're supposed to watch the stars at midnight and draw where different constellations are. There's a list of 'em we need to look for."

"At *midnight?*" I didn't believe my son for a minute. "Well, I tell you what. You'll have to put it off for a night or two. And then you can do it here, by yourself. If you really have such a project, I see no need to do it

241

with someone else."

"But, Mom, it's a joint project! And it's due tomorrow. We *have* to do it tonight."

"Stephen." My voice sharpened. "It's not getting done tonight, period. Not even here. I won't have you so much as standing out on our own back lawn. If I have to, I'll talk to your teacher myself and explain."

"He's not going to listen to you." Stephen hit his leg. "Man, Mom, you just —"

"Can it, Stephen." Jenna gave him a look to kill.

My son, my son. A giant fist squeezed my heart. Why did he have to be so awful? So self-centered? Couldn't he for once act like he cared about anyone but himself?

Kelly looked like she was going to cry. Jenna patted her on the leg. "This will be over soon. With so many people watching out for this guy, he'll be caught. And your mom's going to be a hero again."

Stephen made a sound in his throat. "Yeah, well that's great. Let's just hope she doesn't get killed in the process."

Kelly made a little strangled sound. I wanted to put an arm around her and cuff Stephen at the same time. What his thoughtless words did to his sister.

Calm, Annie, stay calm.

"I'm going to be fine, Stephen, now stop it." I reached over to massage his shoulder. He drew away.

"I'm scared, Mom." Kelly scuttled around the coffee table to sit by me. I drew her close.

"I know. It's all kind of scary. But you told me how you pray, remember? You can pray hard about this."

Stephen gave a little snort. He turned his head away, looking out the front windows.

"Believe me, I will." Kelly eyed her brother, her disdain clear.

I thought of Kelly's words as I crossed the street a short time later to talk to Dave Willit. Down the road I could see the unmarked sheriff's car, parked on the Willit's side of the street and facing my direction. Without the deputy's presence, I would not have been walking the short distance alone.

Dave met me at the door, and I stepped into his foyer, the typical remorse nibbling at my heart.

"Hi, Annie." He smiled at me, his expression full of warmth. Dave's face was thinner than before Lisa died; I knew he'd lost weight. Still, he remained a handsome man. Sometimes I could almost see a gossamer shroud of sadness about him. Yet at the same time he possessed a strength, an inner steadiness that I found vaguely disarming. I'd commented on it once, and he'd responded it was the strength of walking with God, surely nothing for which he could take credit.

"Erin's in her bedroom, doing homework. After you called I told her you and I were going to talk about the case you're working on. I asked her to stay put."

"Good. Thanks." I folded my arms, suppressing a shiver.

"You cold?"

"No. I just . . ."

He looked at me, through me, into my soul. Though he said nothing, I sensed he knew of my discomfort in his house. That he wished he could erase it like a fallacious answer on a blackboard, but didn't have a clue how to begin.

Neither did I.

He gestured for me to sit in the family room. My mind flitted back to a day ten months ago when we'd sat in this very place. These very chairs, in fact. Less than two weeks and yet a lifetime after Lisa had died.

I licked my lips, staring at a piece of lint on the carpet. "I can't bear to do this to you again, Dave. You or Erin. But I feel I should tell you what's happening. Then you can decide how much you want to tell Erin. I've instructed Kelly to say nothing, but you know how best friends are. Hard to keep a secret." I managed a wan smile.

"You're right about that."

With halting words, I told Dave everything. I'd meant to give him a gutted overview. But the more I talked, the more I wanted — *needed* — to talk. Even as I did I felt selfish, unleashing my problems and fears on this man. But his expression — his eyes holding mine as I spoke of the dead roses, my interviews, the call about Kelly, the phone trace — unwound it all from me like thread from a spool.

"It'll all be over with soon, though. I'm going to do the drawing right away and . . . they'll find him."

These words had become a mantra. Perhaps if I said them enough I'd believe it was true.

Dave rubbed his jaw and gave his head a little shake. "You continue to amaze me, Annie."

Huh?

"Believe me, I can understand how scared you are. And angry." Dave's gaze grew distant for a moment. I could feel the white-hot coals of his memories. "Yet here you are, clenching your teeth this second time until you see another murderer snatched off the streets."

"I don't feel like I have much of a choice," I half whispered.

"That's what I mean. You just forge ahead and do what needs to be done." He ran a hand over his eyes. "You can count on me helping you in any way I can. I know it's all terrifying. But I'll be here, I'll do whatever you need."

His sincerity pierced through me. "Thank you."

We talked about details. How Jenna would be taking the kids to school tomorrow, with the unmarked sheriff's car following. How we would also pick them up. That one of us would watch the girls cross the street at all times until Bland was caught. Dave said that he would tell Erin, because her not knowing while picking up the vibrations of something amiss would only frighten her more. I related exactly how much Kelly knew. He promised to tell Erin no more than that. For now the unmarked car would remain our secret.

When we could think of nothing more, we sat silently, each lost in our own thoughts.

He cleared his throat. "Annie, I've been wondering . . . May I ask where you are with

God? Last summer, you told me you'd promised to seek Him."

Another difficult topic. "True. That's why I've been coming to church."

"But you haven't yet decided to accept Christ into your life, right?" He pulled back. "I'm sorry if I'm asking you —"

"No, no, that's okay." For what this man had been through, and my part in it, he deserved to ask me whatever he wanted. "I'm just . . . I've come a long way. I used to not even know if I believed in God. But I do now. And I've listened carefully to all the sermons so I can understand. Christianity is a new concept to me, you know? I wasn't raised in church at all."

"I know."

"So now I can accept that Christ died for me. That when He came alive again He conquered evil. I mean, I don't really understand how this all works in a cosmic sense."

Dave smiled. "Neither do I. Or we'd both be God."

"Suppose so." I rubbed my palms together. "And I understand that if I ask Christ to forgive me for all the wrong things I've done, He will. And then I'll belong to Him, and I'll go to heaven." I smiled self-consciously. "There. How'd I do?"

"Great." Dave fixed me with a look like a proud teacher to a student.

"Good. Well. I . . . guess I have it then."

He waited a long beat, but I said no more.

"Can you tell me what you're waiting for? You have to admit Jesus is handing you a pretty good deal."

"I do. But . . . Okay." I forced myself to face Dave. "It's the 'belong to Him' part. I've heard over and over that He wants to be Lord of my life. In a way, that's kind of scary. Because if Christ is Lord of my life, then I'm *not.* My decisions aren't my own anymore. What if He wants me to do things I don't want to do?"

Kindness creased Dave's face. "That is frightening to think about." He focused on the seam of the couch cushion, rubbed it with a finger. "But since we've gone this far, do you mind if I respond?"

"No, go ahead."

"Okay. Let me ask you a question, but it's not one to answer aloud. When you look at your life, Annie, this life that you are running under your own steam — is it working?"

I glanced away, the question seeping into my soul.

"See, for my own life, I know I couldn't do half as good a job as God does, because

He's the one who created me. He knows my talents and weaknesses better than I do. It's like the Bible says when it talks about the potter knowing better than the clay how to form the jar."

The words jingle-jangled, distant sleigh bells in my head. The sound was joyous and fresh — and vexing.

"Well. I'm grateful for your courage to speak your mind, Dave. Lots of people wouldn't. I promise I'll think about all this. Okay?"

"Good. That's all I can ask."

With an apologetic shrug I pushed to my feet. "I'd better be going. I need to start drawing now, work as long as I can tonight. Thank you again for talking to me."

"You're welcome. And thank you, Annie, for all you're doing."

Dave ushered me to the door and stood in his threshold like a soldier, watching me walk across the street until I slipped into my house with a small wave.

CHAPTER 20

Six-thirty P.M.2

He drove with his left hand, checking the map in his right. Lack of sleep zinged a forced adrenaline through his veins. He hadn't eaten for hours. No matter. "With focus, human needs are overcome."

Jack Hurst in *Cry of the Slain.*

There was the road.

He turned right off the small highway and saw homes ahead. Grove Landing. A second turn, and he was on Barrister Court. He did not know the house number. But one newspaper article had mentioned her huge log home at the end of the cul de sac. Beyond the street lay forest.

Wait.

His foot pulled off the gas.

Up there, on the right. A man sitting in a car, between two houses.

He could only see the back of the man's head. Looked like the guy was watching Annie Kingston's house.

Why?

Who was this man?

Scenarios and possible reactions ticker-taped through his mind.

This man would see him as he drove past.

He cursed, then pulled over. Held up the map, pretending to consult it while glaring at the man through the tops of his sunglasses.

See that? The guy's head turned slightly. Maybe checking the rearview mirror. Maybe watching him.

Fire raced beneath his skin — his premonition of danger.

This was no ordinary man.

This had all the markings of a protector in an unmarked car. Private security guard? Plainclothes law enforcement?

The man's right arm moved, as if seeking something on the passenger seat.

Reaching for pen and paper to record his license plate?

Instinct smacked him in the chest. He lowered the map, pulled back out on the street. Hit the button to roll down his right window. Stopped alongside the mystery car, gesturing.

The man stared out his open window.

"Sorry to bother you." He spoke in an English accent. "I seem to be quite lost. I thought this road went through and could point me back to the highway. Apparently not."

The man surveyed him. "Where are you trying to go?"

Such tension in the man's shoulders, suspicion in his voice.

"Back to the freeway actually. I'm staying at the Holiday Inn on the south side. Do you know it?"

The man tilted his head. "Yeah. Go back the way you came from. Turn left, then when you come to the end of that road, left again. That'll head you back toward Redding."

"Thank you, much gratitude."

He eased away. Rolled up the window. Felt the man's eyes upon him as he turned around on the street. He passed the car again. Smiled. Waved.

The man raised a hand.

Law enforcement. Definitely.

He headed toward Redding.

A scene flashed in his head. The tortured faces of his wife and sons as police cars surrounded his home.

Like Bremer Slate's downfall in *Death Moon*.

No.

No.

He narrowed his eyes. He would ditch his car. Take off the blond toupee. Use his backup ID to get a rental car. Put on the black wig.

He'd spent twenty years hiding under law enforcement's nose. They would not stop him now.

CHAPTER 21

A distant side of my brain registered the sound of water running from the master bedroom suite. Jenna must be taking a shower. What time was it? Ten? Eleven? I couldn't bother raising my head to check the office clock. I'd taken my watch off when I started hours ago.

The kids would already be in bed. Jenna informed me at dinner that she would see to that. I was to hit my office, close the door, and plunge into my drawing task, which I itched to begin. And once I did, I wanted no interruptions.

If I could find the endurance, I planned to work all night.

Except for the vague sound of water in pipes, the house felt eerie in its silence. My own breathing, the swish of my sleeve, the moving of materials — all seemed amplified. But I noticed this intermittently, as if my mind surfaced from the depths to breathe, then sank once more. Down in the murky waters of concentration, I focused on Bill Bland until I could almost touch him, feel him, smell him. The professional artist within me re-created his face. The projector in my head revisited the scenes of the murders in vivid color.

I'd started with Bland's driver's license photo — the most recent picture I had. In fugitive updates, acceptable practice includes enlarging the best picture you've got of the suspect, if that will help increase accuracy. I used the basic grid system. A driver's license picture was ridiculously small to start with, requiring me to draw the gridlined face numerous times until I could increase it to the necessary size. But I would take no chances. This update would be the best I could possibly make it.

Laying tracing paper over Bland's photo, I made a small-scale grid, then traced his features upon it. Next I created a larger grid on a second sheet of paper, redrawing the face onto it, using the smaller grid as guidelines. Bland's features were soon four times as large as on his license photo. Repeating this step again, I increased the picture another 400 percent. Now his basic features were the size I wanted.

From my days as a courtroom artist I'd

learned two important principles.

One, people's faces are not perfectly symmetrical.

Two, proportions are the key to recognition.

Bland's traced features, as they appeared twenty years ago, helped solidify his unique proportions. The challenge in creating an update was in knowing which of these proportions would remain the same and which would modify with age.

Now I worked on aging Bland's face, using the tinted paper and graphite pencils. Little by little the image in my head was emerging. The wrinkles in his forehead and around the eyes. The deeper groove underneath his bottom lip, created by the nervous habit of lifting his chin. The softening of his already nondescript jawline.

The projector whirred in my head, and flash — I could see

Bland's face as his chin jerks up and sinks down, his lower lip pushing into the top one. Bland stands in the Tarells' hallway, greeting his employer with controlled intent, moments before the meeting begins . . .

■ ■ ■

Flash to

a close-up of the same mouth twenty years later, speaking into the phone, ordering a dozen dead roses . . .

Time ticked by, and Bland's features emerged. My heartbeat sent a whoosh through my ears. My pencil scratched against paper. Outside, Grove Landing lay in darkness, the blinds of my office shutting out the night. I'd closed them long ago. Somewhere in the Redding area, Bill Bland lurked. I knew my house was under surveillance, but the thought of those windows at night, like one-way mirrors, had driven me to pull the slats tight.

The longer I worked, the more close the air in the office felt, as if a woolen blanket of oppression descended from the ceiling. Every motion, every sound I made, seemed magnified. A strange sense stole over me, as though Bland and I were two actors onstage, our movements spotlighted, black emptiness between us. That darkness was growing smaller, smaller as we neared each other . . .

The nerves in the back of my neck began to tingle.

Help me do this right, God. Please.

Minutes passed. I felt my heartbeat. The warmth of my fingers clutching the pencil. The dryness of my throat. For some time I'd needed a drink, but hadn't stopped to get one. My apprehension of the unseen Bill Bland and my concentration on the man appearing on my paper blended together, fusing me to my chair, to that time and place. Energy fizzled through me, overriding muscle aches and tiredness. I knew then that I would work all night, that I would not — *could not* — rest until my task was done.

CHAPTER 22

Night — the darkness his cover. The forest smelled musty.

He pulled back a camouflage sleeve to check his watch. Its face glowed a sickly green through the goggles. Almost midnight.

He waited in the woods beyond the cul-de-sac. He watched. His backpack lay on the ground a few feet away.

An unmarked car still sat on the street. But a different man. Much bigger. Different vehicle. They'd changed shifts an hour ago.

House under surveillance. And burglar alarm likely.

Best entrance — back lower-level sliding door.

He would seek the moment of weakness. Like Darell Fleck in *Twin Mortal.*

The Kingston house was dark, except for those first-floor windows. Bedroom? Office? Annie Kingston up late, working on her drawing?

No. She would not be ready to start it so soon.

A faint sound. Off to his right, from the back of the house.

He watched.

A figure stealthily walking up the side yard.

His muscles gathered. Backup security? Had he been spotted?

He slid behind a large tree.

The figure rounded the house's front corner, headed down the sidewalk. Male. Baggy jeans. T-shirt. Spiked hair.

This was no security officer. Maybe a kid. Teenager. Annie Kingston's son?

He looked back to the unmarked vehicle.

The man inside had disappeared.

Where? So fast?

He stared at the car. Was that the top of a head behind the wheel? The man ducking?

The teenager slunk down the sidewalk. Not even noticing the unmarked vehicle.

Other movement. Far down the street.

He eased from behind the tree, leaned forward.

A car. Moving up the road. No headlights.

It drew even with the teenager. The kid crossed in front of it, opened the passenger door. An inside light flicked on. Another male at the wheel. Another kid. The first teenager climbed inside the car.

A reconnaissance. Annie Kingston's son sneaking out of the house.

From the back.

From the sliding glass door.

Darell Fleck's moment of weakness.

The car with no lights pulled a U-turn, headed out. He looked back to the unmarked vehicle. Was the man there to watch the kid?

The man sat up. The car engine started.

He pressed behind the tree as the car turned around in the cul-de-sac, headlights washing over the forest. The man stuck a round light on his car roof. In the goggles' green tint, it flashed a muddy brown.

This was not security. This was law enforcement. Here, outside city limits — the Sheriff's Department.

His Sheriff's Department.

His mind clicked through possibilities.

A teenager, sneaking out. About to be arrested? Drugs?

He curled his lip. *His* sons would never stoop to such despicable behavior.

He eased on his backpack and quietly trekked toward the rear of the Kingston house.

Chapter 23

My shoulders hurt; my fingers cramped. I laid down the piece of chalk and sat back, turning my neck from side to side, flexing both arms back until my spine popped. Sighing, I glanced at my office clock. Twelve thirty-five. I could hardly believe how much I'd accomplished. At this rate I would be done before too long. Bland's features were in place; they just needed the final applications of color. Wouldn't it be great for the drawing to be complete by the time the kids had to leave for school? Jenna and I could drive them into town, then take the update straight to the Sheriff's Office. After that, maybe I'd manage to get some sleep.

I kneaded muscles at the back of my neck. Bland's eyes glared at me from the paper, as if daring me to complete him so he could come to life and finish me off. A sudden shiver clutched my spine. I pushed away from my drawing table and rose. My legs needed stretching.

Breathing deeply, I paced the perimeter of the area rug.

My throat felt so dry. I headed toward the door, intent on padding to the kitchen. When the knob was halfway turned, my phone rang.

The sound jangled through me. I froze, nerves pulsing.

Bland.

My eyes fastened on the drawing, a ridiculous notion filling my head. Did some supernatural power emanate from it? As if the features summoned the man himself.

A second ring.

I stared at the phone.

From the other side of the office wall, I heard footfalls. Jenna had jumped from bed, awakened by the receiver in her room. The sounds crossed toward the hall. Her door opened.

Third ring.

I forced myself toward the desk.

My office door opened. "Answer it!" Jenna's hair was tousled from sleep, her eyes wide.

Fourth ring — interrupted. I raised the receiver to my ear. Jenna hurried to press the button on the recorder.

"H–Hello?"

"Annie, it's Ralph Chetterling."

Chetterling. My knees weakened.

"Hi." The greeting squeaked from my throat.

"Were you up?"

What is this, a social call?

"Yes. Working."

"Good."

He cleared his throat, and I sensed hesitation. Something was very wrong.

"Look, I have some unpleasant news for you. I picked up your son a few minutes ago. He was sneaking out of your house to meet up with a friend, and under the circumstances, I could not let him go and endanger himself. The friend's name is Jeff Waite. Evidently they had this all planned. Jeff drove here to get Stephen."

My brain could not process the news. I gripped the phone and blinked.

"Annie?"

"Yeah. I'm here."

Jenna watched me like an eagle on a hunt. I shook my head and mouthed, *It's not Bland.* She slumped in relief.

"What — where was Stephen going?"

"I'm not sure what they had planned. An all-night party on a Monday night seems a little unusual, and the boys aren't talking.

264

But there's an extenuating circumstance here, I'm sorry to say."

He paused again. I leaned against the desk, preparing myself.

"When I pulled the car over I searched it. The interior smelled of marijuana, and Jeff appeared under the influence. I found joints in the glove box, plus a bag of marijuana and the rolling papers. Stephen had only gotten in the car a minute before, but he had some joints on him as well, in his jeans pocket. My guess is that he brought them with him."

My legs began to tremble. All thoughts of Bill Bland fell away, replaced by a new, worse fear — a mother's fear for her child facing the consequences of his own foolishness. I could hear the empathy in Chetterling's voice, the careful unfolding of information that he knew would rock my already shaky world. "What are you going to do, Ralph?"

"Annie, I have no choice but to have them taken in for possession of an illegal substance. Stephen had under an ounce, so it'll only be a misdemeanor. We'll charge him, and then let him go into your custody. Jeff faces additional charges if he tests out for operating a vehicle under the influence, plus he's clearly got over an ounce. He's looking at a felony."

Stephen . . . arrested. *My son,* with a drug charge. Images blew through my head. Stephen in court. Stephen, with his rebellious smirk, unwilling to listen, unwilling to change. Bent on self-destruction. A dry wind kicked up those images, gusting them down a muddied path into the future, a path that twisted and narrowed onto treacherous cliffs.

I couldn't form a reply.

"Look, is Jenna awake?" Chetterling's voice pulled me back. "Maybe you can call her to the phone. I know this is difficult as a parent. Believe me, I went through the same thing raising my niece."

"Yeah. Jenna's standing right here." I held the receiver out to my sister. "It's Stephen."

"Stephen?" She scrunched up her face.

"No, I mean — just take it."

As Jenna said hello I stumbled around the desk to fall into my leather chair. The wind in my head picked up again, swirling pain and guilt and anxiety into a dust storm until I could barely hear Jenna's end of the conversation. *This wouldn't have happened if I were a better mother. If I knew how to handle my son. If Vic hadn't walked out on us all.*

What was I going to *do?* Part of me

wanted to kick Stephen, to lash back and hurt him as he was hurting me. Another part wanted to wrap my mother's arms around him and never let go, to save him from himself. Did he even begin to realize how *stupid* his actions were tonight? Not only the drugs and sneaking out, but now, after he was warned about Bill Bland. How could Stephen ignore that? Did he think he was indestructible?

God, help me. I can't handle this!

Minutes passed. Jenna's voice wove in and out of my thoughts. Then slowly the gist of her conversation began to sink in. I raised my head to watch her, the questions she posed thrumming my nerve endings.

"What if we didn't come get him? What if we let him sit in juvenile hall for a night or two?" Jenna paused, listening. "I think so too. It would teach him the kind of lesson he needs to learn."

No, Jenna, no! I couldn't let my son sit in jail. It was dangerous there; who knew what would happen to him? I couldn't do it. I *couldn't.*

Think of something else, Annie, anything else. You can't deal with this —

The back door.

Out of nowhere, that realization seared

through me. A frightening thought, yet a saving grace, for it gave me a reason to get up, get away, leave Jenna's voice and the decisions behind.

On autopilot, I headed across the room.

"Could you hold on just a minute?" Jenna spoke to Chetterling behind me. "Annie, where are you going?"

"Downstairs."

"Why?"

"The sliding door. Stephen snuck out of it. Which means it's unlocked. He must have slipped up here first, turned off the alarm. I have to go lock it. The door, I mean."

"Can't it wait a minute? We have to decide what to do with Stephen."

"No, it can't wait."

"Annie —"

"No!" I whirled on her, furious. "I can't! I have to go!"

Tears biting my eyes, I stumbled from the office.

CHAPTER 24

The kid had left a light on in the bedroom. It was enough.

He flipped up the night goggles.

His eyes flicked around the huge rec room. Couches near a fireplace. TV. Computer area. Messy. Probably the kid's —

Footsteps above.

He hurried over to press against the wall of the stairwell. Listening. He must not be pushed into impetuous action. He must wait. Plan.

Where to hide?

A latch clicked open at the top of the steps.

He slid along the wall and pulled open a door that had to lead to a closet beneath the stairs. Smothering blackness reached out to him. He stepped inside and flipped down the goggles.

"I don't know, Jenna, I just don't *know*." A woman's voice.

Jenna. The sister.

His mouth tightened. She wasn't supposed to be here.

He needed Annie alone.

Light spilled from the stairwell. He pulled the closet door shut without latching it.

Footfalls down the stairs.

Silence.

He waited.

CHAPTER 25

I turned on the rec room's overhead lights.
The place was a mess, Stephen's stuff
strewn everywhere. He'd left a lamp on in
his room. I headed toward it, stopping at
the threshold to survey the chaos of his bed
and floor.

If I searched his dresser, would I find drugs?

No, I would not search. Not now, maybe
not ever. I couldn't bear to think what I
might find.

Wading through shirts and pants, I crossed
the carpet and turned off the lamp. Then
back into the rec room, toward the sliding
door. Outside, the night loomed black as
sin. Somebody out there could be watching
me, so easily visible in all this light. In a
flash I pictured

myself, backlit and vulnerable, watched by
Bland, hulking in the forest. He sees me move
toward the door, check the lock, the palm of

one hand resting against glass. I push the latch into place. Then bend over to pick up a sawed-off broom handle, laying it in the groove behind the sliding door for extra security . . .

Nerves pricking, I stepped back from the door. I was spooking myself.

"Are you done down there? Come on!" Jenna's voice echoed through the great room. She should be quiet. She'd wake Kelly.

I hovered near the couches, stalled by ambivalence. The room weighted with an oppression that raised the hair on my arms. What was it? Stephen's lingering teenage angst? Still, I could not bring myself to mount the stairs, return to the office. Deal with the decisions his actions had forced upon me.

God, what am I going to do?

I covered my eyes with both hands. For a moment I simply stood, wondering where God was, wondering if He really existed, really cared, as I'd come to believe. If so, why was He letting all this happen?

"Can you tell me what you're waiting for?" Dave's question tremored through my soul.

What right did I have to continue running

my own life, then blame God when things went awry?

Oh, forget it.

I lowered my hands. Filling my lungs, I turned to go back to the office.

My eyes half focused on the stairway wall. The closet door wasn't closed all the way. Now what? Why had Stephen been under there? It held paint, various other items for the house, nothing of interest to him.

What if he was hiding something in there?

With a sigh, I moved toward it. My fingers grasped the knob.

"Annie! I need you up here, *now!*"

Great.

I leaned my head against the door, fighting with myself over what to do. I could check the closet, just for a minute. Put Jenna off for just one more minute —

"Annie!"

Please, Jenna. Can't you let me be?

But I knew this wasn't Jenna's fault. I *did* need to handle the situation with Stephen. Now.

"Annie, are you —"

"Okay! Okay, I'm coming."

With a halfhearted shove I pushed the door shut and trudged back up the stairs.

Forty-five minutes later, Jenna and I sat in the television room, talking. We'd moved from the office because I couldn't stand to be in there with Bill Bland's picture staring at me. Nor could we sit in the great room, due to the way voices echoed up to the second floor. Amazingly, Kelly had not awakened. No point in pushing our luck.

My sister urged me to let Stephen cool his heels in juvenile hall for at least a night. "You can still change your mind, you know. It would give him a good taste of the kind of life he's choosing."

She was right. *And* she wasn't a mother. Jenna had no clue what that would do to me, knowing my son was behind bars.

I couldn't go through with it.

We watched the clock, waiting for Chetterling to call and say the booking was complete. It was taking some time. The detective insisted on returning to his surveillance out front, which meant calling a deputy to drive out and get the boys. We knew the boys had been picked up some time ago, Jeff and Stephen handcuffed in the deputy's backseat. Time and again that scene played upon the screen in my mind.

Time and again I forced it away.

When the call came, Jenna would leave to pick up Stephen. I'd elected to stay home with Kelly. I simply couldn't bear to see my son held in custody.

"Are you still going to try to work tonight?" Jenna rested in an armchair, her feet up. She'd gotten dressed, run a quick comb through her hair. Only Jenna could manage to look beautiful with no makeup after one in the morning.

I closed my eyes, pushing my thoughts back toward Bill Bland, to my immersion in his features, his life. The connection remained, but on some deep, distant level, like a telephone line fraught with static. "I have to finish it. Besides, it's not like I'd sleep even if I went to bed."

"Might be hard to concentrate."

"You're telling me."

"You could try again in the morning."

"Jenna, listen. If I lie in bed, I'll think about Stephen. And those thoughts are far more terrifying than Bill Bland's threats. Bland is someone who can be stopped as soon as he's caught. But stopping Stephen . . . how do you get through to a kid who won't listen?"

I felt her answer, even though she would

not voice it again: *You put him in jail, just like Bland.*

She sighed. "Maybe you should try sending him to live with Vic. Get him away from these friends here."

"I already took him away from his druggie friends in the Bay Area, remember? Doesn't seem to matter where he is on the outside; Stephen just gravitates to guys who are like him on the inside. I can't take him away from himself. Besides, you know Vic wouldn't take Stephen, not to save the kid's life. Sheryl doesn't want to be bothered with my children; she's made that perfectly clear."

Jenna was silent for a moment. "We have to think of Kelly too. She's a good girl. We can't allow drugs to be around her, all that bad influence. Stephen, with his immoral friends around his younger sister. Makes me shiver just to think about it."

We. Silently, I thanked God for my sister. She would stick by me in this, all the way. Even if she didn't agree with my decisions.

"I know. The only good news is, we live away from Redding. Stephen's friends can't just walk up to the house, you know. They have to have a car."

"Don't most of them?"

"I suppose. Still, it's better than living in town, like we did in the Bay Area. Remember how his friends flocked around all the time? I never knew who'd be showing up, and at what hour."

"Well, one thing's for sure. You've got a friend in Detective Chet—"

The phone rang.

"There he is." Woodenly, I reached for the receiver. Then pulled back my hand. "Wait. What if it isn't? I should take it in the office, by the recorder, just in case."

Jenna put down the armchair footrest. "You stay, then. I'll get it."

Tucking my feet under me, I hunched on the couch, listening to her steps across the hardwood floor.

CHAPTER 26

She'd turned off the bedroom light. He kept the goggles down, binocular capability turned off.

The phone rang, not five feet from where he stood. He surveyed it, waiting.

Footsteps upstairs.

He slunk back toward the closet.

A second ring.

The footfalls sounded directly overhead, then continued past the stairway.

The third ring cut short.

He focused on the cordless phone. He must know what was happening upstairs. Dare he risk listening to the call?

With long, silent strides he neared the receiver. Picked it up. Pushed *talk.*

" . . . still doesn't want him taken to juvenile hall." A woman's voice. "I tried to talk her into it, but she won't budge."

"It's understandable." A man. "Hard thing for a parent, knowing your kid's in jail."

"I know. So I'll be going to get him."

"Is Annie going with you?"

"No. We'd have to bring Kelly, and Annie doesn't want to wake her up."

"Makes sense. Just check the doors one more time. She relocked the one Stephen used, right?"

"Yes."

"Tell her to turn the alarm back on after you leave. She knows I'm still outside here. She can call me anytime."

"Okay, I will."

They said good-bye. Hung up.

He clicked off the line.

Darell Fleck would croon. A second moment of weakness in one night.

He calculated. How long for the sister to drive to Redding, get the kid, and return?

Thirty minutes. Maybe forty.

Was that enough time to convince Annie Kingston?

He smiled.

CHAPTER 27

"Now turn the alarm back on as soon as I close this door." Jenna's last words before she disappeared into the garage. "And remember, Chetterling's out front."

My sister was beginning to hover like a mother hen. "Okay, don't worry. I'll be fine."

She nodded, gave me a grim smile, and left.

I walked to the keypad on the kitchen wall and punched in our code. The alarm light turned from green to yellow.

Fatigue washed through me. I leaned against the kitchen table, procrastinating. I couldn't seem to drag myself back to work. As soon as I got myself in gear, Jenna and Stephen would be back, and I'd have to deal with him.

I didn't want to deal with him.

Maybe I should wait until tomorrow to talk to Stephen. Besides, what was there to say? Why should I expect him to listen?

Sighing, I sank into a chair, then pushed back to my feet to make some tea. I dumped a bag into a mug and stuck it under the boiling hot water faucet. I turned the handle, listening to the hiss of water hitting porcelain . . . then frowned.

Was that a sound? Coming from the great room?

I turned off the water. Cocked my head, standing very still. *Kelly.* All the commotion had finally awakened her.

Silence.

My mug made a faint click as I set it on the tile. I turned, crossed the kitchen on cat feet, looking up a floor over the banister toward my daughter's room. Before me, the great room was dimly lit by two floor lamps turned to their lowest wattage.

The corner of my eye caught movement to my right. I swiveled to look.

A camouflage-clothed figure emerged from the TV-room threshold.

Every muscle in my body froze. My blood congealed. My brain flashed a brilliant white, then buzzed in crazed reaction.

An alien.

A soldier.

SWAT team member.

A man. Some weird gadget on his head,

its lenses flipped up. A long-barreled gun in his right hand. He moved toward me saying things I couldn't comprehend. The words rolled through my ears, disjointed, garbled, as if I heard them underwater.

Bill Bland.

The features leapt at me. Everything I'd imagined, each one I'd drawn, right down to the look of arrogance — *except he's not wearing glasses* — come to life, in the flesh, advancing on me, right here, right now.

My doors were locked, the alarm turned on. Had he risen from the drawing I created?

"Annie Kingston."

My name, uttered low. I fastened my eyes upon him and couldn't breathe.

He fixed an intense stare upon me. "You know who I am?"

No response formed.

"I can see that you do."

His voice had a chilling quality. Steeled. Utterly cold.

My lips opened. "Wh–what — ?"

Kelly.

Upstairs, safe in bed. My young teenage daughter, whom this murderous man had watched at school.

My heart frosted over. Nothing mattered

but my daughter's safety. Nothing. Whatever this man wanted from me, he could have.

God, if You've ever been there, don't let her wake up!

The gun pointed at my chest. "I must talk to you. You must listen."

What? I flailed to understand him. To connect fragmented thoughts. My eyes flicked toward Kelly's room. Immediately I pulled my focus back, but it was too late. Bland turned his chin a few inches, sliding a look up to the second floor, then back to me.

"Your son is gone. But you have a daughter at home."

I could feel my heart slamming through my shirt.

"And your sister's gone."

Could I run upstairs to Kelly's room and lock the door? Would he shoot me in the back? Then kill Kelly too?

"I am also a parent." His voice remained hard, controlled. "*My* family comes first. Understand?"

What should I do? God, help! Here I am, facing death again!

Bland checked his watch. "I have little time. You will listen carefully."

Sudden righteous anger rattled through my veins. How *dare* this man expect me to listen to him? After he'd broken into my house? Stalked my children, threatened me?

Somehow I found my voice. "They're looking for you. They know you're here. What makes you think stopping me will keep the TV show from airing? They'll only want you all the more."

His chin jerked up — the movement I'd heard about so many times. He narrowed his eyes. "You speak nonsense."

Panic sizzled up my spine. *Think, Annie!*

What if I fled out the front door? Chetterling would spot me in an instant. But I'd be on the outside of my own home, and Bland would be on the inside — with my daughter. What if he locked me out? He could use Kelly as a hostage.

Annie, come to your senses. He has a gun.

"Sit down." Bland pointed behind me, toward the kitchen table.

Did he know Jenna would be returning soon? How *could* he?

I backed up, not taking my eyes off him. Groping for a chair, I lowered myself into it. Bland followed, pulling out a seat. He set the gun beside him on the table, well out of my reach, then took off his backpack and placed it on the floor. He sat with legs spread, hands on his thighs. The goggles remained on his head. I faced him, floating in a netherworld of disbelief.

"I know you're drawing me for *American Fugitive.*" He spoke rapidly. "I'd been watching the news online. Expecting it. The show is too successful. It forces me into action."

Just wait until Chetterling and his men are forced into action. You're going to pay.

"I know all about you. I know what you can do." He pierced me with a stare. "Say something, let me know you're listening."

Jenna, hurry! "I'm listening."

"I didn't kill Tarell and Dessinger."

I won't have to finish my drawing. He'll be caught tonight. This will all be over.

"I've brought the proof to you."

I gaped at him.

His face hardened. "I *suggest* you not look at me like that. You will believe me by the time I'm through with you."

I managed a nod. Could I keep him talking until help came? "You didn't kill the men. I hear you. And you didn't steal from Tarell's company?"

Bland jabbed a glance at the clock, then sprang to his feet. I flinched, but he strode past me to the door leading to the garage and locked it. Then resumed his seat in front of me.

My arms trembled. Chetterling was so close. What if I threw open the door Bland just locked and set off the alarm?

No. I'd still be a hostage. So would Kelly.

"Yes, I stole company funds. Edwin discovered it. The man was greedy, in debt. His brother had been killed in a car accident, which left him the only heir to the family fortune. He wanted it all — *now.* And he did what was necessary to get it."

My eyes pulled toward the front kitchen window. I resisted the urge to check outside.

"Edwin let me hang in the wind until he made his plans. Then he told his father about the funds. I was summoned to the house for a confrontation. Only later did I realize this was Edwin's idea, not Don's."

Bland leaned forward, his body rigid, eyes narrowed.

"Listen closely, because I'm going to tell you what happened that night — the night Edwin killed his own father."

CHAPTER 28

Bland's words rapid-fired as he kept an eagle eye on the clock. He was lying, of course. But as long as he kept talking, as long as I humored him, he wasn't hurting me. If I could just find a way to get to Chetterling.

"Edwin came to my office around noon that day. Told me Don wanted to fire me for taking the funds. But good old Edwin had convinced his father to hear my side of the story. I was to be at the Tarell house at eight." Bland stared at me, almost through me, a coldness settling in his eyes, as if he pictured himself in the scene he was creating.

" 'It's your lucky day, Bland,' Edwin says. He has a deal for me. He's 'a little short on cash.' He tells me to go to the bank, withdraw all the money, take fifty thousand for myself, and give him the rest. I'm to tell Don at the meeting that all the money has been spent. 'Then I'll go to bat for you,' Edwin says. 'Convince my father to keep you on.' "

Bland's voice hardened as he mimicked the words he attributed to Edwin. But he didn't fool me. *Twenty years. He's had twenty years to make this up.*

" 'And if I don't do all that?' I say." Bland curled his lip. "I hated Edwin. Since the day I met him, I saw him for what he was. 'Then you'll get nothing,' Edwin tells me. 'And you'll be fired.' "

I glanced toward the great room. *Please, Kelly, stay asleep.* Bland pressed his fingers against the side of my face. "Look at me when I'm talking to you!"

I recoiled at his touch, then slowly forced my eyes to his. He drew his hand away.

"First Susan divorced me. I had to find quick money to stay in my own house. Then Edwin wanted to use me. Well, I won't be manipulated. Not then, not now. I tell him I'll take whatever money's left to the meeting and offer it back. Plead for mercy. That I'll take my chances with his father over him any day. 'Maybe I'll even tell your father how you tried to bribe me,' I say." Bland scoffed. "Edwin dares me to try. I won't do it, and he knows it. We both know Don will never see the truth about his own son.

"So I withdraw the money. Put it in a briefcase in the trunk of my car. Just before Edwin leaves at the end of the day, I inform him he'll get his share *after* he's convinced Don to go easy on me.

"That night in Don's study, Edwin sits in a chair facing the fireplace. He's already placed his suit coat on the arm of that chair, like he's staked it out. I walk over to the mantel. Don stands near his desk, and Dessinger takes the couch. Don confronts me about the money. I tell him I took it; I had no choice. I look at Edwin, waiting. His forehead beads with sweat. He looks so nervous. I think, *Something's not right.*"

I willed myself not to show disbelief at Bland's claims. So perfect, how he'd rewritten the scene. He knew about gun trajectory. He knew he'd have to claim Edwin sat in the chair from where the gun was fired. I wanted to yell at Bland to stop it; did he think I was this stupid? But I would do nothing unnecessary to anger this clearly unstable man.

"Of course, something *wasn't* right." Bland's voice dripped with disdain. "Edwin reaches into his coat pocket and pulls out a gun. Shoots Dessinger. Yells 'No!' real loud,

I'm guessing so his mother will hear, then kills his father. I freeze in terror." Bland's fingers curled. "Before I can pull out of it Edwin leaps at me and hauls me back across the room. We both hit the floor. He's on top of me, trying to press my fingers against the grip of the gun so it'll have my prints. I fight him. The gun gets knocked to the floor. Edwin's mother runs in. Now he has a witness to watch him shoot me in self-defense after I supposedly killed the two men. So now I'm fighting for my life. I grab the gun by the barrel and hit him in the head. He collapses off me, and I run. If he catches me, I know I'm dead."

Bland's voice continued, angry and bitter. "I race away, trying to get my head together. I know Edwin will call 911. Tell them his lies. And now that I've run, I *look* guilty. They'll be searching for my car. Arrest me on sight. But if I can just get some time, I can think everything through. Edwin's not as smart as I am. He's missed something, I know it. He *will not* win."

Bland jerked his head, glaring at me from the corner of his eye. I had barely moved during his entire story. My body was so tight my muscles felt like they would crack. Bland lashed out a hand and grabbed my jaw. "Are you listening to me?"

His fingers dug my flesh into my teeth, squeezing an answer from me. "Y–yes. I'm listening."

He stared at me another long moment, then pulled back his hand. "All right. In my garage back then I had an old Chevy I bought before the company funds came my way. I hadn't even registered it with the DMV. So I ditch my car a few blocks from my house and run for the Chevy. This buys me some time.

"I drive to the back parking lot of a strip mall. Everything's dark. I hunker down in the car and think. Nothing can be left to chance. I have the gun. I haven't touched the grip. Edwin's prints should still be there. But that's all I have. It's his word — and his mother's — against mine. She heard him yell *no.* She saw me hit him with the gun. Don Tarell is dead. Tarell — Redding's finest citizen. Close golf buddy to the chief of police. I've been forced to use company money. They'll say that's motive. *No one* is going to believe me. Edwin will come up with some excuse to explain his prints on the gun instead of mine. He'll claim I wiped mine off, that he must have touched the gun during our struggle. Because of everything else, they'll buy his story. So I have to find something besides the gun. Some piece of evidence that will save me."

He straightened, flexing his jaw. "And I do."

Bland checked the clock, and my gaze followed. Jenna would be back soon.

Jenna, please hurry.

He focused on my face, eyes narrowed. His chin jerked up. "Your time is running out."

CHAPTER 29

I stared at Bland, mind scrambling for some response. He raked a glance out the front kitchen window.

"What . . . happens when my time runs out?"

"We'll have to leave."

We. I shook my head. "Please, no."

"That's the backup plan, you understand. You can avoid it if you pursue justice. If you agree to convince the authorities to test my two pieces of evidence."

I licked my lips, desperately trying to follow his logic. *Two pieces of evidence?* "I'll do whatever you want me to do. Is one piece of evidence the gun?"

"Yes."

"How could you keep it all this time?"

"Very carefully."

"Is it in your backpack?"

He scoffed. "It's in a box in the forest directly behind your house. The box flaps are opened enough to prove it's not a bomb. The gun barrel's stuck in Styrofoam to preserve the prints on the grip. They *must* take utmost care with it."

The sheer arrogance of this man. Now he was telling the Sheriff's Department how to handle evidence? "What makes you think the fingerprints are going to be there after twenty years?"

A black expression stole over Bland's features. He leaned forward, chin down, staring at me through the tops of his eyeballs. Searching, laying open my soul. "You don't believe me. Do you?"

I couldn't answer. He would hear the lie in my voice.

Slowly, he pressed back in his chair, jaw working. "This isn't the attitude I expected from you."

"But . . . . it doesn't matter what I think, does it? As long as I put your evidence in the right hands?"

"It matters a great deal. *You* are someone they trust. They'll listen to you when you tell them, 'There's a complication. Bill Bland has evidence that proves his innocence. I insist you test it.' "

"Okay. I will. I promise. What's the second piece?"

For a long time he assessed me. Then he bent toward me until his face practically touched mine. "I don't believe you."

I couldn't bear to have him so close. My head pulled away as far as it could. "I will, really!"

"No. I see into your mind." He straightened, hands on his thighs. "You've deceived me. You led me to think you were one character, but you are really another. You aren't Valery Ness, the unwitting pawn. You're Lee Strait, the masked antagonist." He rose from the chair, looking down his nose at me. "Get up."

My heart fluttered into a mad dance. I couldn't find the strength to move.

"Get *up!*"

Somehow I rose, holding on to the chair for support.

He reached for his gun, leveling it at me. "We're leaving."

My muscles turned to water. "N–no. Please."

"I have no alternative. We're out of time, and you aren't on my side. So you force me to give you more responsibility. Once they see that I'm innocent of murder, you must convince them to drop charges for kidnapping. They'll do it. They'll count my twenty years as time enough paid."

Kidnapping. "I'll take your things to the Sheriff's Department today! You can trust me!"

"No, I can't. I'll have to deal with the evidence myself now." The hard resolve on his face struck my chest like a cold fist. "I didn't bring this gun for you. So don't make me use it." With one hand he slipped on the backpack. "Go. Downstairs."

"Where are we going?"

"Go."

My feet moved.

"Wait." Bland pressed his fingers into my arm. My mind flashed a gory scene of the gun going off point blank against my skin. He looked at the alarm keypad, where the telltale yellow light glowed. "Turn that off."

I froze.

"Do you want to do this alone, or do I have to wake up your daughter?"

"No!" Tears bit my eyes. "I thought you said you were a *father.*"

"I am." His answer seethed. "And *my* family comes first. Now turn off the alarm."

I stumbled to the keypad and punched in our code. The light turned from yellow to green.

"Good." He pulled me away. "Let's go."

Propelled before him, I searched the

corners of my mind for a way out. I knew a victim should never allow herself to be isolated from others. That spelled almost certain death. But what could I do? There was no escape. And even if I could escape, I would never abandon Kelly.

"Downstairs." He pushed me toward the basement door, made me open it. Leaning around me, he flicked on the stairway light. "Go. No, wait." He moved backward, pulling me away from the steps. "You have a cell phone?"

His words hardly registered. "Yes."

"Where?"

"I don't know. In my purse."

"Where is it?"

"I don't . . . I can't . . ."

His hand flashed out, sinking fingers into my shoulder. "Answer me!"

Please don't wake Kelly!

"In the office."

"Get it. Hurry."

We scurried across the hardwood floor and into my office. With shaking fingers I withdrew the phone from my purse. Bland snatched it and dropped it into his pocket. He didn't even glance toward my work area, where the drawing of his own face lay.

"Now downstairs."

I barely felt my legs as we descended. Someone else moved my feet, someone else filled my lungs with air. We hit the carpet, and he pushed me harder. "Go."

My hands fumbled with the lock on the sliding glass door. He thrust me aside and unlocked it himself, watching me all the while, then tried to draw back the door. It moved only a few inches. He pulled harder.

"What's wrong with it?" His voice rose, rage twisting his features. "What have you done to the door?"

"It's — it's the broom handle behind it." I pointed a quivering finger.

With a curse, he threw it aside, then yanked open the door. "Out!"

I tottered over the threshold onto our deck. Bland pulled the door shut. "Wait." He flipped the goggles over his eyes. "Out there." He pointed with his chin.

Our feet clattered over wood, then onto the lawn. Straight on through the backyard, the lights of my house fading as we reached the trees at the edge of my property. There I hesitated, ransacking my brain for a last-minute, luminous idea that would save me.

"Move!" His hand thrust against my spine.

We lurched into the forest, its darkness swallowing me like the cavernous maw of a monster.

CHAPTER 30

She stumbled over a root and nearly fell. He pulled her up. With the goggles, he could see. She couldn't.

"Stop."

She halted, muscles tense under his fingers. Served her right. Her loyalties hadn't been adequately swayed. She deserved the fear.

"Don't move." He slipped off his backpack and set it on the ground. Reached inside and pulled out the plastic bag containing his second piece of evidence. Put his gun in the backpack. He didn't need it now. She wouldn't run in this blackness.

He straightened, checked the sky. A bare hint of a moon. Cloudy. But rain wasn't likely this time of year.

The faces of his family flashed in his head. Beth. Nine-year-old Scott. Twelve-year-old Eddie.

All this for you.

Carefully, he placed the plastic bag on top of the box.

"What is that?" The woman's nervous whisper grated on his nerves.

"My evidence. Edwin's gun is in the box."

"What's in the bag?"

Anger zinged up his spine. "Stop the questions!"

She pulled in a hitching breath.

"They'll find it when they search for you." Bland watched her green-tinted face as she absorbed his strategy. He could see she longed to ask another question but wouldn't. Good. She was learning.

He'd reward her with the genius of his plan.

"To get you back, they must test my evidence. Now."

CHAPTER 31

The minutes blurred into eternity. Chaotic thoughts ran through my head, and tears trickled from my eyes. The darkness blanketed me, the scent of rich earth mixed with my own sweat. Even as my eyes adjusted, I couldn't see very far ahead in the cloudy night. Bland served as both my captor and guide, pushing me faster than I could safely move. Again and again I tripped or ran into scratchy bark. I could feel his anger building, as though it was *my* fault that his first plan hadn't worked.

Had Jenna returned home yet? Surely she had. My mind shoved in film of her frantically searching the house, calling Chetterling. Kelly would wake up. Even Stephen would be scared.

How long before they discovered the unlocked sliding glass door?

Oh, God, comfort my family.

"This way." Bland jerked me left. My right

elbow grazed a tree trunk.

Trudge and breathe, trudge and breathe. With every step, sounds intensified — my heartbeat, the whoosh of blood in my ears, Bland's voice, night rustles of the forest — as if a giant hand turned up the volume.

Keep calm, Annie. Stay alive. And keep praying.

Was that a break in the thick canopy of trees ahead? A ribbon of road?

Bland began to curse, pulling me back and forth along the edge of the trees. We veered left, then right, then left again. The more we stumbled around, the tighter he clutched my arm.

My foot hit a rock, and I went down hard on one knee. Bland yanked me up. My throat felt coated with dust. I dared not ask what he was looking for.

Then I knew. His car.

Deep within me, something rolled onto its side, curled into a fetal position. Bland was going to kill me, right here. He couldn't find his getaway vehicle, and I was only slowing him down.

Where are you, Jenna? Where are you, Chetterling?

"There." Bland pushed me out of the trees, onto the dark road. "Go."

There sat his car. In a burst of clarity I sought data about it. White. What kind? I peered at the back of it as we scuttled to the passenger side. A sticker for Enterprise rental. Ford logo. License plate . . .

We were moving too fast. I feigned a trip and went down on my knees. "Ungh." Breath whooshed from my mouth. I pressed my hands against the asphalt, steadying myself, eyes cutting left.

4ASG592

"Get up." Bland shoved his hands under both my arms and lifted.

"I'm trying."

4ASG592

I repeated the digits and letters, searing them into my mind as Bland pressed me inside the car. He slung his pack and night goggles into the back and slid into the driver's seat. Soon we were barreling down the road — away from Redding.

4ASG592. 4-Annie-silly-girl-592.

"Put your seat belt on."

I threw him a nonplussed look.

"Put it on!"

I fastened myself in.

God, please get me out of this alive, and I'll let You run my life. I promise.

"We will drive for a while. Then we will

call the Sheriff's Department."

4-Annie-silly-girl-592. "But . . . I don't know if I can get cell phone service out here."

Headlights crested a hill in the distance. Bland waited until the car passed.

"We'll drive till you do."

I pressed a hand against my forehead. Surely I was dreaming this bizarre night. I'd fallen asleep at my drawing table, cheek pressed against Bland's face, his criminal stream of consciousness flowing into mine . . .

New tears burned my eyes, tiredness and anger leaching strength from my limbs. How had Bland staged this so-called evidence that proved his innocence? What if his scheme actually worked?

"I'm going to tell you the rest of the evidence." Bland clipped his words. "Then you'll see that you've judged too quickly. The plastic bag. It contains the shirt Edwin wore the night of the murders."

Edwin's shirt?

"It will have blowback. Small particles discharged when a gun is fired. They kick back and get lodged in your hands and sleeves."

He claimed to have Edwin's shirt? But

how could he have known Edwin threw it out?

More headlights. Bland watched them approach and pass, then checked the car's taillights in the rearview mirror.

"As I sat in my car that night, planning, I realized I needed the shirt. I considered turning myself in, handing over the gun. Telling the sheriff's detectives to check Edwin's shirt. But I couldn't be sure, after our fight, if Edwin's prints could still be lifted from the gun. I knew the police wouldn't listen about his sleeves. They'd arrest *me.* He'd go home.

"I drove to Edwin's neighborhood, cruised by his town house. No lights. He was still at his mother's. Spouting his lies. But I noticed something on the street. Garbage cans, ready for pickup the next morning. That was the break I needed. I called Edwin's home number from a pay phone. Left a message. Told him I had the gun — with his prints. Told him about his shirt. Said they'd no doubt be asking for it in a day or two, just to cover all their bases. Did he know they'd find discharge on its sleeve? That he couldn't wash all of it out?

"Back to Edwin's neighborhood. I parked in a little alley and stole to his street. Finally, he came home. Within fifteen minutes, he was dragging out his garbage can."

I pressed back in my seat, thoughts reeling. Clearly, Bland had been at Edwin's town house that night. Because Edwin *had* thrown that shirt away in the garbage can. Could Bland's story possibly be true? Could Edwin, full of his own guilt, have felt compelled to tell a detective later why the shirt was missing — when he hadn't even been asked about it?

Wait. Maybe Bland was telling the truth about this, but he still committed the murders. Or maybe there was a third explanation I couldn't imagine right now.

My head spun, fear and lack of sleep shunting my brain. I *knew* Bland had killed those two men. He'd certainly shown his lack of conscience to me. He threatened me. Stalked my daughter. Broke into my house.

4-Annie-silly-girl-592

"You listening?" Bland hit my arm.

Pain pounded my muscle. "Yes." *But not with my heart.* "Could I ask a question? If you want me to understand . . ."

His lip curled. "Go ahead."

"Does Edwin know you have the shirt?"

"No."

"Why didn't you go to the Sheriff's Department when you got it?"

"That's *two* questions!"

I shrank in my seat, heart pounding. Was he going to hit me again?

Bland threw me a disgusted look. "I planned to turn myself in that night with the gun and shirt, but then I turned on the radio. News. About me. My abandoned car had been found. They didn't know what I was driving. They said I was armed and dangerous. *Armed and dangerous.*" Venom coated his voice. "I pictured trigger-happy cops and deputies. I would be surrounded. Probably shot. I couldn't take the chance. The situation couldn't be controlled. I chose to run."

Bland suddenly slowed the car. *Why?* Terror sliced through me. Did I now know too much? Stopping could be fatal. As long as he was driving he couldn't kill me.

"We need to stop and make the phone call. It's dangerous to talk while driving."

He was worried about *dangerous?*

The car slowed further, until the speedometer read thirty-five. "There." Bland pointed with his chin to a sign for a turnabout. He pulled into it and shut off the engine and lights. Darkness poured over us like tar, smothering and sticky. My heart caught in my throat.

I could make out Bland's black form as he dug in his large camouflage coat pocket for my cell phone. "We'll ask to talk to the man parked out front of your house."

My jaw loosened. How did he know about Chetterling? "He won't be there anymore. He'll be looking for me."

"Good, then that's who we want. What's his name?"

I told him and gave him the number to the Sheriff's Department. Then watched, helpless, my eyes slowly adjusting to the darkness, while he dialed. "Here." He thrust the phone at me. "You ask for him."

My fingers quivered as I held the cell to my ear.

"Shasta County Sheriff's Department."

"H–hello. I need to talk to Ralph Chetterling. Right now. Tell him it's Annie Kingston."

"Ms. Kingston." The woman's voice repeated my name with thinly veiled excitement. "We've been looking for you."

But will you find me in time?

CHAPTER 32

"Where are you?" the woman asked.

"Enough!" Bland snatched the cell from my fingers. "This is Bill Bland." He paused. "Don't worry about her; she's fine. You hear who I am? Bill Bland. Tell that to your detective. And have him call me back right away on this number." He looked to me. "What is it?"

I whispered the digits. He repeated them. "I'm hanging up now. I expect his call immediately."

He frowned at the phone, seeking the disconnect button, then pushed it.

"Five minutes. After that, we leave. Cell phone calls can be tracked."

Bland's icy determination settled over me like a winter fog. The air in my lungs thickened. I lay my head against the seat and forced myself to stay calm.

"You know this man? Chetterling?"

"Yes. I've worked with him a few times."

"Good."

I knew what he was thinking. Chetterling would want to protect me —

The phone rang.

He punched the talk button. "Bland."

I heard Chetterling respond. His voice, distant but distinct, rolled out in the calmest tone I'd ever heard him use. Even separated by miles, darkness, and deceit, I felt comfort in listening to it. "I hear you're with Annie Kingston, Mr. Bland. Is she all right?"

"She's fine."

"I'd like to talk —"

"Quiet! You need to do what I say. You need paper and pen. I have information for you."

"All right. Wait just a minute."

Where are you, Chetterling? In your car? At my house? Does Jenna know I'm okay?

4-Annie-silly-girl-592

"Ready, Mr. Bland."

Bland related a truncated story of the shirt and gun, telling the detective where they were now located. "Test them immediately, and Annie Kingston will be returned to you."

The way he talked — as if he had the right and power to move the universe. The precariousness of my situation washed over me. What did he expect to do with me while a lab tested his evidence? What if that took days? What if the results weren't what he wanted to hear?

"We already have your items, Mr. Bland. They were found by deputies searching the woods for Annie. They have not been compromised. But you have to understand how important it is to us that Annie is safe."

"It's important to *me* that my evidence is safe."

"Understood, Mr. Bland. We'll take care of it. I do suggest that you and Annie come in now. We'll want to know she's safe while we run your tests."

Bland scoffed. "I bring her in and you won't run anything. She stays with me until you're done."

"We'll do the testing as soon as we can. But right now it's the middle of the night. We'll have to wait until tomorrow to get your items to the lab, and then I don't know how long —"

"I can tell you how long." Bland's voice rose. "You think I didn't research this ahead of time? Think I'd try to pull this off without planning?"

"No —"

"The problem with you detectives is, you

don't know about forensics. You need to spend a little more time with your lab buddies. So here are the facts. Are you *listening?*"

"Go ahead." Chetterling sounded unflappable.

"One. A twenty-year-old latent can be lifted from that gun. The grip is custom wood, smooth enough to hold a print. Two. The discharge in the shirt fabric will also still be present. Both of these tests are relatively simple — that, even *you* should know — and can be done in a matter of hours."

"I see. No doubt the results will turn out as you said. Now if I could talk to An—"

"One more thing, Detective. Since I know you're playing me. You think I staged that shirt. I'll prove I didn't."

"I'm listening."

"On the tag of the shirt the dry cleaners wrote 'E, space T A R' for Edwin Tarell. I tracked down the cleaners. A mom-and-pop shop still in business. Called Scotty's. They can verify their writing."

The back of my neck prickled. I pressed against the car door and watched Bland with wary eyes. His planning was so detailed. He was so sure of himself.

Maybe his arrogance will prove to be his

downfall. Hadn't Susan said something like that? What had he overlooked?

"Most important will be the DNA. I waited over ten years for science to catch up with my needs. You'll find blood on the shirtsleeves. Probably Don Tarell's. I can imagine Edwin staging his sobs over the body, clinging to the father he so loved." Bland's sarcasm could have been cut with a knife. "You might have to exhume the bodies to get their DNA. The tests take a couple weeks. You'll get a match."

Could that be true?

Even if the DNA did match, did that prove Bland's innocence? There had to be a hole in his story. My overloaded mind searched in vain for what it might be.

"All right, Mr. Bland. We'll check all this out. What you need to do now is bring Annie Kingston back safely."

"Are you *deaf?* I'm not bringing her back until you test the evidence!"

"You're going to keep her until DNA testing is done? That's a long time to deal with a hostage."

Bland snorted. "After twenty years? Two weeks is nothing."

Two weeks? God help me, I would never make it that long.

"How can we know she's safe?"

"I'll let you talk to her. Every day."

"Mr. Bland. Just bring her back. Stop running. Surely you're tired of it. A man like you, accused for twenty years of a crime he didn't commit? If I were you, I'd want it over with."

"You're playing with me again!" Bland's shout raked through my ears. "I'm not talking to you anymore. Just do what I say!" He punched off the phone and threw it on the floor.

We sat in silence, my heart thumping. I couldn't begin to guess what he would do with me now.

Bland hit the steering wheel hard, then yanked the key out of the ignition and shoved open his door. I cringed in my seat as he paced beside the car, cursing, fighting to control his fury, clearly losing. After a few long moments he flung himself back inside and started the engine. Without a word he flipped the headlights on and scratched out of the turnabout.

We drove.

Time passed. Twenty, maybe thirty minutes. With every curve in the road, Bland's anger grew until it became a live and writhing creature. He hunched behind the wheel, cursing Edwin Tarell, cursing life.

God, help me. Help my children. Just let me see Kelly and Stephen again.

Would Chetterling and Delft run those lab tests as they'd promised? What if they didn't but said they had just to encourage Bland to let me go? How could Bland know they would tell him the truth?

I longed to ask where we were going, what he would do with me. How he expected to hide from the law now. Thank God he hadn't seen my drawing of his face. He'd have ripped it to shreds. Chetterling no doubt took it immediately. By now copies were being made, circulated. The drawing wasn't in full color, but under the circumstances, it was usable.

They would catch Bland. I just needed to stay alive until they did.

Bland glared at me. "You could have made this easier. My first plan failed because of *you.*"

I saw a hairpin turn loom ahead, his foot hard on the accelerator, the road suddenly precarious beneath our wheels.

"Watch out!"

I braced my hands against the dashboard, every muscle clamping down. Bland whipped his head around to gauge the road and veered. Not far enough. Our front tires crunched off pavement, my side mirror barely missing a wayward tree branch.

My scream reverberated through the car. We bumped over rough ground and bushes, our headlights bouncing, searing the forest. A redwood tree rushed toward us on the driver's side. Bland smacked on the brakes. The final second stretched toward eternity. We wouldn't stop in time.

The front tires banged over something solid. My stomach jumped up to my throat, my head snapping. My shoulder hit the window. The force from whatever we rolled over began to slow us down. We skidded . . . skidded . . .

The tree came closer.

A final slide . . .

We hit something else on the ground and crunched to a stop — inches from the tree. Bland shot forward, his forehead hitting the steering wheel.

Earsplitting silence.

I couldn't move.

Precious seconds passed. I gasped for breath, assessing myself, realizing I wasn't hurt. I turned toward Bland, noting for the first time his lack of a seat belt. In his anger he'd forgotten to put it back on. He was raising his head from the wheel. Not badly hurt, but dazed.

Escape.

My thoughts blurred. Should I do it? Run into the forest, in the middle of nowhere? No purse, no money. What then?

Annie, just go!

Bland groaned, one hand against his head. Desperately, I fumbled with my seat belt. Unlatched it. Reached for the door.

Goggles! With them I could see in the forest. I could run. Bland wouldn't be able to find me. Where were they? Hadn't he thrown them in the backseat?

I swiveled around, and by a providence that could only have come from God, saw the goggles tossed from the impact of our wreck up on the console. I grabbed them and flung myself out the door.

CHAPTER 33

I ran for my life, dodging trunks, half tripping over logs. The goggles were too big for my head, but I had no time to stop and adjust them. With one hand I held the gear in place, crashing through the eerie, green-tinted forest. I didn't care about the noise I made. I only wanted to put distance between myself and Bland. The car headlights were still on, bright over immediate trees, then quickly waning. I aimed in a diagonal away from them.

Vaguely, I heard a car door slam, followed by Bland's bellow of rage. Then silence. Still I ran, my mouth open, breath jagging in and out. Utter panic pushed me through the dense brush. If he caught me, he would kill me.

Bland fell silent. What was he doing? A limb reached out, catching tiny end branches in my hair. I ducked and pulled away. Terror pushed strangled sounds from

318

my throat. I flung myself behind a tree, then leaned out, seeking a straight shot of sight to the passenger side of Bland's car. Its headlights were visible — two fuzzy green spots across my goggle lenses. Bland was nowhere to be seen. My fingers fumbled around the side of the goggles. Wasn't there something that would make them magnify? I found a tiny dial and turned it. Instantly the car leapt into close-up. I could see an open rear door, Bland leaning inside the backseat, rifling through something. His body jerked this way and that, his movements erratic.

He was looking for the goggles.

I watched, praying.

After an extended search he emerged from the car, smacking a fist against the door. He strode a few feet away, swiveling his head in search of me, yelling my name. As if I would return just because he demanded it.

Even with the magnification, I couldn't make out his facial expression. But I could imagine the fury upon it. What would he do now? I hadn't thought to take his car keys. But maybe that was a good thing. *Please, God, just let him give up on me. Let him drive away.*

I hadn't taken the time to locate my cell phone, somewhere on the car floor. I consoled myself with the notion that there wasn't any service out here anyway.

Bland paced the side of the car with the ferocity of a caged lion, cursing. Back and forth. Back and forth. When his anger played out, he rested, breathing heavily, against the door. No doubt scheming his Plan C. He was assessing, unwilling to be pushed into impulsive action. How could he gain control again? He couldn't find me in the dark. He couldn't waste time here, with detectives fanning out in search of him . . .

Bland gingerly felt his bruised forehead, then swiveled to crash his fist against the top of the car. He hung there for a long moment. Then, determination arching his shoulders, he straightened, stalked around the front of the car, and threw himself into the driver's seat. His door slammed.

I held my breath. *Please let the tires not be flat.* The engine gunned, as if he was testing it in neutral. Slowly, the car backed up, bumping over a small fallen branch and the uneven forest floor. The headlight beams swung over trees and downed branches. I pressed myself behind the tree until I heard the tires meet asphalt, the faint squeal as Bland smacked the car into drive. Leaning out once more, I watched him shoot forward, continuing to head away from Redding.

His brown-tinted taillights disappeared around the hairpin turn.

Nauseated relief rose in my stomach. I sagged against the tree and whispered tear-singed thank-yous to God.

But my grateful prayers were short lived. Soon the night closed around me, the lingering precariousness of my situation threatening to steal my breath once more. I stood alone in the woods in the middle of the night. Not even sure what county I was in. No one knew where I was. I had no purse, no money, no cell phone . . .

Come on, Annie, keep yourself together.

Summoning all my willpower, I concentrated on preparing myself for what lay ahead. I adjusted the goggles to fit my head. Then fiddled with the magnification dial, familiarizing myself with its maximum power, how to snap it on and off quickly.

The darkness snatched at me, but I had to capture *it,* make it my friend. I reminded myself that Bland could much more easily spot me in daylight. I needed to find help — before dawn.

Getting lost in the forest would be the

worst thing I could do. I needed to follow the road back to civilization.

I slunk through the forest, aimed in a wide angle toward the road, away from the direction Bland had gone. What if he'd rounded that corner, turned off his car and lights, and sat waiting, the spider ready for the fly? I wanted to head that way, too, in case a house lay up ahead. I couldn't remember passing a house until this point. But I had no choice. I had to head back from where we had come.

Hitting the road, I strained with every fiber of my being to listen. Cicadas chirped and the sound of my own pulse filled my ears. The asphalt stretched emptily before me, tinted a deathly green-gray. Looking like the road to hell. I shuddered, realizing for the first time the chill of the night.

I desperately needed a drink of water.

Drawing my arms across my chest, I started down the barren road.

Minutes bunched around me, sodden with the fear of Bland's return. All I could do was put one foot in front of the other. I rounded the first curve. Then a straight section. Another bend.

Walk. Breathe. Loose pebbles crunching beneath my shoes.

The stillness of the forest ululated through me, to the hollows of my bones. With each step, I imagined Bland materializing out of the night. My mental projector kicked on, throwing out scene after scene in frantic sequence. Flash! a

close-up of his hand on the gun, trigger finger ready. The camera pulls back to show his hulking figure in the woods, watching my approach. The gun rises. A shot cracks the night. Without a sound, I fall . . .

Flash! he

rolls slowly down the road behind me, headlights off, patient. Knowing he will catch me. He drives with his left hand, the gun in his right, ready . . .

I screamed in my own head for the film to stop. Shivering, I hunched through the void, every sound echoing in my ears. How long had I been walking? Thirty minutes? An hour? Time had vanished, consumed by the incessant scuff of my feet.

The sky mocked me, clouds obliterating the stars and moon. The sickly green of my world turned smothering, claustrophobic. I was a refugee, abandoned on some unknown planet where perpetual half-night stretched for eternity. Where the threat of death hovered just beyond my reach, its vaporous, fatal fingers poised to pluck.

The distant chirr of cicadas stopped.

I froze.

Fright gripped my throat with an iron hand. I held my breath, nerves acrawl with the frenzy of a million insects. They milled and swarmed down my arms, my legs, in the cavities between my ribs.

The night turned jokester, strewing colors and lights at the outer reach of my vision. I whirled toward a metallic gleam to see — nothing. Wrenched my head the other way to a flash of movement that vaporized before my eyes could land upon it.

No Bland. Come on, Annie. Move.

Shush-shush. My shoes against asphalt. My heart clattered against my ribs, the wind kicking up a faint keen through the trees.

I tried to occupy my mind. Anything to keep the scenes from flashing.

Had Bland used my cell phone to call Chetterling? Or had Chetterling called him back? What would Bland say when they talked? He would lie to them. Tell them I was with him. Tell them I was safe. It would buy him time.

Was Chetterling at our house with Jenna?

What was happening with my children? They must be petrified. Kelly would be crying, shaking. The mere thought pulled fresh tears into my eyes.

Kelly would call Erin. No. Not necessary. All the cars and deputies and dogs would wake the entire neighborhood.

Bushes rustled. I halted, air backing up in my lungs. My ankles trembled, fingers digging into my thighs.

An animal?

Bland.

I cocked my head, moving my ear to the right, to the left. Then turned all the way around, acutely aware of the vulnerability of my back. I searched the road, the woods. Nothing. Again. Just the wind and the thwack of my heart.

Forward, Annie.

I forced one foot in front of the other.

Please, God, help me. Just get me back to my children.

Something in the distance. A vague light. Before I could react, headlights crested a hill. I leaped with wild instinct off the road, stumbling toward a grove of trees, and threw myself on the ground.

The headlights grew closer.

Only then did I remember that the car was coming from the opposite direction of Bland. What if it was someone else? The driver could help me.

But how to know if the driver could be trusted? What if it was a man alone? Why should I trust a strange man on an empty road in the middle of the night?

What if it was law enforcement? What if I hid only to see a sheriff's or police car go by? I would be *sick*.

I could rush out onto the road, wave my arms.

They would never see me. Not in this darkness.

The lights approached. Ambivalence wrapped a rope around me, played tug-of-war. I hugged the ground, fighting against the desperate desire to race back to the road and wave my arms, praying to God that the person would save me.

Beams cut a swath through the green darkness. I could hear the car engine, tires singing. Panic swept through me, and I dug fingers into the earth as if any second it might fall away, leave me exposed.

The car sped past. Solid dark color. Not Bland. Not law enforcement.

My lungs jellied. I lowered my head to the

earth, throat tightening. *God, help me. Please, just help me get home.*

The tears would be held back no longer. I don't know how long I lay there, crying. Once I started, I couldn't stop. Couldn't quiet myself. If Bland had hulked by on foot, he would have heard me for sure.

Finally, head throbbing, I lurched to my feet. I had to keep going. For my children. Had to.

4-Annie-silly-girl-592

My brain treated me to the scene of a policeman spotting Bland's license plate. Stopping the car. Bland coming out with his hands raised.

Next shot: *Choog, choog. Copies of my drawing spitting out of a machine. They are picked up, passed through impatient hands . . .*

Vengeance smeared my soul. I couldn't wait to see Bland behind bars. Couldn't wait to testify against him.

I stumbled along, my mind a leaky pan. Thoughts out of focus. Stress and enervation took its toll, and my limbs began to wobble. I yearned for rest.

The road forked. Which way should I go? I couldn't remember from which direction we'd come. I should try the other way, hope for a house . . .

Come on, Annie, which way?

I veered right.

The shirt . . . The gun . . . How could Bland have staged his evidence? What had I missed?

So tired. Maybe I should rest for a while. Just lie down, sleep a little. When I woke it would be morning. Bland would be far away by then. Or he would be caught. I would be safe.

My head sagged, so heavy.

I forced myself to keep going. My insides shook like gelatin.

In the distance, something swam in half focus. My brain wouldn't register the shape. It bobbed before me, amorphous and blurry. The blurriness confused me; I wasn't crying anymore. I didn't think I had one drop of moisture left in my body. I felt like a lake bed scorched by the sun.

The thing drew closer. I watched it, obsessed with my need for water, sleep.

Keep walking. Just keep walking.

Some minutes passed. Then, like a weakened laser, the object's meaning beamed.

Mailbox.

My breath hitched. Mailbox . . . meant a driveway . . . meant a house.

Keep walking.

Somehow I managed to pick up speed. But the mailbox seemed to draw no closer. Would I never reach it?

Why couldn't I even swallow? My throat snagged on its own dryness.

The world fuzzed at the edges. The next thing I remember, I stood by the mailbox, peering down a driveway at a small wood house. Tinted green, like my world. No lights on.

God? Please get me there.

I started down the vast sea of unpaved driveway, rocks rolling like waves beneath my feet. What if no one was home? What if they wouldn't come to the door?

I couldn't sort out answers. Logic had fled my mind, ghosted away like a spirit riding the wind.

Just take the next step.

The house loomed before me. It had a porch. Three stairs. No railing. My leg lifted, toes hitting the rise of the first stair. *Lift a little higher.* I felt the first step, hoisted myself up. Took the second. The third. Wood squeaked as I forged a path toward the front door.

What if someone heard me? What if they met me with a shotgun?

What if Bland lived here?

That stopped me cold. My hand, raised to ring the doorbell, hung in the air.

I struggled for coherent thinking. *Could Bland live here?*

Who knew? All I knew was I needed sleep. And a glass of water.

Somebody's finger rang the bell. Somebody's ear heard the distant chime.

I swayed before the door.

An upper window lit up. Then nothing.

Maybe I should leave. Maybe I'll find another house soon . . .

Another window shimmered. A sound from the house. Someone walking down creaky stairs?

The goggles. I would look like some kind of monster. With one hand I slipped them off. Vaguely, I heard them clatter to the porch.

Footsteps. Kind of a scuffle. Like my slippers on the hardwood floor of our great room.

"Who's there?"

A male voice. I drew back. A strange man wouldn't be safe, would he? Alone in his house?

My mouth opened. No response formed.

"Who is it, Clay?"

A softer voice. Female.

330

"I don't know."

A woman. A couple.

My body listed to one side. I put out a hand against the door, steadying myself.

"Who *is it?*" The male again.

My mouth answered. "Annie Kingston. This man . . . I was kidnapped. Do you have any water?"

Something clicked. The door pulled back a few inches. Wary eyes looked me over. Another head appeared — the woman, gawking at me.

"For heaven's sake, Clay, let her in."

The door receded, opening up the house like a yawning cavern. I thought it would swallow me whole. The two figures undulated before me.

My foot moved across the threshold. Then somehow I just folded over on myself. The floor rose up to meet me, almost in slow motion. Next thing I knew, my bleary eyes were blinking at a pink fuzzy slipper. My lips parted. There was something I had to tell them. Something very important . . .

"Four. Annie-silly-girl. Five-nine-two."

My lids weighted. Callused hands cradled my head as blackness enveloped me.

"Four . . . Annie . . . sil . . ."

CHAPTER 34

My first waking sense was of voices above me.

"I think we should call an ambulance, don't you?" a woman said.

"Don't know. What if she can't pay for it? It's a long way to the hospital. We don't even know who she is."

"Wait. She's coming to."

I remembered sinking to a hard floor, but now I lay on something soft, a cushion behind my head. And something over me. A blanket? My head rolled to the right, my eyes opening. A lemon-colored blur wavered before me. I frowned, then blinked a few times. The blur crystallized. A large yellow flower. Green leaves. The fabric on the back of a couch, inches from my nose.

"Hey, there."

Who was talking? Did I know these people? Where was I?

In a sickening rush, it all came back.

I dragged in a shuddering breath, turned my head toward the sound. "I need water." The words sounded cracked and broken.

"Sure, honey, I'll get it right now."

Footsteps hurried away. I tried moving my head to follow them, but my neck felt made of lead.

"Don't worry now, she'll be back." The man again.

I looked toward him, vision still bleary until my focus could readjust. There. Gray hair, bulbous nose, deep-set eyes. Prominent ears. Near seventy, perhaps.

The woman returned, glass in hand. "Here you go."

I was too shaky to hold the glass. She helped me sit up, then held it to my lips. I wanted to guzzle it but couldn't. I took slow, even sips until half the water was gone, then shook my head to say "no more." The woman pulled the glass away.

They introduced themselves as Clay and Shirley Welron. Then asked my name, where I lived. What was this about a man kidnapping me? Did I want to call someone?

"Yes, please." I was feeling better now, alertness returning. Able to sit up completely, I finished the water. Shirley took the glass to the kitchen for a refill and returned. Clay picked up a phone from an end table, stretching its long cord to lay it beside me. He stood back, hands clasped and mouth working, watching as I dialed. Shirley hovered, fingering her red cotton robe. It occurred to me that my arrival must have frightened them badly.

Jenna answered on the first ring. When she heard my voice, she burst into tears. I'd never heard Jenna cry like that. My heart pinched until I thought it would break in two. My chin lowered to my chest, eyes waiting for tears that wouldn't come. My body must have been more stressed and exhausted than I'd realized.

"It's okay, Jenna, I'm okay. Really."

"He didn't hurt you?"

"No."

"You sure?"

"Yes, I'm sure. But he took me at gunpoint. And he wrecked the car, and I had to escape into the forest. Is that bad enough for you?"

"Oh, Annie." Jenna's ragged breaths morphed into a laugh of desperate relief.

"Is that Mom?" Kelly's voice filtered through the line. "Let me talk to her, let me talk to her!"

Muted noise followed — the sound of a hand being placed over the receiver, the jar of the phone moving from person to person.

"Mom!"

"Kelly, honey, yes, it's me. I'm all right."

For a moment she could say nothing over her sobs. I soothed her, saying I would be home soon, that I wasn't hurt, that I was so sorry to scare her. Sudden fresh tears formed within me, spilling down my cheeks.

"Mom, just come *home.*"

"I will, honey, I will."

"It's been terrible. We've been so worried, Erin and her dad too. They came over when all the sheriff's cars got here. And then Erin stayed while her dad helped look for you."

Dave, out in the black forest, looking for me. I pictured him searching, and my heart clutched.

"Kelly, can you put Jenna back on now?"

"Okay. I love you."

"Love you too. So very much."

I asked Jenna about Stephen. He'd been downstairs, she said, but ran into the office when Kelly shouted the news that I was on the phone. Did I want to talk to him?

Suddenly, I had no idea what I would say to my son. What could he possibly be feeling after all he'd done? He was the one who'd slipped into the night, left the sliding glass door open . . .

"Of course I want to talk to him."

At that moment my eyes locked with Shirley's. She and Clay had retreated across their living room and now perched on matching chairs, trying not to listen, hanging on every word. The look of empathy on Shirley's round-cheeked face — as if she sensed the gap between me and my son. Somehow I knew it was an expression founded on experience. I don't know why that split-second unspoken communication between us strengthened me, but it did. Perhaps merely because I saw that she'd survived the ordeal.

I gave her a weak smile.

"Hi, Mom." His words sounded strained.

"Stephen. Oh, it's so good to hear your voice."

"It's good to hear you, too." He hesitated. "I'm . . . glad you're okay."

I closed my eyes, feeling his pain writhe just beneath the surface. The catch in his breathing told me what he couldn't put into words: he couldn't forgive himself for what he'd done.

"Stephen, everything will be all right. Do you hear what I'm telling you? *Everything.*"

"Yeah. Okay. Well, the detective wants to talk to you."

"Is he right there?"

"Yeah."

"He *is?*" Why wasn't Chetterling out looking for me?

"He's been here, talking to people and getting deputies and search teams out and stuff. Here he is."

Phone shuffling noise once more. Then Chetterling's voice. "Annie!"

The happiness in his tone tightened my throat. "Hi."

"Boy, you don't know how glad I am to hear your voice."

"I'm glad to hear yours too."

"Where are you, other than in someone's house?"

"I haven't the slightest idea. All I know is we headed east on little back roads."

"Okay. Maybe you'd —"

"Ralph, listen. First, be careful. Bland's armed with a good-sized gun. Second, you got a pen? Write this down before I forget it. Four-Annie-silly-girl-five-nine-two — 4ASG592."

A pause. "Got it. Tell me that's a license plate."

"It is."

"California? Sounds like it."

I squeezed my eyes shut, visualizing the plate. "Yes. It's a white car. Four doors. A Ford. And it's an Enterprise rental."

"Great. We're on it. How long ago did you see him?"

I frowned, focusing on my knees. For the first time I noticed how dirty my clothes were. "I don't know. I sort of . . . lost track of time."

"That's all right. Don't worry, we'll get him. I'll put out this plate right away. And your drawing is already being faxed around the state."

No reply would form. The sheer thought of Bland behind bars made me almost sick with revenge.

"Annie? You there?"

"Yeah. I . . ." A wrench clamped around my throat. My body seemed to sink right into the cushions, as if my last bit of energy had trickled away. "Ralph, just get me *home*."

I huddled on the couch, drinking water, shivering on and off, while Clay gave Detective Chetterling directions to his house. I'd ended up in Lassen County, not far outside a small town. Chetterling asked Clay if they'd let me rest there until he came to pick me up. No doubt the Lassen County Sheriff's Department would be glad to bring me home, he added, but statements needed to be taken from the Welrons, and he preferred to do that himself. Coming up Highway 299 — a much straighter drive than the back roads Bland had evidently taken —

Chetterling could arrive in about ninety minutes. Meanwhile, Sergeant Delft would work at the Redding office, fielding all the information about Bland to other law enforcement.

By the time I'd said a final good-bye to Chetterling and my family, my eyelids would barely stay open. I lay down on the couch, mumbling about getting a few minutes' rest. Shirley's gentle hands tucked a blanket around me.

Sleep rolled in like a midnight fog.

CHAPTER 35

I stumble through black-green woods, branches reaching out to grab me, roots rising up to trip me. Bill Bland pursues me, breath hot on my neck. Kelly sobs in the distance, and Stephen calls my name. I cannot find them. Their sounds echo ahead of me, then behind, then to my side. Another voice joins, speaking in a low drone. I cannot understand what it is saying . . .

The forest shimmers, compacts. I rise above it, up and out, into light that glows red against my closed eyelids. Voices waft through my ears, my head. A woman . . . a man . . .

Chetterling.

My eyes blinked open to daylight. I turned my head, looking across the Welrons' living room and beyond to see the detective seated with them at the kitchen table. He closed a notebook and glanced at me.

"Good morning, sleepyhead."

Never had his voice sounded so good. Chetterling's presence meant safety. My home. My children.

"Hi." Sudden embarrassment washed over me. I pushed myself to a sitting position, then winced as my head thumped in protest.

I wanted to leave right away. Chetterling agreed to take my statement at my house so we needn't delay the reunion with my family. Both Stephen and Kelly had begged Jenna to let them stay home from school, he informed me, and she'd relented. But before he and I left, Shirley and Clay insisted we eat breakfast, especially me. Chetterling sided with them. If I didn't eat, I'd probably just faint again, and did I want that?

Somehow I managed to down a piece of toast and two glasses of water. Plus a couple aspirin.

On my way out the door, I couldn't thank the Welrons enough. They waved away my gratitude, insisting they'd been glad to help.

"When that man that took you comes to trial, you'll see us on the stand." Clay stood on his porch with hands in his pockets, a vindictive gleam in his eye.

Chetterling and I spoke little on the trip home. I must have dozed on and off, because it didn't seem to take very long. When we did talk, it wasn't about Bland at all. Worries about Stephen had risen to the surface.

"You'll receive a notice in the mail about his court date," Chetterling explained. "It'll be one of those general times for juvenile court, and you'll just have to go and wait your turn."

The thought of watching my own son face a judge seemed otherworldly. "But they won't send him to juvenile hall, right?"

"Not for a first offense. He'll likely get probation."

"What if he doesn't straighten up? What if he keeps making wrong choices and ends up in the hall?" My words caught on a hook of fear.

"Annie." Chetterling threw me an empathetic glance. "That's always possible, but there are a number of steps between here and there. If probation doesn't work, Stephen could be put on weekend work detail or house arrest. If he refused to comply with either of those two things, he'd be taken immediately to the hall. But the juvenile court system is not about retribution. It's about trying to turn kids around before they find themselves adults and in *real* trouble."

All those years of my sitting in court-rooms, sketching the defendants and lawyers and judges, covering the tragedies of people on the wrong side of the law. Now I would sit in court for a member of my own family. Surely I would be judged as well. What kind of mother was I if a child under my roof made these kinds of choices?

"One thing you've got to avoid, and that's beating up on yourself."

Chetterling had certainly learned to read me well.

"Believe me, I did the same thing when I was raising my niece. There I was, *in law enforcement,* and not able to keep her out of trouble. Annie, you do the best you can with kids. You teach them morals, model a right way of living, and still they're going to do what they're going to do. Some never give their parents any problems. And some nearly put their parents in a grave. I've seen it all. I've also seen kids from terrible homes, kids that you wouldn't give a chance in the world, be model citizens." He shook his head. "Sometimes you just can't explain life."

"How is Nicole now?" Chetterling, a private man, had spoken so little of his niece. I didn't even know how old she was.

"Great. Totally turned around. She's married, has two young children." He shot me a rueful smile. "I look at those kids and tell her, 'Just wait, your time's coming.' Thought scares her to death."

As well it should.

Tiredness overcame me once more. I lay back against the headrest and closed my eyes. The next thing I knew, we were pulling up to the curb at my house.

Never had home looked so *good.* Despite my exhaustion I bounded out of the car and up my front walk. Kelly and Jenna met me on the porch. We group hugged, all three of us breaking into tears. Kelly clung to me, crying long and hard.

Stephen was waiting in the great room. I marched over and claimed a hug before he could decide whether he wanted one or not. His arms went around me and held on tightly. "Mom, I'm so glad you're back."

I squeezed my eyes shut, shuddering a muted sob. "And I'm glad *you're* back."

We pulled apart, my hands still on his shoulders. He couldn't look me in the face. Dropping his gaze to the floor, he mumbled, "I'm sorry for leaving the door open."

My heart lurched. Maybe, just maybe, he'd learned his lesson. Maybe he really would turn around now. "We'll talk later. But you can know one thing for now. You *will* stop doing what you've been doing. 'Cause I'm not going to let you tear your own life apart."

He nodded.

Greetings over, there was so much to do, and I possessed the energy for none of it. I wanted to keep hugging my family, answer their questions. Assure them that I hadn't been hurt, that things would soon be all right because Bland would be caught. And Kelly insisted I call Dave because he'd been so worried. He'd taken Erin to school that morning, but promised to call and tell her when I arrived home.

I shot a look at Chetterling. He'd touched base with the Sheriff's Department — the Office, as he termed it — in a long phone call. I knew he'd heard some new information, and I *had* to know what it was. But I wouldn't question him in front of the kids. Chetterling now stood ready to take my statement. I would have to tell him the whole story. Everything I could remember, both for Bland's future day in court (please, God!) and to help locate him now. The very thought of relating all those details weighted my limbs.

"Kelly, would you call Dave for me? He's probably seen the car out front anyway. Tell him I'm fine, and I'll talk to him later. But right now I have to meet with the detective. Okay?"

"Okay." Solemn-faced, Kelly headed for the telephone in the TV room. I watched her go. *What have I done to my daughter? When will she ever feel safe again?*

Stephen hung against the fireplace, gauging my every move. He didn't look at Chetterling, whose presence surely caused more than a little ambivalence within him. The detective who'd picked him up for drug possession, and the same one who'd brought his mother home in one piece.

"Annie." Jenna turned her back to Stephen and spoke in a low tone. "Chetterling is waiting to talk to you."

"I know." Standing zombielike, I tried to work my brain enough to decide where we should go. Stay in the great room? Kitchen table?

"Maybe you should go to your office." My know-me-like-a-book sister gave me a gentle nudge. "That way you can talk in private."

I took a deep breath. "Will you come too?"

"If you want."

"Yes. Please." Maybe some of her strength, her stamina, would flow into me.

I looked past her shoulder toward my son. "Stephen —"

"Yeah, I know. You have to talk to the detective."

Was that tired empathy in his voice — or returning sarcasm? I gazed at him, the fifteen feet between us suddenly feeling like a canyon. What was it going to take to bridge it?

Minutes later Chetterling, Jenna, and I sat in my office, the detective at my desk so he could take notes, and the two of us before him in matching chairs pulled over from the wall. Chetterling also had a tape recorder running so that nothing I said would be missed.

"Okay." I bit the inside of my cheek. "First I need to know what you heard when you called the Office."

"Right."

He adjusted his position, elbows on the arms of my leather chair. A small motion, but it seemed fraught with weariness. Only then did I realize he'd gotten even less sleep than I had. He'd been up all night, looking for me.

"First, a detail regarding the media. As you know, they can be a real pain in the neck."

Oh no. Not more reporters. I *hated* publicity. "They found out I was kidnapped."

"I'm afraid so. Took them awhile. They listen to law-enforcement radio chatter to pick up stories, but this all happened in the middle of the night. This morning, however, when we knew you'd been found, and bulletins for Bland's arrest were being circulated . . . there was no way to keep that quiet. Delft said calls have been coming into the Office from all over the country. I'm talking national news, Annie. Things might be pretty intense for a while."

Chetterling didn't have to spell it out for me; I'd been around reporters during my stint as a courtroom artist. I knew what they would do to get a story. And my kidnapping could easily woo them as a major one. An artist, creating a drawing for *American Fugitive,* becomes the target of the fugitive herself . . .

I groaned. This had *sensationalism* written all over it.

"One thing we have managed to keep under wraps, however," the detective continued, "is all of the information about the shirt and gun Bland brought us. For obvious reasons we don't want that in the news right now."

Agreed. But what a hole in the story.

Without that motivation made known, Bland would look all the more like a pure maniac. *Everyone* would want him caught. The thought almost made me smile.

"But if your phone starts ringing, I'd like you to answer it." Chetterling indicated the extension with a movement of his chin. "You don't have to answer reporters' questions, but we do still have the recording device plus a trace on your phone, and just in case it's Bland . . ."

Jenna made a disgusted sound in her throat. "He'd have some gall, calling here now."

"Agreed, but just in case."

"Okay, okay, we'll answer the phone." I waved a hand at him. "I don't care about this. I want to know what's going on with Bland."

Chetterling nodded. I had to admit the man was patient. "His car's been traced to an Enterprise agency right here in Redding. It was rented to a man by the name of Joseph Strong from Nevada. The agency made a photocopy of his driver's license because it was from out of state. Delft had them fax over the copy to the Sheriff's Office. The picture matches your drawing."

"That's great!" Jenna lashed a fist in the air.

I leaned back, feeling weak. *Joseph Strong from Nevada.* So that was the man Bland had become. They could catch him now. Surely they would.

Chetterling puffed out his cheeks. "Now it gets convoluted, I'm afraid. Joseph Strong isn't an established ID. No such address in Nevada. Bland must have used it as a backup. And the rental car was returned sometime very early this morning. Sitting right there in the agency parking lot, keys inside. With, by the way, your cell phone on the floor."

I closed my eyes. I couldn't believe it. He'd slipped away again. And we still didn't know the main identity he was using. "Let me guess. I can't even have my phone back. You took it to the lab for fingerprints."

"I'm afraid so."

Of course. Just one more thing Bland had taken from me. "Go on." My voice sounded flat.

"We do have another lead. Now, Annie, this one's not going to be easy to hear at first. Yesterday afternoon, when we had that first deputy watching your house, a car drove up the street slowly, like the driver was looking for something. Our deputy was immediately alert, watching in his rearview mirror. Then the car — a blue Ford Taurus — came up even with our deputy, and the man behind the wheel asked for directions to Redding. The guy had an English accent. Our deputy relaxed, thinking it was just someone who'd gotten lost." Chetterling gave a small wince. "We now think it was Bland."

"Here?" Jenna's face reddened. "On this street? And he talked to your *deputy?*" She slapped a palm against her cheek. "That's . . . I can't believe that. He could have been stopped!"

"I know, I know." The detective rubbed his forehead. "Believe me, the deputy's been jumped on. But not half as badly as he's jumping on himself. Still, it may be a little late, but he's coming through for us. As I said, he noticed that the car was a blue Ford Taurus. And he noticed that the plates were from Kansas —"

"Kansas!" Jenna rose to pace the office, fuming. "What Englishman lives in *Kansas?*"

I gave her a worn look. "Jenna. Forget it; it's done. Sit down, you're making me crazy."

She glared at Chetterling, then flopped back in her chair, arms folded.

"Okay." I ticked the items off in my head. "So we have the make and color of the car. And the state —"

"Right. Plus our deputy remembered that the plate started with a *D* followed by a *5.* We've got people running all this now. A Taurus is a popular car, but with all those defining factors, we shouldn't come up with too many. We'll run all the possibilities down, match them to driver's licenses. Then, with your drawing, Annie, we'll get him. I don't want to make promises, but this is a really good lead. It shouldn't take too long."

"I'll believe it when I hear it." Jenna remained defiant.

I could hardly blame her. If I had any more energy, I'd feel the same. As it was, I didn't feel much of anything except exhausted. "Ralph, please call me the minute you pick him up. I don't care what time of day or night it is. I just want to know he's off the streets."

"I will, Annie. I want him off the streets as much as you do."

Silence for a moment. Jenna stewed. I watched the detective open his notebook, pull the tape recorder toward him. "You ready to start?" His eyes avoided Jenna's.

"Yeah. Ready."

Chetterling punched a button on the recorder. He stated the date, time, place, subject, and people present, then indicated for me to start.

I began at the beginning, when Bland first appeared in the house. Wracking my brain, I sought to relate every detail about Bland's version of the Tarell/Dessinger murders.

"You won't appreciate the significance of all this yet until you read the case files." I indicated one of the boxes near my desk. "Even Delft may not, until he gets a fresh read. Because everything Bland told me fit perfectly with the crime, except for who did it. For example, Edwin Tarell told detectives that he stood at the fireplace and Bland sat on an armchair across from him. The direction of the shots indicated that they'd come from that chair. But Bland says *he* stood at the fireplace and Edwin sat in the chair."

"You believe that?" Jenna blurted.

I scowled. "After all he's done to us? Not on your life."

In truth, I couldn't remember when I'd trusted someone less.

"He's had twenty years to perfect his story." Chetterling looked up from his notes.

"Exactly. And he's done it to a fine science, if the tests work out. He's pretty smart that way. But he's also too arrogant for his own good. He sneaks here to try to change my mind about his guilt. Figures he'll convince me in record time to believe him and bring his evidence to you. Then, when I don't believe him — okay, maybe it had something to do with how he'd threatened me, stalked my daughter, and broken into my house — he puts Plan B into effect and takes me hostage to force you to test his evidence. *And,* get this, he informs me that when he's cleared of the murders, I'll feel sorry enough for him to plead for the kidnapping charges to be dropped so he can run home scot-free!"

I squeezed my eyes shut against fresh, angry tears. Jenna pressed her fingers around my arm, murmuring soothing words. But the tremble of her flesh against mine spoke more loudly. My sister's rage matched my own, maybe even surpassed it. If *she* came up against Bland, forget jail; she'd shoot the man and be done with it.

Chetterling filled the awkward silence. "Criminals pull that kind of stuff all the time. Most of them are just plain stupid. But the smarter ones, the ones who've planned everything to a *T,* just get too full of themselves. And the more they get away with, the more invincible they think they are."

The detective waited until I was ready to continue. I'd jumped ahead in my story and had to back up, gathering scattered details. By the time I finished, over an hour had passed. My thoughts would barely process, coagulating in emotional clumps. My throat ran dry, and my mouth felt disconnected from my brain. Twice we'd been interrupted by phone calls from reporters — one each from the AP wire service and NBC news. Jenna had answered the calls with a curt, "No comment." I could hardly believe all this was happening. More than anything I wanted to crawl into bed and hide — for about a year.

Chetterling turned off the tape recorder and closed his notebook. "You need to get some more sleep."

So did he. "No, no, I . . . have to talk to . . . Stephen. And I promised to see Dave."

Jenna put both hands under my elbows and hauled me out of my chair. "You're not talking to anybody right now. You're going to bed."

It was a conspiracy. I tried to voice an argument, but all logic fuzzed over. Didn't they know there were things I had to do?

Had to fix my son. Today. Had to talk to Dave . . .

"Annie." Chetterling towered over me. "Delft took Bland's evidence to the lab this morning. We're checking it out right now. You understand we have to do this. When we pick Bland up, we can't afford to have his attorney accusing us of not following every lead."

"Uh-huh."

"We'll find the holes in his story. All this babble of his won't go anywhere."

"I know."

He gave me one of his rare smiles. "Time to let your sister put you to bed."

I don't remember mounting the stairs. I do remember protesting when Jenna insisted on giving me a sleeping pill.

"Jenna, it's already early afternoon. You give me that, I'll sleep till midnight."

"So."

"So I don't want to be awake all night — *alone* — while you snore away."

We compromised. She cut the pill in half. I downed it and slid into bed, clothes still on. Jenna closed the window blinds and unplugged my phone. "There. No one's going to bother you now."

Within minutes, I fell into an exhausted, dreamless sleep.

CHAPTER 36

Two-fifteen.

He paced the tiny motel room. His limbs jittered from caffeine and sugar and lack of sleep. The detested contacts had been taken off, his black-framed glasses put back on. Still, his eyes hurt.

But no matter. These things, he would overcome.

He considered his situation once more.

She'd taken the goggles.

They would dust them for prints. They'd dust her cell phone too. This would only lead them back to Bill Bland. He'd never been printed in his new identity.

Had she been found? She would draw him from memory. They would use this.

Could she lead them to the rental car?

Not likely she knew enough information.

He sat down on the side of the bed. Sudden, vicious anger tried to burst him apart. He clenched his teeth and fought it.

Nathan Bailing in *Over the Top.* Pushed to the edge, fighting to win.

Timing was no longer under his control. This was unacceptable.

He snatched up a pillow and hurled it against the wall.

No. Overcome . . . Overcome.

He would hide until the evidence tests resulted in his favor. Watch law-enforcement attention turn to Edwin.

This *must* happen before her drawing was circulated.

Edwin's lawyer would argue viciously against the evidence. Claim it unreliable.

This could be overcome. Edwin wouldn't win.

He lifted his mouth in a slow smirk. Edwin on the defense instead of him. What a day that would be.

He must call Beth. Tell her he'd been detained at his cousin's funeral. She wouldn't ask details. She knew better.

Scott and Eddie. His heart twitched. He missed them. They were good boys. *His* boys. They would behave while he was gone. They would be safe.

His home must not be found.

He turned on the TV, searched for cable news. CNN: a political talk show. Fox News: Wall Street information. He clicked through every channel.

Nothing about him. No drawing.

He left the television on, volume low. Resumed pacing.

He glanced at his backpack. The gun lay inside. His last resort.

He would fight.

He would not be taken.

CHAPTER 37

When I woke, my digital clock read six-forty. I'd slept over five hours. For a few minutes I could do no more than gather my wits, blinking bleary eyes at the high wooden beams of my ceiling. Then I thought of all that could have happened while I slept — and pulled myself from bed. Five minutes later I stood in the kitchen. Jenna had made dinner. Stephen moved food around his plate, barely raising his eyes to mine. Kelly jumped up from her chair to hug me for all she was worth.

"Mom, you were on television! We all saw it."

My hand stilled against the back of her head. I threw an anxious look to Jenna. "Tell me it wasn't too bad."

"*National* news, Mom." Stephen sniffed. "They told about how you were doing a fugitive update of the guy, and how he kidnapped you, but that you were home now. They put up his picture, asking people to look for him. And they showed a picture of you."

I stared at my son. "Did the phone ring a lot this afternoon?"

"Yeah, like about a hundred times."

"It's okay, Annie." Jenna scowled at Stephen. "I've handled it. Some of the calls were people worried about you — like from Emily and Edwin Tarell. Edwin was really upset, blaming himself. He wants Bland caught now more than ever. And Vic phoned. The kids talked to him. Anyway, don't focus on that. Just think, they'll find Bland now for sure." She strode to the cabinet for another plate. "Now this television topic is officially closed. Sit down and eat something."

Like an obedient child, I did as I was told. For the next few minutes we ate in silence.

"Jenna, did you hear from Chetterling?" I tried to keep my voice light for the kids' sake. They had clearly been rattled enough by the evening newscapade.

"No. But he promised to call tonight, no matter what."

The four of us spoke little as we finished. Too much to say, I guess, and nowhere to start. Ravenous, I polished off one and a half pieces of chicken. Stephen managed to down half of his portion, then pushed back his plate. "I gotta go to my room and study."

Right. Well, the "studying" could wait. Despite everything, we needed to talk. Although where I would find the emotional energy, I didn't know. Determined, I led Stephen downstairs and told him to park it on the couch. As I lowered myself into a chair, a picture of Bland forcing me out the sliding door flashed through my head. Nerves prickling, I pushed it away.

"Stephen, we have to talk about what you've been doing. And where you're headed."

He slumped on his spine, legs spread, one rocking back and forth. No doubt only the previous night's events tamed the defiance on his face.

"You know you're going to have a court date. Detective Chetterling says you'll most likely be put on probation. Know what that means? The slightest little infraction, and things get a lot worse. They can place you on house arrest or give you work detail. They may even send you to juvenile hall for a few weekends." I pushed my heels into the carpet. *Juvenile hall.* Just speaking the name sent a flutter through my stomach.

"Yeah, I know."

"Is that all you have to say? 'Yeah, I

know?' How about 'Wow, Mom, I was really stupid, and I won't do it again'?"

He shrugged. "I won't."

"How do I know that?"

"Because I just told you."

"You've told me lots of things before, Stephen. You haven't stuck by any of them."

"This time it's different."

"Why?"

Silence.

Go ahead, Stephen, say you're sorry again. Admit your stupidity caused us all a lot of fear and pain.

He flexed his jaw and considered the coffee table. I watched him, my laced fingers tightening.

"Well, let me tell you this. I'm going to give you a little help. First, I'm taking away your computer —"

"No!"

"Oh, yes."

"But I have homework to do on it."

"Fine. When you have homework, you can sit at my computer in my office. And I'll be around to watch, making sure you're not chatting with your friends."

I couldn't help coating the last word with a derisive tone. Stephen clutched his elbows and glared at me.

"Second, I'm taking out the phone down

here. You want to make a call, you can come upstairs."

"Mom, you can't —"

"Yes, I *can*." I leaned forward. "I can do anything it takes to keep you from ruining your life, you understand? I can and I will. What I won't do is sit back and pretend not to look while you throw yourself down some drug drain with a bunch of no-good friends."

He scoffed at me. "You're not going to be here anyway, Mom. You're gonna get yourself killed. Then I'll be able to do whatever I please."

The words scorched like a firebrand. I pressed back against the chair, breathless, my mother's heart still sizzling. Stephen glowered out the sliding door, eyes narrowed.

He doesn't mean it. He's just scared.

"Is that really what you want, Stephen? To be rid of me?" I couldn't keep the tremble from my voice.

He flipped me a disgusted look.

And something within me snapped.

"Fine." I shoved from my chair, seething. "Guess what — it's not going to happen. You're stuck with me. Because I love you. But I don't like what you're doing to your-

self or this family. You were a total idiot going out last night, Stephen! When you *knew*
you'd be in danger simply walking the
streets. Didn't you even *care?*"

"I didn't think about it. And I said I was
sorry!"

"Then how about acting like it?"

His face contorted. "I care, I care, all
right? I'm *sorry* for what I did. I'm sorry for
sneaking out, and I'm sorry for being your
son, and I'm sorry I'm such a disappointment to everybody!"

He rocketed from the couch and stalked
toward his bedroom.

"Stephen, don't you walk away from —"

He whirled around. "There's nothing to
say! Take my computer, take the phone. I'll
be a good boy and not do anything ever
again, okay? Now leave me alone!"

Three strides and he crossed his threshold,
slamming the door. Within seconds rap
music throbbed through the walls.

I leaned against the armchair, tears
scratching my eyes. Stephen's guilt was
plain enough, but why did it have to wrap
itself in such nastiness? Why couldn't he
just hug me and say he was going to change,
and then *do* it?

God must be punishing me. After all, I'd

desperately promised last night to let Him lead my life if He would save me from Bland. And I hadn't kept that promise.

So what? Even if I made good on it, even if I became a card-carrying Christian, that was no guarantee things would improve. Would Bland be caught before he hurt somebody else? Would Stephen turn perfect? Would I never be in danger again, and would Sheryl magically poof away, leaving Vic free to come back and love me like he used to —

What was I thinking? I hated Vic.

I dropped my head in my hands. I couldn't handle this. I couldn't raise Stephen, couldn't find the day-to-day energy or wisdom to deal with him. What if he did end up in jail? What if I had to watch my son led away in handcuffs, visit him behind bars? The mere thought turned my muscles to water. I *couldn't* manage it.

What was I going to *do*?

When you look at your life, Annie — this life that you are running under your own steam — is it working?

Dave Willit's words to me . . . was it only yesterday? It seemed a lifetime ago.

"Oh, God," I whispered. "It's not. It's not working at all."

Hunching over the chair, I let the tears flow. I cried and cried, not even bothering to do it quietly. Stephen would never hear me over his music anyway. Some time passed before I was sobbed out. Tired, I headed for the bathroom to splash my face and blow my nose. Then I took a good, long look at myself in the mirror. Past the red eyes and splotchy cheeks. Into my own, sorry soul.

By the time I turned away, I'd made a decision.

First things first. With resolve, I unplugged the keyboard to Stephen's computer and unhooked the telephone. With these in hand, I slowly climbed the stairs.

CHAPTER 38

I informed Kelly and Jenna that I needed to go see Dave. Kelly wanted to come with me. I hesitated, contemplating the conversation I expected to have. Not exactly one I wanted to engage in with kids around. On the other hand, her presence would keep Erin busy.

"Okay, Kelly. Just stay in Erin's room with her and let us talk."

Then I had to deal with Jenna, who insisted that the two of us couldn't cross the street unescorted, even though we continued to have twenty-four-hour surveillance on our house. Most likely Bland had run far away from here by now. Still, Jenna hissed out of Kelly's earshot, the man was full of surprises. What if he killed the on-duty deputy, sped up the street, and forced us both into his car?

"Jenna —" I shook my head — "you've been watching too many crime shows."

"I don't *need* crime shows, Annie. I live

with *you*."

I raised defeated hands in the air and headed for the door. "Come on, Kelly."

Jenna trotted after us — with her purse. Which contained her gun. I forced my thoughts away from her deadly weapon by wondering what she'd think when I told her my real reason for seeing Dave. I'd never talked to Jenna about my search for God, although she knew we'd started attending church. Wasn't quite sure what she'd think of me. We'd simply never discussed religion of any sort, much less Christianity.

Not until we stood safely on the Willits' porch did Jenna turn around. "Tell Dave I expect him to walk you home."

I couldn't resist saluting her retreating back.

Erin and Dave knew we were coming. Erin wasted no time answering the doorbell and flinging herself into my arms. She erupted with crying, her shaky words muted against my chest. "I'm so glad you're okay."

I held her, smoothing her hair, muttering empty words of solace. Her tears soaked into my heart. When she pulled away, Dave hugged me too. His green eyes were misty as he stood back, hands on my shoulders. "You sure scared us."

My throat tightened. "I know. I'm so very sorry."

"Nothing to be sorry about, Annie. I just thank God you're safe."

The girls headed for Erin's bedroom. Dave offered me something to drink, which I declined, then invited me to sit down in his family room. We settled in the same chairs in which we'd sat yesterday. My thoughts flitted over all that had occurred since then — the terror and tears that had urged my return to this spot. But a small voice whispered that my presence wasn't due merely from the events of the past thirty hours. The seed had been planted ten months ago. I just hadn't tended it very well.

I leaned forward, focusing on my crossed ankles. Now that I was here, shyness settled over me. Where to begin?

Dave leaned back in his chair, waiting. I could feel his eyes upon me. And I sensed something more — that he seemed to know why I'd come. A moment passed. I hoped he would break the silence, make small talk. But he wouldn't rescue me.

"Well." I curled my fingers around each other. "I suppose you've heard all that happened."

"Yes. Jenna was good enough to call when you'd been found. Plus, of course, I got to see you on the news tonight."

Terrific. "I guess I really ruined your night's sleep, huh."

"You didn't ruin it. I chose to help search, and then after we knew you were with Bland, I stayed up to pray for your protection."

I glanced at him, surprised. "The rest of the night?"

He nodded. "Not only me. I called Pastor Storrel and Gerri Carson when I first heard you were missing. They prayed all night."

My mental projector spun out the scene of that eerily green-tinted road, the moonless sky, my stumbling, plodding feet. Had God been with me the whole time, watching over me because of those prayers?

"That's amazing, that they would do that for me."

"They love you, Annie. We all do."

How to respond to that? I watched my fingers lace and unlace.

"I'm glad you called Gerri. She knows how to pray. She was meeting with me, you know, after . . . last summer. Answering my questions about God. She's the reason I started going to church. After a while, though, I stopped meeting with her because I just wasn't ready to . . ."

I returned to the fascination of my hands.

"And now?" Dave's voice was gentle.

I sighed. "My life's a mess, Dave. Another crazy man's chasing me. My son's just been arrested for drug possession. He's a mean and hateful teenager, and I feel like I'm totally losing him. Plus I walk around with this stain of guilt all the time. Everything's my fault — my divorce, Stephen, the tragedy on this street, everything. Even though I know in my head that's not true, I can't seem to shake it. I'm just tired. I'm forty-one years old and don't seem to know what I'm doing or where I'm going."

I slumped back in my seat. There. I'd blurted out the whole wretched mess. Amazing that it could be encapsulated into one meager paragraph.

Dave grinned.

Grinned.

I stared at him.

"Annie Kingston, those are the wisest words I've ever heard you say."

I must have missed something.

His expression softened. He leaned toward me to place a hand on my knee. "Finally you're where God's wanted you to be for a long time. At the end of your rope. Realizing this world is too difficult to navigate alone. And you're right — it is. Because God didn't design us to sail it by ourselves.

He wants us to let *Him* guide us."

Dave was being so kind. He could have said so much more. He could have pounced on me for holding back from God all these months. I managed a rueful smile. "I'm kinda shipwrecked already."

"No, you're not. Let me put it to you this way: God's handled a lot worse."

I looked into his eyes. "If I ask Christ to become a part of my everyday life, my problems aren't going to just magically disappear, are they?"

One side of his mouth curved. "Afraid not. Look at me and my struggles. But that's not the question. The fact is, this world is full of evil. Until Christ comes to earth again and gets rid of it forever, we're stuck with the consequences of sin. In the meantime the question is: do you want to face the evils of this world alone or with Christ's help? When you think about it, the answer's obvious. It's like asking: would you rather stumble around in the dark or turn on a light?"

"But what if I don't always feel it?"

"Feel what?"

"God beside me. What happens when things still go wrong, and I feel lousy and alone?"

Dave took a deep breath, gazing out his

family room window. "Tell me, Annie. *Do* you believe that God is all-powerful? That He wants to forgive you of your sins and be a major part of your life?"

"Yes. I do."

"This is a solid truth to you?"

"Yes."

"Do you believe God's truth changes from one day to the next?"

I pondered that. "I guess not. I mean, if He changed His mind every day, where would we be?"

"Exactly. God's truth is final. Eternal. The facts written in the Bible are strong enough, sure enough, to carry us through this world and into eternity. They will *never* change, no matter what." He spread his hands. "Think about it. What if God's truth *did* rely on your emotions? Would you want to serve a God whose truth depended upon how you feel?"

What a horrid thought. "I see what you mean."

He smiled at me, and I smiled back.

"Will you let me pray with you now?"

"That's what I came for. Despite all my arguments."

Dave looked happier than I'd seen him

since before Lisa was killed. "Then let's do it."

He bowed his head, closing his eyes, and I did the same. "I'm going to pray some verses from Psalm 51, if that's all right with you — a psalm of repentance. You can just repeat them after me."

"Okay."

With Dave's leading, I spoke these words to God — words that a psalmist had written hundreds of years ago, but that applied to my life as if they'd been composed yesterday:

Have mercy on me, O God, according to your unfailing love. According to your great compassion blot out my transgressions. Wash away all my iniquity and cleanse me from my sin. Surely you desire truth in my inner parts. You teach me wisdom in the inmost place. Cleanse me with hyssop, and I will be clean; wash me, and I will be whiter than snow. Create in me a pure heart, O God, and renew a steadfast spirit within me. Restore me to the joy of your salvation and grant me a willing spirit to sustain me. O Lord, open my lips, and my mouth will declare your praise.

Surprisingly, I *did* feel something while repeating those words. A sense of peace in knowing that I was doing the right thing.

"Anything else you want to say to Christ right now, Annie?"

I hesitated. "Yes. Just that . . . Jesus, help me. You know I've got all sorts of problems, and I feel overwhelmed. But I'm going to give those problems to You, like I'm supposed to. And I'm going to trust You to show me what to do." I swallowed hard, then whispered, "That's all."

"Great. And I say a hearty amen!"

"Amen."

We raised our heads. I looked at Dave questioningly. He stood up, pulled me to my feet, and hugged me. "Welcome to God's family."

His smile was contagious.

"Thank you. For everything."

I could hardly believe what I'd done. On one hand the occasion seemed so momentous, which it was. I'd just changed my eternal destiny. On the other hand, it had been so simple that I wondered why on earth I'd waited forty-one years.

We talked awhile about Stephen. Dave promised to help me pray for my son. Finally, I rounded up Kelly to leave. He walked us out to the porch.

"Oh, Dave, I almost forgot. Jenna says you have to walk us home."

He shot me an amused look. "Bossy sister, huh?"

"You have *no* idea."

As we crossed the street, I draped my arm around Kelly's shoulder, a grateful chant running through my head. *Thank You, Jesus, thank You, Jesus, thank You, Jesus . . .*

Jenna met us at the door. She thanked Dave for bringing us back and playfully tugged at Kelly's hair. But I knew my sister too well. I could see the pinch around her mouth, the furtive eyes. Once Dave had gone I hovered in the great room, biting my tongue until Kelly drifted away to watch TV.

"What is it? Chetterling? Reporters?"

"Chetterling. He wants you to call him back." She headed into the kitchen. "I'm turning on the alarm. Everyone's in for the night."

I followed, a rock sinking in my stomach. Jenna wouldn't make eye contact with me. *Please, God, not so quickly. Let me hold on to that feeling of peace a little longer.*

"Bad news?"

Jenna punched in the code before she answered. "Go call. I'll let him explain."

I stared at her for a moment. Then turned

to head for my office with heavy, dreading steps.

CHAPTER 39

Office door closed, I lowered myself into my desk chair. I reached for the phone, then stopped. Was this one of those times when I should pray first? I stumbled over a quick plea to God for help, then picked up the receiver.

My fingers trembled as I dialed Chetterling's direct number.

"Okay, Ralph." I didn't even say hello. "Lay it on me."

His reticence wafted over the phone line. "Did you get some sleep?"

"Yes, I'm fine. Now tell me." I was beginning to sound as snippy as my sister.

He inhaled deeply. "All right. Good news first. After the news shows, calls poured in about Bland's photo. And his license plate was traced. We now know the name he's using. Tom Smith. And we know his address — in a small, rural town in Kansas. Deputies have been out there, talking to his wife, who knows nothing about his past. Bland wasn't there. His wife said he'd taken off on a trip to a cousin's funeral and hadn't returned. The media has gotten hold of this information. Local cameras followed officers to Bland's home, then quickly disseminated the film. I just got a call from CNN. But that doesn't matter, Annie. What matters is, Bland will now have nowhere to hide. With his current identity and his picture posted everywhere, it's only a matter of time."

Finally. After twenty years. Emily and Edwin's faces shimmered in my mind. How achingly gratified they would be to see Bill Bland in handcuffs.

"So what's the matter, Ralph?"

"It has to do with the shirt and gun."

I stared at my drawing board across the room. Twenty-four hours ago I'd toiled there, drawing Bland's face. Now something in Chetterling's tone made me sense my work was all for nothing. "You're done testing them?"

"Those tests don't take long, and the lab gave them priority. Now I really expected this to amount to nothing. But it hasn't turned out that way. The shirt checks out as Bland claimed. Discharge residue from a gun was found in the right sleeve. The blood on the sleeves is consistent with Don Tarell's blood type. Fortunately Delft saved a blanket that Emily Tarell put over her husband's body. Some of his blood seeped onto that. With a couple weeks to do a DNA analysis, we'll be able to definitely say whether the blood on the sleeves matches the blood on the blanket, but at this point it seems fairly certain that answer's going to be yes. The owner of the dry cleaning shop identified his writing on the inside tag of the shirt. Plus we've got Bland's story of how he got the shirt fitting together with Edwin Tarell's story about throwing it away. So I don't doubt this is *the* shirt."

I closed my eyes. "But it doesn't prove anything, right? Even if it's the real shirt, Bland could have put it on later and fired some other gun."

"True. Although we can match a bullet to a gun — and I'll get to that in a minute — there's no way to match discharge to a particular weapon. So this shirt in itself is not compelling evidence."

"But the gun?"

"That's the most surprising part. I'd have bet the shirt off my own back that we wouldn't lift a latent off that thing after so many years. But we did. Bland preserved it well. The print is Edwin's. He had prints taken at the time of the murders so the techs could distinguish what print was whose at the scene, and two experts agree that this latent matches his. *And,* here's the real problem, the latent looks like it was left by someone holding the gun to shoot it — fingers wrapped around the grip."

The mental picture flashed before me. "Edwin *held* the gun?"

"That's what the print tells us."

"But . . . that doesn't match his story. He said he tackled Bland and the gun was knocked away. He never mentioned picking it up. In fact, Bland picked it up by the barrel and hit him with it."

"I know." Chetterling scraped out the words.

This couldn't be. Something had to be wrong here. "Are you saying you think Bland was telling the *truth?*"

"No. But I am telling you we've got evidence we can't explain."

"So? Let them fight it out in court."

"That's just it, Annie, it may be too much to allow us to get to court. Delft and I met with the D.A. late this afternoon, told him everything we had. He's not even sure that he can charge the guy with the homicides."

"What?" I shot forward in my chair. "Look

at all you've got! Bland *disappeared* for twenty years, for heaven's sake. After stealing from Tarell's company."

"I know, I know. It's heavy circumstantial evidence. But that's all it is — circumstantial. On the other side is this hard evidence. The gun used in the crime. No doubt about that because we matched its bullets. And the shirt worn when the gun was fired."

"You said the shirt meant nothing."

"By itself it means nothing. But you add it to the print taken from the gun, and how's a prosecutor going to explain that in court? Bland's attorney would have a heyday with it, even with the obvious chain of evidence problems. Especially since the star witness against Bland is the man whom the evidence implicates."

"Chetterling —" I pushed to my feet — "you're not telling me Bland's going to get away with this! *Please*."

"Annie, we'll get him. We've just got to find a way to explain all this."

"But he *threatened* me! He did everything he could to keep me from drawing that update; isn't that evidence enough?"

"It'll help a lot. But we've got to be able to 100 percent pin those threats on him. Right now we've got no witnesses as to who left that money at the florist shop, or who called you. We can't prove he did it. Yet."

"Oh, no. No, no, no." I paced over to my drawing table, smacking my hip with the heel of my hand. My throat threatened to close like some steel door. "I won't accept this. Not now, not after everything that's happened. What about Bland kidnapping me, doesn't that count for anything?"

"Of course it does." Chetterling's voice ran steady, and I could have punched him for it. I didn't want steady and soothing right now; I wanted fighting mad. "We've got him on kidnapping charges and other counts, no doubt about that. Even in the worst-case scenario, he'll still do jail time."

Tears pricked my eyes. "There will *be* no worst-case scenario, because he is going down for these murders if I have to drag him off to prison myself!"

"Believe me, Annie, I feel the same way. And I promise you we'll get him. But I just wanted to warn you that things may not go easy, even once he's in custody."

"What about the embezzlement charges?"

A sigh seeped over the phone. "That's another problem. We've known about it, but it didn't matter much until now. Charges for the embezzlement should have been filed twenty years ago. But in the aftermath of the murders, it simply was overlooked. Now it's long past the statute of limitations to file."

I worked my jaw, letting this new ridiculous piece of information seep into me. "They were never filed."

"No."

"And just whose fault was *that?*" Probably Delft's. He'd handled this whole case from the beginning. Or maybe the district attorney. But Chetterling wouldn't name names.

"Annie. It's done. There's nothing we can do about that now. It doesn't matter anyway. We're *going* to convict him on the murder charges and the kidnapping and everything else."

I barely heard the words. "I just can't believe this. Twenty years Bland has to plan his story, to doctor this evidence. And now he's actually going to get *away* with it? Arrogant, guilty-as-sin Bland is going to slip away after killing two people?"

"Listen to me. We'll find a way to make our case. We're still working with the D.A. When we bring Bland in, we'll do our best to get him to confess."

"He'll *never* confess; you should know

him better than that! He'll go to his grave saying he didn't kill those two men."

"Well, then, his grave is just where he'll go, because this is a death penalty case."

"Don't placate me, Ralph!" My voice cracked. I tilted my head back to view a blurry ceiling. "I know a few things about the court system, remember? If you've got a shaky case, there's a good chance the D.A. won't go for the death penalty, and you know it."

No response. I'd finally succeeded in beating Chetterling down. "Okay." His voice ached with weariness. "I think you need to go to bed, get some more sleep."

"How do you expect me to sleep now?"

"We'll keep pursuing Bland. I can assure you of that."

I lowered my chin, rubbed the back of my neck. Chetterling sounded so dogged with determination, despite his tiredness. He probably still hadn't slept — and now may not see his bed tonight, either. He must be beyond exhausted. And there I was, attacking him, as if he hadn't done everything he could to help me. I pressed a thumb and fingers against my temples.

"Ralph, I'm sorry. I don't mean to be so . . . It's just that every time I turn around, I get hit with something else. I'm beginning to think this is never going to end."

"I know. And I'm sorry. You've been through a lot. You know we're doing all we can here."

"Yeah. I know that." I drifted over to sit on the edge of my desk. "You going to talk to Edwin Tarell tomorrow? See if he can explain that print?"

"This can't wait. We're pulling him in right now."

"Now, *tonight?*"

"Yes. He insists on it. He's mad as a hornet at Bland and wanting to set things straight."

I focused on the wall, thinking of my family's needs, of Stephen. I really should stay home. But an inner voice nagged. "Let me come in and watch his interview."

Chetterling hesitated. "Why?"

"I don't know. Because I have to. Because I'm the one who heard Bland's claims and may think of some important point. After all, this interview's got to work so we can charge Bland, right? Because I'm going to go crazy pacing this house not knowing what's going on."

"Annie, you need to stay home and safe right now."

"Oh, right, my home is really safe! Isn't

this where Bland showed up, when I was supposedly being guarded?"

Silence.

Oh, Annie. I winced at my cruelty. I'd hit him below the belt. "Ralph. I'm so sorry. You didn't deserve that; I know you were off chasing my son —"

"Don't worry about it." His tone had flattened. "We're all under pressure."

"Really, please. Forgive me." Good grief, and I'd just become a Christian. Is *this* how I was supposed to act? Someday I would make it up to this man.

"Forget it, Annie."

Miserably, I gazed at my drawing table. If Bland's fugitive update were still sitting there, I'd be tempted to rip the thing up. I couldn't stand even the memory of his face.

"So. Are you going to let me come?"

Another long sigh. "I can't seem to tell you no, even when you beat me up."

Dear Chetterling. I managed the barest of smiles.

"But I don't want you driving in by yourself, and Jenna can't bring you because someone's got to stay with your kids."

"I'll . . . work that out. I'll send the kids over to Dave's."

"All right." He sounded defeated. "You'd

better hurry; we're not waiting for you."

"I'm on my way."

389

Chapter 40

He sat frozen on the motel room bed, staring at the TV. Every muscle clenched, but his insides puddled like melted wax.

His driver's license picture on CNN's "Breaking News." Tom Smith. They knew his name.

His wife's terrified face filled the screen. Bland groaned.

More scenes of chaos. Sheriff's Department cars, lights spinning, surrounding his house. Beth hugging Scott and Eddie, the boys' faces blocked out. Beth shaking her head in frantic denial, cheeks tracked with tears. Sheriff's deputies entering his home.

His home.

Cut to old film of Emily Tarell shortly after the murders, grief-stricken. Photos of Don Tarell and Peter Dessinger. Of Edwin, talking to deputies.

Edwin. He should have blown the man's brains out when he had the chance.

No word about the shirt and gun.

Not one word.

They were paying no heed to his evidence. Get that?

None.

Ice clogged his veins. Long after the story was finished, he stared sightlessly at the screen. Stark memories filled his head. Memories of stealing from Tarell Plastics. His last look at baby Nick. Running away from the murders. Researching fake IDs. Meeting Beth, the births of Eddie and Scott.

A life built. A life taken away. Everything now gone.

Everything.

Anger rose, burst like fireworks, and died. Fear flamed, sputtered, then was gone. Then sadness. Aching and deep. He sat and stared at the TV until that, too, trickled away.

With focus, human needs are overcome. Jack Hurst, *Cry of the Slain.*

With focus . . .

But he was not Jack Hurst now. He was Rolf Weitz in *Cradle.* Trapped. No way out. Forced into final, desperate action.

He would not be taken.

He forced himself to calmly review his final plan.

He must get to them before his Taurus was spotted.

The TV was nothing but noise. He turned if

off. Crossed to his backpack. Opened it and pulled out the gun. Grasped it. Reveled in its hard, brutal comfort.

Outside, he unscrewed the license plate from his car and traded it for his backup.

Darkness descended as he drove out of the parking lot and headed north.

CHAPTER 41

Dave agreed to stay at our house, bringing Erin with him. No doubt my request was an upset to their school-night routine, but he hadn't hesitated.

I would have bet a night's sleep that Jenna would argue about going, concerned as she was for my safety. But she also wanted Bland charged for his crimes and was as rattled as I about Chetterling's news.

Within ten minutes of my call to the detective, we were on the road.

By the time we hustled into the Sheriff's Department building, Edwin Tarell was just sitting down with Sergeant Delft in the small, sterile room where Sam Borisun had been questioned. Edwin sat tall, shoulders back, righteous indignation setting his jaw.

"You two can stand here. Watch and hear, like you did before." Chetterling indicated the one-way window. "If you think of something, write me a note and have a deputy knock on the door. When we're wrapping up, please go around the corner until Tarell leaves. He's mad enough as it is, and I can hardly blame him. Probably best if he doesn't know you watched the interview."

"Okay." I glanced at Delft through the glass. "How's the sergeant?"

"Frustrated out of his mind, but determined to get to the bottom of this."

Jenna raised her eyebrows at me as Chetterling entered the little room. Her lips were firmly set, one hand pushing back her hair. My sister's nervousness matched my own. Something had to give here.

Chetterling introduced himself to Edwin. They shook hands. Chetterling lowered his giant frame into a seat at one end of the battered table opposite Delft, Edwin between them. The detective leaned back in his chair, legs apart and arms crossed.

"I apologize right up front if I sound impatient." Edwin's voice was tight. "I'm so angry I could *spit.* The mere thought of Bland having even the remotest chance of getting away with killing my father! At this point, I'm telling you, I'd love to shoot him myself."

"We understand." Delft's words were clipped as he plunked his forearms on the table. "And we apologize, too, for having to put you through this. No doubt we'll clear things up. We want to be in the best position possible with the D.A. when Bland is picked up. So we're grateful you were willing to come down so quickly."

"Absolutely."

"All right. Just to cover all legal bases, we have to inform you that you have the right to remain silent. Anything you say can and will be used against you in a court —"

"*What?* Wait a minute! What are you reading me my rights for?"

"Really, sir, it's merely for legal purposes."

"That's ridiculous; you don't read rights to a witness!"

"Mr. Tarell. You *are* a witness to your father's and Peter Dessinger's murders. But at this moment, whether any of us like it or not, there's evidence that implicates you as well. We have to discuss that evidence. And I want to do everything by the book. So I must read you your rights."

Edwin cut his stare from Delft to Chetterling. The detective spread his hands, as if to say *Don't blame us.*

"Fine." Edwin chewed the word. "Go ahead. But if things get out of hand, I'm calling a lawyer."

Delft gave him a penetrating look. "You telling me you need a lawyer?"

"I . . . no. Of course not."

Jenna and I exchanged a glance. This interview was getting off on the wrong foot. *Please, God, help these men work together.*

Miranda rights completed, Delft forged ahead. "As we told you, early this morning we obtained two items from Bland that he claims are evidence from the murders. Now we'll give you the details. One is the shirt he said you wore that night. The other is the gun that was used."

Edwin blinked. "I told you he took the gun. But the shirt?"

"You threw it in the garbage can that night, remember?"

"Of course."

"Bland claims he was there. He saw you — and pulled it out of the trash."

Edwin sat very still. "He says he pulled it out of my garbage can?"

Delft nodded.

"He was there? Right *there?*"

"Apparently so."

"Wait a minute, I'm not buying this. How do you know it's my shirt?"

"We have numerous pieces of evidence to identify it. Blood DNA tests will tell us for certain in a few weeks, but we expect that blood is going to match your father's. Besides, you tell me. If Bland *wasn't* at your house that night and *didn't* pull your shirt out of the garbage can, how did he know you threw it away?"

Edwin brought a hand to his forehead. "Whoa. This is . . . I can't believe this. I'm lucky I didn't get shot. He could have killed me too." He rubbed his head, then looked to Delft. "So what's the rest of his story?"

"He says he wanted evidence that would prove *you* killed the two men. Bland says he called that night to tell you about discharge from the gun that would be on the sleeve. And you fell right into his trap, throwing away the shirt. He was waiting to pick it up."

Edwin hit both palms against the table. "That's insane! I threw away that shirt because I couldn't stand to look at it. Like you said, it had my father's *blood* on it."

Delft nodded. "I know."

"These are just Bland's claims," Chetterling soothed. "Doesn't mean we believe them."

"I should hope not." Edwin's cheeks flushed.

Delft arched his back. "We ran the shirt through some lab tests. We did find gun discharge on the right sleeve."

Edwin's head tilted. He stared at Delft through the corner of his eye. "You've got to be joking."

Delft didn't respond.

"The sergeant's not acting very friendly," Jenna whispered.

I glanced at the camera mounted in a top corner of the room. "They're probably thinking ahead to Bland's trial. They'll want to show the jury how well Edwin held up when confronted with these claims."

Edwin eased back in his chair. "Okay. All right. Why are you two so upset about this? It's obvious Bland staged it. At some point he put the shirt on and fired the gun. He has had *twenty years*."

"Yes, that's what we expect." Delft hit his clasped hands against the table. "So frankly, I'm not too worried about that. What does worry me is the gun. The lab lifted a print from someone who was clearly holding the weapon to fire it." The sergeant paused. "The print is yours."

Edwin stared.

"Problem is, this doesn't support your statement. You told us you knocked the gun from Bland's hand. You never mentioned picking —"

"You trying to tell me you found *my* fingerprint on that gun, after all this time? I don't believe that!"

"It surprised us too. But Bland preserved the gun well."

"After twenty — No. No way." Edwin pointed a finger at Chetterling. "What is this? Why is he doing this to me?"

"Look." The detective leaned forward. "We're on your side. We want Bland behind bars as much as you do. As you know, Sergeant Delft has spent two decades looking for the man. Now he's practically in our hands, and we get these surprises. I don't want the D.A. telling me he can't press charges because of some clever mock-up of Bland's. But we can't explain this fingerprint. You told Delft you never held that gun. Now we're giving you a chance — before Bland is caught — to tell us how it got there."

A picture of Emily Tarell filled my head. *"For twenty years, Annie, I've prayed for justice . . ."*

Come on, Edwin, give us something.

Edwin held Chetterling's gaze for an extended moment. I could see the rise and fall of his breathing. Could sense the drawn-out, agonizing breakdown of some protective wall. Then, slowly, he folded his arms.

His eyes dropped to the table.

I gripped Jenna's arm, fingers sinking through her sleeve. What was this?

Edwin raised his chin. Gave a little shrug. "All right. This was always a minor point, but now that it's become so important to you."

His tone mixed impatience and defensiveness, as if the situation were entirely the fault of these two men.

"Twenty years ago, I changed one little part of the events." Edwin looked Delft squarely in the eye, as if to prove this admission wouldn't lessen his dignity. "I was young, scared, and riddled with guilt. Everything happened so fast. I couldn't have stopped Bland. All the same, I felt, as I still do today, that I should have. Should have pulled off some supernatural stunt and saved at least my father. I told you when Bland took aim at my father, I jumped at him, but he got off the shot before I hit him. Actually, I didn't jump Bland. I had no time. It was the other way around. A split second after he shot my father, he swiped the edge of his jacket over the pistol grip, rubbing off his own prints, and launched himself at me. He so took me by surprise that he was able to yank me back across the room to where he had stood and knock me down. Then he grabbed my hand and forced my fingers around the gun. He pointed the gun toward the wall and pushed my finger against the trigger, trying to get me to fire it. I fought for my life. I didn't realize what he was trying to do at that moment. Later I did — he was trying to stage evidence. But then I only knew I had to save myself. When I fought back so hard, he grabbed the gun by the barrel and pulled it away from me. I managed to push him off, and ended up on top of him. I was trying to get the gun back; believe me, I'd have shot him. But I ended up knocking it out of his hand. About that time my mother came through the door."

Delft's eyes hadn't left Edwin's face during the entire story. Now he exchanged a long look with Chetterling, then rubbed his jaw. "So let me get this straight. Bland kills Dessinger. Then shoots your father. Then wipes off the gun, attacks you, and presses one of your fingers against the grip."

"Yes."

The sergeant spread his hands. "Why? Why didn't he just kill you?"

Edwin leaned forward. "No, no, don't you see? That never would have worked! This was all part of Bland's wild scheme. If he killed *me,* he'd be the only suspect. He'd never get away with it. But if he made it look like *I* did it, then his problems would disappear. Amid all the chaos of my killing my own father and Peter, who'd think to file charges for his embezzlement?"

Delft absorbed the answer. Chetterling flexed his jaw, both hands spread flat against the table. I knew Chetterling well enough to practically read his flip-flopping thoughts. He wasn't buying the story, but neither did he believe Edwin shot those two men. Still, one point had come to pass. In the chaos, embezzlement charges *hadn't* been filed. Had Bland really been cunning enough to foresee this?

"What about the residue on Bland's own sleeve?" Delft asked. "He had to know we'd test both of your shirts. Residue would be on his hand too."

Edwin shook his head. "All I can think is that he had a matching shirt in his car. Somehow, before the police arrived, he planned on changing into it. He knew Mom and I would be busy trying to revive the men. And washing his hands would have been easy."

Delft sniffed. "Mr. Tarell, I have to tell you the truth. This story sounds a little far-fetched."

"And Bland's story doesn't?" Edwin

expelled a puff of air. "Look at what he claims! He hangs around my town house when he knows everyone's looking for him and waits for me to throw away my telltale shirt? After he's called me and tricked me into doing just that? Come on!" Edwin swiveled his head from one man to the other. "By the way, have you forgotten he's been on the run for twenty years? While I've been right here in town, being a good citizen? And if that doesn't do it, how about his threats toward Annie Kingston? How about the fact that he kidnapped her at gunpoint?" Edwin pushed to his feet. "I can't *believe* this! I can't believe you two even brought me down here. This is outrageous!" He paced to the wall, then swung back. "Why don't you just stop wasting time and go find Bland?"

Oh, boy. This was not going as I'd hoped.

My tired brain worked to sort through everything. I had to agree with Delft — Edwin's story was hard to believe. But Bland *couldn't* be telling the truth. Particularly after all he'd done to me. And seeing Edwin now — the anger and frustration that tightened his arms, creased his face — I had to believe his version over Bland's.

Delft and Chetterling watched Edwin,

poker expressions in place. "Mr. Tarell." Chetterling indicated the table. "Please sit back down. Let's work through this."

Edwin glowered at both men in turn, then slowly took his seat.

"All right." Delft shifted in his chair. "Why did you lie about this?"

"Because —" Edwin closed his eyes, as if amazed they couldn't understand. "Because my father was *dead*. Because I was in the room when it happened. And I didn't move fast enough to stop it. And there was my mother. How was I going to explain to her that I'd done nothing? That I'd stood there, frozen, while Bland jumped me. When she ran into the room, I was on top of Bland. She automatically assumed I'd attacked him in self-defense. I just . . . let her think that. And then when I had to make my formal statement to you, I didn't want to change my story."

Delft drummed his fingers. "A man like you ought to know that lying to law enforcement about events of a crime is serious business."

"I do know that."

"Yet you've let this story remain for all these years."

Vaguely, my mind registered a car honk-

404

ing out front. Hadn't it been going on for a while?

"I — Okay." Edwin held up both hands. "Yes. I lied to you. Do you want to hear me say that word? I lied, and I let the lie stand all these years. But so what? It's a minor point! It doesn't change the fact that Bland is guilty. All he's done since then should convince you of that. The man deserves to rot in hell!"

"Well, he just might deserve that," Delft retorted, "but now we've got a fine mess on our hands. What if your lie — the lie you told to save your own face — ends up allowing Bland to go free?"

Edwin tilted his head. "Oh, come *on.* That's not going to happen. This little detail against everything Bland's done?"

"You're our star witness, Mr. Tarell." Delft's voice sharpened. "Imagine Bland's defense attorney questioning you about your *little* lie on the stand. He'll tear you apart. He'll tell the jury, 'Hey, the guy lied about this, what makes you think he's not lying about everything else? And by the way, the hard evidence of the shirt and gun backs up my client's claims!' This is assuming, of course, that we can charge Bland in the first place."

The honking continued. Who *was* that?

Edwin's indignant expression remained, but his cheeks paled. "This can't be that serious."

"I'm afraid it is." Delft pierced him with a long stare. "And we don't like surprises in court. So in case you do get to testify against Bland, you'd better come clean right now. Any *other* lies you've told us?"

Edwin's face darkened. He smacked his palms against the table. "That's it! This conversation is over."

Once more, he was on his feet.

"Oh, Jenna —" I pushed her — "we'd better go. He's coming —"

A deputy trotted around the corner, aiming for the interrogation room, an instinctive hand hovering over his weapon. With hardly a glance at us, he skidded to a stop and threw the door open. Chetterling's head whipped around. Edwin drew to a halt.

Noises from the building's entrance escalated. More honking. Voices, shouts, someone else running.

I froze, watching the detective and deputy exchange a few words. Chetterling's face slacked. He motioned to Delft.

"What's going on?" Jenna leaned toward the glass.

"I don't know." Whatever it was, it

couldn't be good. And I didn't want to face one more thing on this never-ending day. "But we have to get down the hall before Edwin comes out of there. I don't want him to see us."

With nervous glances over our shoulders, we slipped around the far corner, toward Delft's office. Behind us, multiple pairs of feet hustled from the interrogation room.

"What's happening?" Edwin's demand filtered to my ears.

"Bland's here!" I heard Chetterling answer, his voice fading as he headed toward the entrance. "He's barricaded in his car with a gun. Says we'd better listen, or he's going to kill somebody."

CHAPTER 42

Confusion twisted through the air, disconnected sights and sounds bombarding Jenna and me as we huddled in our corridor. Sharp voices and commands tumbled from the entrance. The few personnel in the building hurried down the hallways. Distantly, I heard Bland yelling. What was he saying?

I couldn't believe he was here. *Here.* All they had to do now was capture him.

"Last time he was willing to take down four people." Sergeant Delft's words ran through my head. *"Just how many do you think he'd be willing to take down now?"*

Dull dread filled me as a premonition sank talons into my head — a knowledge surely as strong as Emily Tarell had felt twenty years ago. Someone was going to die tonight.

Oh, God, please don't let any of these men

die. Please don't take Chetterling!

Bland's voice raged on. Noises in the building fell to muted footfalls, lowered voices.

My purse dragged at my shoulder. I set it on the floor. Jenna set hers down too. We looked at each other, shell-shocked. "What do we do now?" I hugged my arms across my chest.

"I don't know. But I have to see what's going on."

"We're safer here."

"Yeah, but . . . can you stand just waiting here, not knowing?"

I envisioned gunshots, yells, the desperation of not knowing who had fallen.

"No."

"Let's just ease our way a little closer."

Jenna slipped back down the hall, pulling me behind her. We rounded the corner — and ran into Edwin. He jumped, then regarded us with delayed reaction, emotions from the last hour still playing across his face.

"Annie! What . . . what are you doing here?"

"We just came to talk to Sergeant Delft. But he was in a meeting."

"Oh. Well. I came to see him too."

We stared at each other.

409

Bland was still yelling. What was happening out there? "Uh, Edwin, this is my sister, Jenna."

"Hi. Glad to meet you." Edwin's distracted gaze roamed toward the front of the building.

More distant shouts. My breathing hitched. Bland this close to me — again. Even without seeing him, I could feel the malevolence of his presence. "This is . . . What do we do now?"

Edwin saw my pinched face, and his expression softened. He touched my hand. "Annie, forgive me. With all this going on . . . It's so good to see you here, and safe. I'm so sorry for what happened to you. It's just what I was afraid of — Bland getting to you."

"It's okay. Thank you."

He nodded, then swallowed, a hardness creeping over his features. "I'm going down there until I can see outside. It's been twenty years since I've laid eyes on that face. And you want the truth? I hope Bland gets himself killed."

"I can understand that." Jenna sounded matter-of-fact, no doubt remembering her own vengeful thoughts. "Let's just hope he doesn't kill somebody else first." She turned toward the building's entrance. "Let's go too, Annie."

"But it could be dangerous."

"We'll stay out of the way." She gave me a nudge, and we eased down the hall, Bland's voice getting louder as we approached.

In the lobby, Chetterling, Delft, and three deputies pressed behind walls, away from the vulnerability of the glass doors. "Stay back and out of the way." The sergeant pushed his palm toward us. "Bland's car window is partly open, and he's got a gun."

We ducked behind the wooden partition of the receptionist's area. I crouched down until my ankles started to shake, then lowered myself to the floor. Prayers chain-linked through my head. *Please, God, let them catch him; please, God, keep everyone safe.*

"I want to talk to Chetterling!" Bland's muffled yell was raucous. "I demand to know what happened to my evidence!"

Peeking around the partition, I had a straight line of view through the front doors. Streetlights dimly illuminated the parking lot. Bland's car sat in the center, its flashers pulsing into the night. His window faced the building. Sheriff's Department cars were gathering near the street entrance, their red and blue lights washing the semidarkness. No doubt the deputies had slipped from

411

their driver's seats to hide behind their vehicles, weapons drawn and pointed at Bland's car.

What did Bland think he was *doing?* I didn't care a whit for the man, but he had a wife and kids. Who apparently had no knowledge of who he was or what he'd done. I thought of my Kelly, Stephen, their stunned faces at the betrayal of their father three years ago. How much deeper the devastation of Bland's family to learn he was a wanted killer.

"Annie, get back here." Jenna yanked at my shirt, pulling me fully behind the partition.

"They've all got guns." Edwin leaned against a back wall, facing me and Jenna, his jaw set. His breathing came quick and hard. His eyes closed briefly, as if he fought to convince himself this was really happening. "I say go for it. Shoot him and be done."

I watched him as an almost palpable anticipation began to seep from his pores. After what he'd been through, I couldn't blame him. I envisioned a scene a few hours from now: Bland in handcuffs; Edwin calling his mother with the news, tears of weary relief and vengeance in his eyes.

I leaned my head back against the partition. "But they can't just rush out there; they might get themselves shot."

"Cut the lights." Delft's voice.

Seconds later the building fell into darkness. An automatic, deep shudder overtook me. For a moment I was back in the forest, huddled and waiting, all alone.

I forced the thoughts away, concentrated on my vision as it strained to adjust.

Jenna pushed into a crouch, then slowly stood to her full height. I tried to pull her back down. She waved me away. "He can't see us now." Edwin rose up beside her. He offered me a hand. I hesitated, then let him help pull me to my feet. We stood side by side, his fingers lacing protectively through mine.

"It'll be okay, Annie." He squeezed gently.

Dim illumination spilled in from the doors and windows. The various car lights outside flashed white and blue and red against the walls. Chetterling was putting on a bulletproof vest, his movements disjointed and jerky under the surreal strobe effect. A bullhorn flashed visible, then not, visible, then not, on the floor beside him.

I frowned through the pulsing lights. Delft hunched near a window. He checked outside and emitted a soft curse. "The media's here."

The detective shrugged his shirt back on. "What do you see?"

"White news van on the other side of our cars."

"How'd they get here so fast?" Jenna whispered.

"They listened to the radio chatter." I couldn't take my eyes off Chetterling. He was going out there. Out to try to save Bland's life, after all the man had done.

Please, God, protect him.

Chetterling spoke into a radio, coordinating his movements with men in the parking lot. His intended shield: a sheriff's car close to the entrance. Two deputies inside moved into position by the door, ready to cover him. I knew the deputies outside would cover him as well.

"I demand to see Chetterling!" Bland yelled again. "I have to talk to him!"

Bullhorn in hand, Chetterling hunkered down. Someone pulled back the door, and he slipped outside.

A deputy quickly secured the door open, in case Chetterling had to return in a hurry.

Delft checked through the window. "He's in place."

I rose to my tiptoes, staring at Bland's car, trying to make out his form. Only the top of his head was visible as he hunched down in the front seat.

"Somebody talk to me *now!*" Bland's voice rose. "I know reporters are here. I want them to tell the world how you ignored my evidence. I want my family to know!"

I caught a glimpse of his head as he leaned toward the passenger window.

"Do you hear, newspeople? Do you know I brought the Sheriff's Department evidence that proves I didn't do those two murders? I brought them the shirt that Edwin Tarell wore and the gun with his fingerprints on it. And what have they done with them? Nothing!"

"Mr. Bland!" Chetterling's deep voice boomed through the bullhorn, echoing off the cars and nearby buildings. "This is Detective Ralph Chetterling. I'm here to talk to you."

More patrol cars were pulling into position on the street, both from the Police and Sheriff's Departments. Bland disappeared beneath his window.

"Chetterling! What have you done with my evidence? You promised me you'd test it."

"We did test it, today. It all checked out, Mr. Bland, just like you said it would."

"Then why wasn't *that* on the news? Why's

everybody chasing me?"

"You've got to come in. Then we can talk. You're not doing yourself any favors, sitting out there with a gun."

"How do I know you're telling me the truth?"

"You can trust me." Chetterling's words bounced across the lot. "You trusted me with your evidence, didn't you? And I took care of it, like I said I would."

Silence. I could hear Edwin breathing. He still held my hand. The pulsating colors were lasering right through my head, to the back of my brain. I closed my eyes.

"Then why haven't you arrested Edwin Tarell?"

"We *did* arrest him. The news you saw went out too soon. We just got through questioning him."

"*What?* How dare he say I'm in custody!" Edwin's whisper was hoarse, his fingers tightening in mine. "It'll be all over the media."

Edwin was right. He didn't deserve this. "I know, but they'll clear that up later. Chetterling's just trying to get him to surrender."

"Who needs him to surrender? Why don't they just *shoot* him?"

He turned to me, and I saw hatred glitter

in his eyes. The intensity chilled me. It occurred to me then — Edwin's fear of what
he would face if Bland went to trial. Sneer-
ing questions from the defense attorney,
publicly having to admit his own lie. The
anxious hours spent waiting for a verdict.

"If you arrested him," Bland cried, "why
didn't I see *his* face on the news?"

Movement at the far end of the parking
lot caught my eye. Two officers, ducking
behind cars, sneaking in closer. A second
later, voices filtered from the blackened
hallways behind us. Three men, with the
vests and rifles of a SWAT team, filtered
around the corner.

"Delft," one said softly, "we're here."

Time ticked by, surreal and swollen. Voices
collided in my head — Chetterling and
Bland outside, Delft consulting with his
men, Edwin's whispers of vengeance. The
SWAT team faded away into shadows, seeking positions. Then Delft was barking commands into a phone. He hung up, hovering
over the receiver. Outside, the lights pulsed,
figures skulked, and my skin pebbled. Again
I felt the sickening knowledge that this
scene could only end badly. Holding tightly
to Edwin's hand, I tried to pray.

"Bland!" Chetterling again. "Come on
out. We'll talk face to face, no guns, no

distance between us."

"I want to see the test results first! And I want to see Edwin behind bars."

"How do you expect me to show you these things when you're barricaded in a car? Come out. Then we can show you everything."

A phone rang. Delft snatched it up, his words an undertow to the current of the standoff outside. Carrying the receiver, he edged toward the door, softly calling Chetterling's name. "We got his wife on the line." He held up the phone. Chetterling scurried to get it, shoulders hunched, head down, then returned to the shelter of the sheriff's car.

"Bland, your wife is on the phone. She wants to talk to you. Listen, and you can hear her." Chetterling held the receiver to the bullhorn. A woman's voice, tinny but distinct, wafted over the parking lot, pleading with her husband to give himself up, to keep himself safe for the sake of their sons.

"I didn't do it, Beth!" A sob shook Bland's voice. "I didn't kill those men. You have to believe that."

"I do believe you, I *do.*" His wife's words cracked. "Just get out of that car so they can talk to you. Everything will be all right."

I brought a hand to my mouth. This was

terrible. I could feel the woman's pain.

Edwin scoffed. "Don't feel sorry for him, Annie. So he has a family. So did my father."

"I feel sorry for his family, not h—"

"And look what he did to *you.*" His grip tightened around my fingers. "Kidnapped you. Threatened you and your kids. 'Stay well, Annie. And alive.' "

I felt too sick to respond. My focus remained on the window, the woman's pleas tumbling over the cars and flashing lights. Bland's answers began to waver, his voice catching. My lungs felt heavy, congealed. Edwin's attitude was beginning to burn my stomach, and Bland's family situation was so pitiful.

Chetterling lowered the phone. "Hear how much Beth loves you, Mr. Bland? Now I want you to open your door and push your weapon aside. Come out with your hands up, and nobody's going to get hurt. I promise you that."

"What about my evidence?"

"It's tested, like I told you. Everything's done. You know those tests don't take long."

Stay well, Annie. And alive.

Edwin's words spiraled through my head. I felt his fingers in mine.

Something . . . what was it? Something

419

about the way he quoted that note.

Something about the look on his face . . .

His blatant desire to see Bland die. To see this over and done with — now.

Stay well, Annie. And alive.

Stay well —

The realization stabbed my heart with the clean force of an ice pick. I pulled my hand from his and sucked in air.

"What?" Jenna leaned around him.

Edwin frowned at me. "What happened, Annie?"

No. I must be wrong. It couldn't be. I was thinking wrong, remembering wrong. *Think, think!* My fingers twisted into fists. I clenched harder, as if to pummel a logical explanation into my brain. Squeezing my eyes shut, I slapped frames of film into my mental projector. Turned it on. Saw myself

standing in my office last Saturday, talking on the phone to Edwin Tarell. Telling him I can't make our appointment. He asks me why. I blurt to him about the dead roses, the note. "A detective is on his way now, and I don't know when we'll be finished, so . . ."

My words trail away. I hear Edwin breathing.

"Bill Bland sent you dead roses? And threatened you? What did he say?"

"Basically to keep away from the case . . ."

"Annie, *what* is wrong?" Jenna's voice.

My eyes popped open. Edwin was staring at me. I couldn't look at him. Couldn't believe . . .

Please, God, no!

I wrenched my gaze away and out the window. Focused on the top of Bland's head as he negotiated with Chetterling. My heartbeat stuttered as I tried to think, *think.* To remember differently.

Edwin laid a hand on my shoulder. "Annie, what?"

I swallowed. When I found my voice it was someone else's. Strained. Thick. "I didn't tell you what was in the note."

"Huh?" He pulled me to face him. I forced my eyes to his.

"I. Did not tell you. What. Was in. The note."

"What note?"

"The threat I got with the roses." My throat constricted, the words flattening. "You just quoted it to me. I never told you what it said."

His face blanched. "Sure you did. You told me over the phone, when you tried to cancel our appointment."

My head swung back and forth, back and forth. "No. I never told you. No."

Our voices ran low. Delft and his men focused on the parking lot, paying us no heed. Jenna stilled, watching us.

Edwin shrugged. "Then somebody else did. Probably Chetterling."

"Chetterling? When did he ever talk to you? I watched him introduce himself to you tonight."

"You *watched?* When?"

How neatly he turned the tables, confronting me, his eyes widening with slow understanding. It was just now registering within him — the clear visibility of the lighted interrogation room through the glass. Our well-timed presence.

"What are you —What *is* this?" He turned a hardening jaw to Jenna. "What are you all trying to do to me?"

Jenna gaped from his face to mine, lips parted.

I could say no more. I could barely breathe. I turned away, my feet moving toward the window, all thought of my own safety chased away. I watched in ascending disbelief, hearing Chetterling's and Bland's voices through different ears, surveying the scene through newly horrified eyes.

"Come on, Mr. Bland, it's time to stop this!" The detective switched the bullhorn from one hand to the other, flexing his fingers. "Your wife is waiting. She wants you safe."

"Tell me all the test results first! Tell the world what you found."

"All right, Mr. Bland. We know the shirt belonged to Edwin Tarell. The gun residue is on the sleeve. We lifted Edwin's print off the weapon. It's all there, Mr. Bland. Everything you said. Now don't throw it all away."

Stay well, Annie. And alive.

Everything happened at once then, those final sizzling seconds that would forever brand themselves into my brain. Edwin sidled up behind me, his fingers around my arm. "What are you insinuating, Annie? Is there some setup against me?"

"You quoted a threat you're not supposed to know." The words convulsed off my tongue. "*Your* shirt shows discharge from firing. *Your* print's on the gun. You admitted you lied to Delft."

"So what? All those things have been explained." Edwin placed his palms against my cheeks. "Annie, please, don't tell me you're thinking . . . This is crazy. Everybody's *accusing* me!"

"Come on, Mr. Bland." Chetterling's voice outside. "It's done now. Twenty years, and the truth's finally out. The world will hear this. Most of all, your family will hear it. I promise you — we found all your evidence!"

"And you've got Edwin?"

"He's here, Mr. Bland. We've already questioned him."

"And you've arrested him?"

"Yes. We have."

Anger creased Edwin's face. He glared through the window at Chetterling, then back to me. I eased away from him, heart thumping.

"How did you know, Edwin? How did you know what the note said?"

"Your wife is still on the phone, Mr. Bland! She's crying. She wants you safe. Your boys want you safe. Come on out now. There's no more reason for you to run."

Silence. Edwin pierced me with his eyes, looking into me, *through* me, shock and fear and dread rippling over his face like wind over water.

"Okay!" Bland's voice rose in triumph. "I'm coming out!"

"Fine, Mr. Bland. Open the door slowly. Slide your gun across the pavement and show me your hands."

Edwin turned toward the window, mouth opening. His expression folded in on itself, his limbs stiffening.

Bland's flashers cut off. His car door opened an inch.

"No. No, this won't happen." The words tumbled from Edwin, desperate denials. "This can't —" He shot me a final stunned, pleading glance, then pushed me aside. *"No!"*

Delft jerked around. Too late. In seconds Edwin pounded past him and through the open front door. "Bland!" He skidded to a stop, stretched out his arms. "It's Edwin Tarell. See? They haven't arrested me!"

The sergeant dove outside for Edwin, tackling him to the ground.

"I'm a free man, Bland!" Edwin shouted through the jumble of arms and legs. "They lied. They're waiting for *you!*"

A deputy sprang to help Delft. They dragged Edwin inside to safety, flipped him over, and pushed his face into the floor.

Bland's car door slammed shut. "I knew it, I *knew* it!" His broken voice ricocheted over the cars and people and blazing beats of red and blue. "You lied, Chetterling!"

"Mr. Bland, listen to m—"

"I'm *not* listening to you! I'm not listening to anybody! You just want me dead. You'll

425

never believe me!"

His body rose into view behind the wheel, curses spewing from his mouth. I saw his contorted features, his right hand fumbling, fumbling. And I knew. My body sprang into action even before my brain could fully register, before Chetterling or any deputy could react.

"Bland, *stop!* " I raced for the door, thinking of nothing, nothing but stopping this man — the man I'd hated, who'd broken into my home and kidnapped me, the man betrayed who'd run from blind justice for twenty years.

He raised the gun.

"No, *don't!* I know Edwin's guilty!" I threw myself outside, pounded and pulsed by a dozen rotating lights. My feet slid and I went down hard, Chetterling springing toward me, Jenna shrilling my name, my flailing hands pushing the detective back toward safety.

"I love you, Beth!" Bland screamed. "I love you, Eddie and Scott!"

"Bland, *stop!* It's Annie Kingston —"

"I *love* you!"

Chetterling shoved me bare inches behind the car, his own body still a target. I strained upward, shouting to the sky, "No, listen to me, I know Edwin's —"

"*I . . . will . . . not . . . be . . . taken!*"

"*Blaaand!*"

A gun blast ripped the worn fabric of the night.

■ ■ ■ ■

SATURDAY, MAY 15

■ ■ ■ ■

CHAPTER 43

Bland, stop! I know Edwin's guilty!

I . . . will . . . not . . . be . . . taken! . . .

For the hundredth time, the scene replayed in my mind. The screams, the pulsing lights, the feel of Chetterling's arms as he pushed me to safety. Night and day, day and night, the film in my head unceasing in its mockery.

"Annie?"

"Mmm." I raised my stare from the grained wood of the kitchen table. My fingers were wrapped around a mug of coffee, now grown lukewarm. How long had I been sitting here?

"I brought in the paper." Jenna's tone ran smooth, soothing. "It's on the cover again; you want to look at it?"

I shook my head. In the last three days I'd read enough, seen enough on the news. Bill Bland's photo and Edwin's and mine intermingled: the triangle of the falsely accused;

the greedy, murderous son; and the artist who'd seen the truth. Too late. The media ran wild, lapping up the story like starving dogs. I'd had calls from papers across the country, every national news station, from tabloids and talk shows. Our phones were now unplugged. Those who knew us could call my cell number.

"It wasn't your fault, Annie." These, my sister's words — and everyone else's — spoken countless times.

"I know."

My head tried to convince me it was true, but my heart sputtered at the consolation. My actions had been stupid. *Stupid.* They'd only placed Chetterling in danger. Only prayer could still the ongoing battle within me, and even then, temporarily. Dave encouraged me to keep praying, assuring that God knew my aching spirit. That He would see me through.

At least my becoming a Christian had been well-timed. I wouldn't want to face these sodden days without God's help.

"I'm going to make you some breakfast." Jenna slid the paper onto the table.

"I don't want any."

"Yes, you do."

She opened the refrigerator door and

withdrew eggs and bacon.

I made a face at her back. "Jenna, stop bossing me."

"Somebody's got to. Look at the messes you get into."

I closed my eyes. "Oh, please, not now. I can't take it."

"Sorry." She placed the food on the counter, pulled a frying pan from under the stove. "But you started it."

She was determined to pull me out of my despondency. To remind me that the world still turned, that the kids and I were now safe. That she was still Jenna.

"Did not."

"Did too."

My cell phone rang. I glared at it before answering. "Hello?"

"Hi, it's Ralph. Just checking in on you this morning."

As he'd done numerous times in the last few days, even though my actions could have gotten him killed. I lightened my tone. "Hi, Chetterling. I'm fine, thank you. Are you working this morning? You of all people deserve a day to rest."

He chuckled. "No, I'm not working. And frankly, it's been so long since I had a day off, I hardly know what to do with myself."

That, I could believe. The man lived and

breathed his duty. "Yeah. I couldn't seem to sleep in either." I reached out to flip the paper over, saw its headline, and pushed it away. "Anything new to tell me?"

"Yes, a few things. Emily Tarell was finally willing to talk to me yesterday. I took a long time going over everything with her."

Poor Emily. I couldn't begin to fathom her latest grief. How I was praying for her. Some day I would talk to her, tell her how this case had pushed me toward Christ. But so far she'd made it clear that she didn't want to see me. I understood, but it pierced. "How is she?"

"Broken. She tried to deny all the evidence, you know. She just couldn't believe it of her son. But when he confessed . . ."

"I can imagine. Oh, I feel so sorry for her."

Jenna broke an egg open and slid it into a bowl, then reached for a second. An omelet. Not that she'd asked what I wanted.

"And how's Sergeant Delft?"

"He's all right. Still has mixed emotions. Hates to admit he was chasing the wrong man. But, under the circumstances, he couldn't have known. He *is* happy to have the case solved."

Edwin Tarell hadn't crumbled easily. He'd clung to his denials like barnacles on a sunken ship until the damning data came in regarding Bland's trip to California. Then fear of the death penalty had worked toward Edwin's undoing. Hours of interrogation and the promise of life in prison had finally unhinged his lips.

Bland hadn't left Kansas until around Sunday noon — more than twenty-four hours after someone placed twenty-five dollars under a pot outside Roses by Redding. In addition to his wife and boys, numerous witnesses in the tiny town swore to sighting Bland that morning — a gas station attendant, a neighbor, the newspaper boy. And the final straw — a witness to the drop-off of the money came forward. It had been dark, but the woman saw a man's face briefly illuminated by a streetlight.

She'd identified Edwin Tarell.

"Also, Annie, Delft finally got through to the producer of *American Fugitive.* They're not updating the segment. They're just canceling it."

"No surprise. They're hardly going to want to show how their own hired artist got the wrong man killed."

"Annie." Chetterling's tone contracted. "It's not your fault."

"I know."

When Edwin cracked, the ancient truth spilled out. On the night of the murders, he'd slipped back inside his town house after throwing away his shirt only to catch sight of a shadowed figure raiding his garbage can. For twenty years, he'd known Bland possessed the telltale piece of clothing, plus the gun with his prints. Edwin had set Bland up; now Bland had outfoxed *him.* All plans to help find the fleeing "killer" fell away. Edwin could only hope Bland would stay on the run.

And it worked — for two decades until the *American Fugitive* show.

Edwin's attempts to force the canceling of my drawing had been acts of sheer desperation. His anonymous call to the *Record Searchlight* about the TV show had helped point suspicion toward Bland.

Chetterling sighed. "Well. I'm going to let you go. Please call if you need me."

His patience made me feel so small. "Thank you, Ralph. For everything. You were always there. You lost a lot of sleep, not to mention putting your life on the line for me."

"Don't worry about it. All part of the job."

Maybe. But holding a hysterically sobbing female wasn't. Which is exactly what he'd done — somewhere amid the chaos of shouts and running feet and Bland's body being pulled from the car. All of it caught on camera for the titillated nation to see.

Jenna poured egg and milk mixture into the pan, then turned to lay pieces of bacon in a dish for the microwave. My sister. Ever competent. Ever in control. She was dragging me out to a firing range next week to teach me how to shoot. No excuses accepted. Lesson to be followed with the purchase of a gun to match her own. Chetterling had backed her up on this. I'd wanted to strangle them both.

I clicked off the line, and against my better judgment, reached for the paper. The story focused on Bland's wife and two sons. Last name Smith — the false identity he'd bequeathed to them. Vaguely, I wondered about the legalities of their keeping it. Neighbors talked about the man they knew as Tom, a longtime accountant at a local hardware store. They'd never have guessed his past. He was quiet, stayed in the background. Had never been real friendly, though. Always seemed to look over his shoulder. Curt. Had strict control over his family. But a fiercely loving father, a loyal husband.

A bookstore owner said he bought a lot of mysteries.

The funeral was scheduled for Monday.

Three deaths — all of them, in truth, Edwin Tarell's fault. He was as much to blame for Bland's suicide as if he'd pulled the trigger himself.

Still. If only I'd moved quicker . . . Realized sooner . . .

"Don't accept that false guilt," Dave had chided me yesterday. The number of times he'd checked up on me the last few days had rivaled Chetterling's. He'd even shown up on our doorstep with a casserole. A man. Bringing two women food. He'd prayed with me in our great room — right in front of Jenna. She hadn't even questioned my newfound faith. Guess it wasn't the time. No doubt we'd have some conversations about it soon.

Jenna fixed me a plate with half of the bacon and omelet and slid it before me. My stomach growled. It did smell heavenly. Serving herself the remaining portion, she sat down at the table.

We ate in silence.

She glanced at me out of the corner of her eye. "What would you say if I wanted to move in here permanently?"

"What do you think I'd say? I've been trying to get you to do that since last summer."

"True. So now's the time."

"To what do I owe this grand decision?"

She gave me a look. "To the fact that you can't take care of yourself."

"Oh. Thanks."

"You're welcome."

I feigned vital interest in chewing a piece of bacon. "What about your consulting in the Bay Area?"

"I'll still do it. I'll work from here."

"And your town house?"

"I'll keep it. No doubt I'll need to stay there when I go see clients."

She had it all figured out. Nice to know she could plan her own life as well as mine. "I'm glad, Jenna. Really glad."

"Good." She paused. "I have another idea."

The way she said it . . . "Oh, boy. Now what?"

"As soon as the kids are out of school next month, let's all take off for Hawaii. We need to loll on the beach. Get tan. Put this horrific week behind us."

Well. Second plan in a row I actually liked. "Sounds wonderful. Let's do it." I stared at my plate, thinking. "Only thing is, Stephen's court date is June 10."

"That's the day before school lets out; I already checked."

Of course she had. "But what if he's put

on probation? I thought he couldn't leave the county, something like that."

"Chetterling said he could as long as you told the court about it, and he stayed with you."

"You asked *Chetterling* about this? Before you asked me?"

"I had to check it out. Make sure it was possible before I got your hopes up."

Good save, Jenna. But she had a point.

"One thing. Kelly's already asking if Erin can go."

So she'd talked to the kids too. "Sure, why not? Always more fun for her to bring a friend."

"True. And, uh, Erin wants to bring her dad."

Ah, so that was it. I leaned back in my chair. "Jenna. That's kind of . . . weird, isn't it? The two of us, and him? What are people going to think?"

"The three of us, with three kids in between. People aren't going to think anything."

I raised my chin, surveying her. Remembering all the times Dave had been over in the past few days. Except for the time we prayed, she'd always found an excuse to leave us alone. "Is this some cooked-up plan of yours?"

"No." She looked offended. "It was totally the girls' idea."

"And you didn't help put it in their heads."

"Of course not."

My tongue ran over my lips. "Uh-huh."

"Stop obsessing, Annie. I don't even know if he'll want to go."

I focused on Dave's house through the kitchen window. The house where his wife, Lisa, had lived. And died. The house where he struggled to raise a daughter alone. The house where I had prayed to become a Christian.

"It's okay, Jenna, if he wants to go." The words formed slowly. Surprising me. "All three of us adults need a good rest. The kids do too." I gave her a look. "Besides, with Dave around, maybe you won't tell me what to do every minute."

She mushed her lips. "Who, me?"

On second thought, I wouldn't count on it.

Movement out on the street caught my attention. I turned toward the window to see a van pull up in front of our house. *Oh, great, now what?* Didn't anybody rest on a Saturday anymore?

"What is it?" Jenna couldn't see the vehicle from her side of the table.

The name on the van suddenly registered. Pretty Petals Florist. Immediate fear spritzed down my nerves. My mouth opened, but I didn't answer. Sitting stone still, I watched a man get out of the driver's seat, open up the back of the van, and withdraw a long white box.

"Oh, no. Oh, Jenna, no."

The tone of my voice plucked my sister from her chair and around the table to peer out the window. She sucked in an audible breath as the man strode up our front walk. Then her shoulders relaxed. "Wait a minute. He's in a marked van."

"Yeah, but —"

The doorbell rang. I jumped. We both stared out the window, waiting.

Jenna straightened. "He's not running away; that's a good sign." She gave a nervous laugh. "Good grief, it's just someone delivering flowers. What's the matter with us?" She started toward the door. "Come on, go with me. They're going to be for you anyway."

Exactly what I was afraid of.

The delivery man stood on our porch with a pleasant smile, holding the long box as if it were gold. He looked from Jenna to me. "Annie Kingston?"

I couldn't help but cringe. "That's me."

He held out the box. "Somebody's thinking of you today, ma'am."

I eyed it. "What's in it?"

"A dozen perfect red roses. Packed 'em myself." The smile would not leave his face.

"Are they alive?"

The corners of his mouth faltered. "Alive, ma'am?"

Jenna gave a little huff. "Just take the box, Annie!" She pulled it from the man's hands and thrust it into mine. "Thank you, sir, very much. She appreciates it. Really." She shot the man an oversized smile and waved him off before shutting the door. "For heaven's sake, Annie!"

"Well, what am I supposed to —"

"Just open it!"

Half out of lingering suspicion and half just to irk her, I took my time carrying the box to the kitchen table. Then, carefully, I untied the yellow ribbon and lifted the lid. The sweet smell of roses wafted into the air. *"Oh."* They were long-stemmed and a deep, velvety red. "They're absolutely beautiful!"

"Well, who sent them? Where's the card?" Jenna crowded in to look.

"Good grief, just a second." I didn't want to hurry this moment. I wanted to bask in it. No one had sent me roses before. Ever. Carefully, I picked one up and admired it.

Held it to my nose. Closed my eyes and took a deep breath. Such a heady fragrance. I ran a fingertip up and down the bud's soft petals. Finally, when I'd had my fill, I passed it to my sister to hold while I lifted out a small white envelope. Inside was a handwritten note.

Annie,
I figured you deserved the real thing this time.

— Ralph

My mouth dropped open. For a moment, all I could do was stare. "*Chetterling* sent me these?"

Jenna's head did a provocative turn until she looked at me sideways. One eyebrow slowly lifted. "Well, well, what do you know? Didn't think the man had it in him. He probably called you this morning because he couldn't wait to hear if you'd gotten them yet."

I gaped again at the card, then laid it down and took the rose back from her. "Oh, Jenna, don't be so . . . . He's just thanking me for the job I did."

"Uh-huh."

Feeling a flush rise to my cheeks, I turned away. "Better get these things in water."

I busied myself with cutting the stems, arranging the roses in a vase. Jenna looked over my shoulder all the while, saying nothing. She didn't have to. My sister can convey plenty without a single word.

My task done, I placed the vase with utmost care in the center of the table, then stood back and admired the flowers. Their scent permeated the room. How could I ever thank Chetterling enough for this gift? All of a sudden, the mere thought of phoning him sent flutters through my stomach.

Jenna stood by the kitchen window, arms folded with the satisfaction of new possibilities, looking back and forth from the roses to me. I turned, intending to ask her if she didn't have anything better to do. But for absolutely no reason, my gaze drifted out the window and across the street. I found myself staring at Dave's house.

Jenna followed my eyes, then gave me a long, penetrating look.

I blinked at her. "What?"

My sister held up both palms and shook her head. "Annie. Even *I'm* staying out of this one."

Jenna walked around me to clear our breakfast dishes from the table. "But —" she couldn't help getting in the last word —

"I do believe you need to call a certain detective."

ABOUT THE AUTHOR

Brandilyn Collins is the bestselling author of *Brink of Death, Eyes of Elisha,* and other novels. She and her family divide their time between the California Bay Area and Coeur d'Alene, Idaho.

Visit her Web site at www.brandilyn collins.com.